Called the "Shakespeare of the novel," HON-ORÉ DE BALZAC (1799–1850) is best known for his masterpiece, *La Comédie humaine,* a chronicle of nineteenth-century French society consisting of nearly one hundred novels and short stories. A man of great appetites, Herculean feats of writing, and immense talent, Balzac is considered to be the founder of the realistic school and was the first to have characters reappear from novel to novel, making him the origi-nator of the modern novel cycle.

Born in Tours, Balzac was studying law at the Sorbonne when he developed a strong interest in literature. After several years writing sensational potboilers, he published his first successful book, *Les Chouans,* at age thirty. Unfortunately, by that time poor business ventures and a taste for Paris high life had plunged him into debt from which he never escaped.

Famous for his zest for life and love, Balzac had only two true *affaires de coeur*—with the much older Madame de Berny, who was his mistress until her death, and with Eveline Hanska, a Polish countess whom he married just months before his own demise. Leaving over forty works unfinished, the robust, hard-living Balzac died at the age of fifty-one. The most famous works in *La Comédie humaine* are *Louis Lambert* (1832), *Eugénie Grandet* (1833), *La Recherche de l'absolu* (1834), *Le Père Goriot* (1834), *Séraphita* (1835), *César Birotteau* (1837), *Illusions perdues* (1837–43), *La Cousine Bette* (1847), and *Le Cousin Pons* (1847).

Ask your bookseller for Bantam Classics by these
international writers.

ARISTOPHANES
DANTE ALIGHIERI
HONORE DE BALZAC
FYODOR DOSTOEVSKY
ALEXANDRE DUMAS
EURIPIDES
GUSTAVE FLAUBERT
JOHANN WOLFGANG VON GOETHE
JACOB and WILHELM GRIMM
HOMER
VICTOR HUGO
HENRIK IBSEN
FRANZ KAFKA
PIERRE CHODERLOS DE LACLOS
GASTON LEROUX
NICCOLO MACHIAVELLI
THOMAS MANN
KARL MARX and FRIEDRICH ENGELS
GUY DE MAUPASSANT
PLATO
EDMOND ROSTAND
MARQUIS DE SADE
SOPHOCLES
MARIE-HENRI BEYLE DE STENDHAL
LEO TOLSTOY
IVAN TURGENEV
JULES VERNE
VIRGIL
VOLTAIRE
JOHANN DAVID WYSS

Eugénie Grandet

HONORÉ DE BALZAC

Translated by Lowell Bair
With an Introduction by
Milton Crane

BANTAM BOOKS

NEW YORK · TORONTO · LONDON · SYDNEY · AUCKLAND

EUGÉNIE GRANDET
A Bantam Classic Book / March 1994

PUBLISHING HISTORY
Eugénie Grandet *was first published in 1833*
as part of Balzac's La Comédie humaine

ISBN 0-553-21429-2

Published simultaneously in the United States and Canada

Bantam Books are published by Bantam Books, a division of
Bantam Doubleday Dell Publishing Group, Inc. Its trademark,
consisting of the words "Bantam Books" and the portrayal of
a rooster, is Registered in U.S. Patent and Trademark Office
and in other countries. Marca Registrada. Bantam Books, 1540
Broadway, New York, New York 10036.

PRINTED IN THE UNITED STATES OF AMERICA

OPM   0 9 8 7 6 5 4 3 2 1

To Maria

May your name, you whose portrait is the fairest adornment of this work, remain here like a branch of blessed boxwood, cut from some unknown tree, but certainly sanctified by religion and constantly kept fresh and green by pious hands, to protect the house.

—DE BALZAC

Contents

Introduction

by Milton Crane

The natural history of man has long been the favorite subject of French writers—novelists, essayists, and dramatists. Almost since the beginning of time, one feels, they have been observing, defining, describing, and classifying the human species in all its bewildering manifestations, isolating and incarnating the peculiar characteristics of the snob, the provincial, the prude, the miser, the lecher, and a hundred other types and sub-types.

The list of eminent social taxonomists that France has given to the world's literature includes such figures as Montaigne, Molière, La Bruyère, Zola, Romains, and Proust. Perhaps the most consciously systematic and comprehensive of these literary sociologists is Honoré de Balzac. His immense cycle of novels, stories, and studies, to which he gave the all-inclusive title of *La Comédie humaine* (The Human Comedy), was designed to do for human society what the great French naturalist Buffon had done almost a century earlier for the animal

kingdom in his *Histoire naturelle* (Natural History).
Balzac himself drew this parallel in his ambitious General Preface to the *Comédie humaine*:

> There have . . . existed and there always
> will exist Social Species as there are Zoölogical
> Species. If Buffon produced a magnificent
> work in undertaking to present in a book all
> of zoölogy, is there not a work of this kind to
> be done on Society? But Nature set, for animal
> varieties, limits within which Society was not
> to be contained. When Buffon painted the lion
> he did the lioness in a few sentences, while in
> Society woman is not always the female of
> the male. . . . The Social State has accidents
> not allowed in Nature, for it is Nature plus
> Society. The description of Social Species is
> then at least double that of Animal Species if
> we consider only the two sexes. And then with
> animals there is little drama, and confusion is
> rare; they attack each other and that is all.
> Men attack each other too, but the differences
> in degree of intelligence make the struggle
> much more complicated. If some scientists
> do not yet admit that Animality overflows
> into Humanity in a prodigious life current,
> the grocer certainly may become a peer of
> France, and the nobleman sometimes descends
> to the lowest social rank. Also, Buffon found
> life very simple among animals. The animal
> has . . . no arts or sciences; while man, accord-
> ing to a law that needs to be investigated, is
> inclined to represent his mores, his thought,
> and his life in everything he appropriates for
> his needs. . . .

So the work to be done must be triple: men, women, and things, i.e., persons and the material representation they give to their thought; in short, man and life, for life is our raiment.

Whether or not one accepts the scientific soundness of Balzac's theory, there is no question that he has left us an incomparable portrait of French life in the first half of the nineteenth century. Like Trollope in Victorian England, like Jules Romains in the Third Republic, Balzac provides more and better information about the personality of middle-class France than many a professional historian or sociologist. This hardly explains, however, his continuing appeal to the common reader throughout the world. One might go so far as to say that Balzac has managed to triumph over his own sociology.

It is easier to affirm Balzac's greatness than to explain it. His genius labored under enormous handicaps. Virtually every critic of Balzac, for example, has complained about Balzac's insensitivity to language. (Emile Faguet, a distinguished critic, scholar, and member of the Académie Française, said of him, early in the present century: "Everyone agrees that Balzac wrote badly. There is no need to correct popular opinion on this point. He did indeed write badly.") A passionate collector of every kind of curious information, he cannot restrain himself from putting it all down, often beyond the requirements of the work. He constantly offends against modern taste by hovering at the reader's elbow, telling him how to react to the events of the story, pointing a moral, drawing a conclusion. And yet Balzac, by the sheer force of his own belief in what he is writing, transcends these gross and palpable faults, which would shipwreck a lesser artist. His genius makes up for what he lacks in talent.

The life of Balzac has been written many times; of the modern biographies, those of Stefan Zweig (1942) and of André Billy (1944) are notable. Balzac was born in 1799 in Tours, the son of a civil servant who changed his name from Balssa to the more impressive Balzac (which his son was presently to ennoble as *de* Balzac). His childhood was saddened by his mother's neglect, of which he complained bitterly in later years. It is hardly surprising, therefore, that he became strongly dependent, while still a young man, on the considerably older Mme. Laure de Berny. She remained his mistress, counsellor, and critic until the end of her life. Balzac's literary success began, after some dozen years of preparation for his art, with the publication of *Les Chouans* in 1829. Thereafter, he made a great deal of money, but spent much more, and was constantly harassed by creditors.

Neither Mme. de Berny, Mme. Hanska (a Polish noblewoman who married him after a liaison that extended over many years), nor any of his other numerous loves could discipline Balzac's extravagant tastes and habits. While at work he would maintain the most Spartan of regimes, writing twelve and thirteen hours a day and living on black coffee and boiled eggs. But when he had completed the work in hand he would indulge in Lucullan debauches: one of his publishers reports that Balzac once ate at a single meal one hundred oysters, a dozen chops, a duck, a brace of partridges, and a sole, in addition to hors d'oeuvres, desserts, fruit, and wine. His other tastes and his expenses were as extravagant as his diet. He might well have said, with Jean Cocteau, "A little too much is just enough for me."

The personality of Balzac, to judge from the accounts of his contemporaries, was extraordinarily engaging. Even persons who had reason to deplore his habits—such as the publishers who watched him spend their advances without delivering the promised novels—were unable to resist his charm. He was the intimate of many of the great writers of his time. Among his closest friends was Victor Hugo, who gave Balzac one of the only two votes he received on the two occasions when he presented himself for election to the Académie Française.

His single-minded concentration on his art and his sense of a priest-like vocation ally Balzac to the great romantics. On the other hand, his work does not deal with the characteristic themes of romantic art, such as the exaltation of love and nature. His themes are those of classical satire and comedy: avarice, ambition, lust, vanity, and hypocrisy. For Balzac it was not love but money that made the world go round. Wordsworth would have found it difficult to recognize Balzac as a fellow-romantic; but Molière would cheerfully have accepted him as a colleague. In still another important respect did Balzac differ from such great romantics as Shelley, Lamartine, and Heine: he was fiercely conservative in politics and religion, maintaining that only the firmest authoritarianism of church and state could control the dangerously anarchic tendencies of bourgeois society. Let a Byron or a Coleridge hymn the French Revolution: the monarchist and Catholic Balzac knew that no price was too high if lawlessness and terror were to be kept from again sweeping Europe.

In 1842 Balzac, the author of fifty novels, conceived the device that, he hoped, would give form and meaning to his entire literary achievement. This was the *Comédie humaine,* a structure designed to describe and analyze all French society in his time. Both his published and his yet unwritten books were to be comprehended under seven headings: Scenes of Private Life, Scenes of Provincial Life, Scenes of Military Life, Scenes of Rural Life, Scenes of Political Life, Philosophical Studies, and Analytical Studies. During the remaining eight years of his life, he constantly reworked these categories and moved books from one group to another.

There is something unavoidably synthetic about Balzac's scheme, which he endeavored to superimpose on books that had obviously been written without thought of a *Comédie humaine*. He may, of course, have been feeling his way instinctively toward this plan throughout his career, but his juggling with the elements of his work argues against the idea. Moreover, his rubrics and even his chapter titles promise a comprehensiveness and objectivity more "scientific" and less artistic than his books in fact are. Like many an artist before him, he was a better writer than a thinker, and it was probably fortunate that he conceived the *Comédie humaine* toward the end of his career, when the artificiality of an outline could no longer mar the spontaneity and originality of his earlier work.

This is strikingly true of *Eugénie Grandet,* which Balzac published in 1834, eight years before he gave it a place among the Scenes of Provincial Life in the *Comédie humaine.* The little provincial idyll of a young girl's first and only love, given too soon to a man incapable of recognizing its worth, is singularly free of the characteristic defects of Balzac's later work. To be sure, it makes a bow to sociology: three of its six chapters, for example, bear titles that are plainly intended to carry a larger social meaning: "Bourgeois Faces," "Love in the Provinces," and "So Goes the World." And the book provides a memorable illustration of Balzac's basic charge against modern bourgeois society, that it is ruled by money.

The character of Eugénie gives shape and direction to the novel, but it is the character of her father that gives it point and savor. Eugénie alone passes from innocence to experience; the rest undergo virtually no development: Charles, the handsome young cousin whose arrival in Saumur sets the events of the book in motion, is already corrupt, as both his Parisian elegance and his Parisian mistress tell us, with much heavy underlining from Balzac; Eugénie's mother merely becomes increasingly defeated and resigned under the weight of Grandet's punishment of Eugénie; and Grandet himself, who is presented whole and of a piece at the opening of the book, is given a rich variety of situations in which to display his character. But the miser can never surprise us by showing us an unexpected side of himself, as Proust's characters so often do; Balzac's characters do not change, they only expand from a central conception.

It cannot be doubted that Balzac's imagination was captured by Grandet, who dominates the novel as Hurstwood does *Sister Carrie* or Falstaff *King Henry IV*. Virtue interested Balzac, but vice fascinated him, as it does us all. In Grandet, as Hippolyte Taine long ago pointed out, Balzac created his own version of Harpagon, the classic miser of Molière's great comedy *L'Avare*. Grandet is not, however, merely Harpagon transferred to the nineteenth century; he is a wholly original creation. Balzac charts his course with precision: during the Revolution, the old cooper bought "legally if not legitimately" the finest vineyards in the district, which had been seized from their former clerical owners. Balzac observes acidly that, although Grandet was regarded as a man with a propensity for new ideas, "actually, he merely had a propensity for vineyards." So he rose in the administration of Saumur; so he prospered, like the Vicar of Bray, under Napoleon and then under the Restoration. Despite the shady origins of his fortune, Grandet was always scrupulously honest; this point is made several times, and Professor Samuel Rogers has wittily said, in his excellent *Balzac and the Novel,* that Grandet "is honest, for all his sharpness . . . because if he were not, he would feel that the pleasure would be gone; it would be like cheating at solitaire."

Grandet is one of the great humor-characters of literature, like the monomaniacs of Ben Jonson's satirical comedies, who are shaped, moved, controlled by a single desire or folly. The first pages of the book introduce us to this cold, pinched creature, who is totally obsessed with money and cannot imagine anyone different from himself. His life exemplifies the maxim that the love of money is literally the root of all evil. How does he tell his nephew Charles that his father is a suicide? "Yes, poor boy, you've guessed it: he's dead. But that's nothing, there's something much worse. . . . He's ruined you. You have no money at all." Later he complains that Charles's mourning is excessive: "That boy is good for nothing. He thinks more of the dead than he does of money." When he blasphemes, Balzac at once explains: "Misers do not believe in a future life; the present is everything to them." (And he adds prophetically: "When this doctrine has passed from the bourgeoisie to the working class, what will become of the country?") Grandet puts Eugénie on bread and water for having given Charles her own money, and causes the death of his wife by refusing to forgive the girl. Avaricious even on his deathbed, he tries to seize the gilded crucifix that the priest is holding out for him to kiss.

The house in which all three Grandets live out their empty lives is likewise an unforgettable creation, which Balzac constructs with loving care, as he does the whole world of his imagination. It is described matter-of-factly, precisely, and comprehensively, as in a superior guide-book—one written by a genius. For Balzac's way is to imagine his people, places, and events as if they already belonged to history, and then to record carefully what he sees and hears. That is why he is so often unable to stop, much as we should like him to. If Grandet receives a letter from his brother, or Charles writes to his mistress, we must read the entire text (*texte intégral et inédit,* as it were). When Eugénie prepares to give her collection of gold coins to Charles to launch him on a career in the Indies, Balzac turns numismatist and annotates each coin fully. When Charles arrives from Paris, Balzac itemizes his costumes, including the significant detail: "He brought every kind of collar and cravat in favor *at that time.*"

Balzac is a most self-conscious historian of his own age, calling our attention to details as if he were an archaeologist explaining the customs of a civilization long dead. (Compare, in this connection, the meticulousness of Theodore Dreiser, surely the spiritual grandson of Balzac as he is the son of Zola, who provides in *Sister Carrie* an entire Hannah & Hogg menu for 1889.) Nowhere is Balzac the historian more successful than in the remarkable story of how Grandet liquidates the debts of his brother, gaining credit in Saumur and Paris as a loving relation while actually making a killing and incidentally fleecing the eager Parisian creditors. (Both André Gide and Martin Turnell have confessed that the details of this intricate machination are beyond their comprehension, though both acknowledge the account of Grandet's speculations to be masterly. Anyone contemplating a career of sharp practice could do worse than consult the *Comédie humaine.*)

Balzac's naïve and almost compulsive determination to record the minutest details of his world gives his creations power to enchant and convince us as they did him. (This is the essence of Balzac's famous "realism," about which so much has been written.) Even the most fantastic events and characters of his novels remain believable. Balzac's own absorption in the world of his imagining is beautifully exemplified in a famous anecdote: The writer Jules Sandeau, one of the small army of George Sand's lovers, called on Balzac and sadly reported the death of his sister. Balzac listened, expressed his sympathy, and finally interrupted his friend: "Come now, let's get back to reality. Whom will Eugénie Grandet marry?"

Of the making of translations there is literally no end, for each age must reinterpret the world's masterpieces for itself in its own language. Mr. Lowell Bair's entirely new rendering of *Eugénie Grandet,* the text of the present edition, conveys in excellent English prose the finest qualities of Balzac's work. As in his translation of Stendhal's *The Red and the Black,* Mr. Bair succeeds in providing the reader with the novel his author might well have written had his language been not French but English.

Eugénie Grandet

I

Bourgeois Faces

In certain provincial towns there are houses whose appearance gives one a feeling of melancholy equal to that aroused by the gloomiest cloisters, the bleakest moors or the most forlorn ruins. Perhaps these houses combine the silence of the cloister, the barrenness of the moors and the desolation of the ruins. The pace of life inside them is so languid that a stranger would think them uninhabited if he did not suddenly encounter the pale, cold gaze of a motionless person whose semimonastic face appears above the window sill at the sound of unfamiliar footsteps.

These elements of melancholy are present in the physiognomy of a dwelling which stands in Saumur at the end of the rising street leading to the castle, across the upper part of town. This street, now little used, hot in summer, cold in winter and dark in several places, is remarkable for the resonance of its cobblestone surface, always clean and dry, for the narrowness of its winding course and for the tranquillity of its houses, which are part of the old town and are overshadowed by the ramparts.

Houses three centuries old still stand firmly there, though built of wood, and their varied aspects contribute to the quaintness which recommends this part of Saumur to the attention of antiquarians and artists. It is difficult to pass in front of them without admiring the massive beams whose ends are carved into fantastic figures which crown the ground floor of most of these houses with a black bas-relief.

Here, wooden crosspieces are covered with slate and form blue lines on the fragile walls of a house topped by a studwork roof which sags with the weight of years and whose rotted shingles have been twisted by the alternating action of sun and rain. There, one sees worn and blackened window sills whose delicate carvings are scarcely visible and seem too light for the brown earthenware pot from which spring the pinks or rosebushes of some poor working girl. Further on there are doors, studded with enormous nails, on which the genius of our ancestors has traced domestic hieroglyphics whose meaning will never be recovered. Here, a Protestant has affirmed his faith; there, some Leaguer has cursed Henri IV; elsewhere, some burgher has engraved the insignia of his municipal nobility, the glory of his forgotten magistracy. The whole history of France is there. Beside a tottering house with roughly plastered walls on which the workman has immortalized his trowel, rises a nobleman's town house. On the semicircular arch above the stone doorway, one can still see vestiges of his coat of arms, shattered by the various revolutions which have agitated the country since 1789.

On this street, the first-floor commercial establishments are neither shops nor stores: lovers of the Middle Ages will find here the communal workshop of our forefathers in all its naïve simplicity. These low-ceilinged rooms, which have no shop fronts, showcases or display windows, are deep and dark, and without inside or outside ornamentation. Their doors open in two solid sections with crude iron fittings; the upper part opens inward, and the lower one, equipped with a spring-bell, is constantly swinging back and forth. Air and light enter these damp caverns through either the upper half of the door or the space between the vaulted ceiling and the breast-high wall in which heavy shutters are set. These shutters are taken down in the morning and put up again in the evening, secured with iron bars bolted in place. The merchant's wares are displayed on the wall. Here there is no deceptive ostentation. Depending on the nature of the business, the samples consist of two or three tubs of salt and codfish, a few bundles of sailcloth, rope, brass wire hanging from the rafters, hoops lined up along the walls, or pieces of cloth on the shelves.

Go inside. A clean, neatly dressed young girl with red arms, wearing a white kerchief, puts down her knitting and calls her father or mother, who comes out and sells you—phlegmatically, obligingly or arrogantly, depending on his or her character—anything you want, whether it be worth two sous or twenty thousand francs.

You see a dealer in stave wood sitting in his doorway, twirling his thumbs as he chats with a neighbor. He apparently owns nothing more than a few old shelf boards for bottles and two or three bundles of laths, but his well-stocked lumber yard on the waterfront supplies all the coopers in Anjou. He knows almost to a plank how many barrels he can sell if the harvest is good. Sunshine can make him rich, rainy weather can ruin him; in a single morning, the price of a puncheon may rise to eleven francs, or fall to six.

In this region, as in Touraine, business is dominated by the weather. Winegrowers, landowners, lumber merchants, coopers, innkeepers and bargemen are all constantly watching for a ray of sunshine. When they go to bed at night they tremble for fear they may learn the next morning that there has been a frost during the night. They dread rain, wind and drought; they want water, heat and clouds to suit their whims. There is a constant duel between the sky and their earthly interests. The barometer successively saddens, relaxes and brightens their faces.

From one end to the other of this street, formerly the main street of Saumur, the words "This is golden weather!" are passed from door to door. And everyone replies to his neighbor, "It's raining gold louis," knowing how many of them a sunny day or a timely rain can bring him. At noon on Saturdays, during the warm weather, you cannot buy anything from these worthy businessmen. Each of them has his vineyard, his little farm, and he goes off to spend two days in the country. There, with everything—purchases, sales and profits— already anticipated, they find themselves with ten hours out of twelve to spend in merry gatherings, gossip, comments and continuous spying. A housewife cannot buy a partridge without the neighbors asking her husband if it was well cooked. A young girl cannot look out of her window without being seen by all the idle groups in the vicinity. Everyone's life is an open book there, just as there is no mystery in these dark, impenetrable houses.

Life is almost always lived in the open air: every family sits in its doorway and lunches, dines and quarrels there. No one passes in the street without being studied. In the old days, in fact, whenever a stranger arrived in a provincial town he was ridiculed from door to door. Hence a number of funny stories, hence the nickname of "mockers" given to the people of Angers, who excelled in this kind of urban banter.

The ancient aristocratic residences of the old part of town line the upper end of this street, which was formerly inhabited by the local nobility. The gloomy house in which the events of this story take place was precisely one of those residences, venerable relics of a time when men and things still had that quality of simplicity which French manners and morals are losing day by day.

After following the windings of this picturesque street, whose smallest features awaken memories and whose general aspect tends to plunge one into absent-minded reverie, you see a rather dark recess in the middle of which is hidden the door of "the Grandet house." It is impossible to understand the full meaning of this provincial expression without giving Monsieur Grandet's biography.

In Saumur, Monsieur Grandet enjoyed a reputation whose causes and effects will not be entirely understood by people who have spent little or no time in the provinces. Monsieur Grandet, who was still called Old Man Grandet by certain elderly people whose number was rapidly diminishing, was in 1789 a well-to-do master cooper who knew how to read, write and figure. When the property belonging to the clergy in the district of Saumur was put up for sale by the French Republic, the cooper, who was then forty, had just married the daughter of a wealthy lumber merchant. Armed with her dowry and all his cash, a total of two thousand louis, Grandet went to the headquarters of the district, where, with the help of two hundred double louis given by his father-in-law to the rabid republican in charge of the sale of government property, he bought for a

song, legally if not legitimately, the finest vineyards in
the district, an old abbey and several small farms.

Since the people of Saumur were far from being
ardent revolutionaries, Monsieur Grandet was regarded
as a daring man, a republican, a patriot, a man with a
propensity for new ideas; actually, however, he merely
had a propensity for vineyards. He was appointed a
member of the administration of the district of Saumur,
and his pacific influence made itself felt both politically
and commercially. Politically, he protected the former
aristocrats and did everything in his power to prevent
the sale of the property of those who had left the country; commercially, he sold the republican armies one or
two thousand barrels of white wine, in exchange for
which he received some superb meadows belonging to
a community of nuns, which the government had been
keeping in reserve.

Under the Consulate, Old Man Grandet became
mayor, governed wisely and did even better with his vineyards; under the Empire, he became Monsieur Grandet.
Napoleon did not like republicans; he replaced Monsieur
Grandet, who was reputed to have worn the red bonnet,
with a large landowner, a nobleman who was destined
to become a baron of the Empire. Monsieur Grandet
relinquished his municipal honors without the slightest
regret. In the interests of the town, he had built some
excellent roads leading to his property. His house and
lands, very favorably assessed, paid modest taxes. Since
the registration of his various holdings, his vineyards,
thanks to constant care, had become the "head of the
region," a technical term designating the vineyards which
produce the finest wine. He could have asked to become
a member of the Legion of Honor.

His dismissal took place in 1806. He was then
fifty-seven and his wife was about thirty-six. Their only

daughter, the fruit of their legitimate love, was ten.

Monsieur Grandet, whom Providence no doubt wished to console for his political misfortune, received three successive inheritances that year: one from Madame de la Gaudinière, *née* de la Bertellière, Madame Grandet's mother; another from old Monsieur de la Bertellière, father of the deceased; and a third from Madame Gentillet, his maternal grandmother. No one knew the amounts involved. These three old people were such passionate misers that for a long time they had been piling up their money in order to contemplate it in secret. Old Monsieur de la Bertellière regarded an investment as an extravagance, finding greater interest in the sight of gold than in the profits of usury. The people of Saumur therefore estimated the amount of money the old people had saved up on the basis of the income they received from their landed property.

Monsieur Grandet then obtained that new title of nobility which our mania for equality can never wipe out: he became the biggest taxpayer of the district. He cultivated a hundred acres of vineyard, which in abundant years yielded seven or eight hundred barrels of wine. He owned thirteen small farms, an old abbey whose windows, arches and stained glass he had walled up for the sake of economy, in order to preserve them, and a hundred and twenty-seven acres of meadowland in which three thousand poplar trees, planted in 1793, grew and flourished. Finally, the house in which he lived belonged to him.

From these things it was possible to judge his visible fortune. As for his capital, there were only two people who could make even a vague estimate of its magnitude. One of them was Monsieur Cruchot, the notary who handled Monsieur Grandet's usurious loans; the other was Monsieur des Grassins, the richest banker in

Saumur, whose profits the winegrower secretly shared whenever he saw fit to do so. Although old Cruchot and Monsieur des Grassins possessed that profound discretion which, in the provinces, engenders confidence and wealth, they publicly treated Monsieur Grandet with such great respect that observers were able to measure the former mayor's capital by the degree of obsequious consideration that was accorded him.

There was no one in Saumur who was not convinced that Monsieur Grandet had a private treasure, a hiding-place full of louis, and that every night he indulged in the ineffable joys afforded by the sight of a large mass of gold. The miserly were particularly sure of this when they looked at the old man's eyes, which seemed to have absorbed the glint of the yellow metal. The eyes of a man accustomed to deriving enormous interest from his capital, like those of a libertine, a gambler or a sycophant, necessarily contract certain indefinable habits, certain furtive, avid, mysterious movements which do not escape his brethren. This secret language constitutes a kind of freemasonry of the passions.

Monsieur Grandet inspired, then, the deferential esteem that was rightfully owed to a man who never had any debts, who, as a skilled cooper and winegrower, could estimate with the precision of an astronomer when he ought to manufacture a thousand barrels for his harvest or only five hundred, who never misjudged a speculation, who always had barrels to sell when a barrel was worth more than its contents, and who could store his vintage in his wine cellars and wait until he could sell it for two hundred francs a cask, when the smaller winegrowers had to sell theirs for a hundred. His famous vintage of 1811, judiciously stored and slowly sold, had brought in over two hundred and forty thousand francs. Financially speaking, there was something of both the tiger and the boa constrictor in Monsieur Grandet: he knew how to conceal himself, lie in wait, watch his prey for a long time and finally leap on it; then he would open the jaws of his purse, gulp down a bellyful of gold and placidly lie down like a snake digesting its prey, impassive, cold and methodical.

No one saw him pass without a feeling of admiration mingled with respect and terror. Had not everyone in Saumur felt the deft incision of his steel claws? For one man, Monsieur Cruchot had procured the money necessary to purchase an estate, but at eleven percent; for another, Monsieur des Grassins had discounted several bills of exchange, but at a frightful rate of interest. There were few days when Monsieur Grandet's name was not mentioned, either in the marketplace or during the evening conversations of the town. For some people, the old winegrower's fortune was an object of civic pride. A merchant or an innkeeper would sometimes say to a stranger, with a certain satisfaction, "Monsieur, we have several millionaires here, but as for Monsieur Grandet, he himself doesn't know how rich he is!"

In 1816, the shrewdest calculators in Saumur estimated the value of the old man's landed property at close to four million francs, but since it must have yielded him, between 1793 and 1817, an average income of a hundred thousand francs a year, it was reasonable to assume that he had a sum of money almost equal to the value of his land. When, therefore, after a game of boston or a discussion of vineyards, someone happened to mention Monsieur Grandet, well-informed people would say, "Old Man Grandet? Why, he must be worth five or six million francs." If Monsieur Cruchot or Monsieur des Grassins heard this remark, they would reply, "You must be shrewder than I am, because I've never been able to find out how much money he has altogether."

If some Parisian spoke of the Rothschilds or Monsieur Lafitte, the people of Saumur would ask if they were as rich as Monsieur Grandet. If the Parisian smiled and disdainfully said yes, they would shake their heads and look at each other incredulously.

The old man's great wealth covered all his actions with a mantle of gold. If at first certain peculiarities of his life gave rise to mockery and ridicule, the mockery and ridicule had now died away. Everything he did was regarded as significant. His words, his clothes, his gestures and the blinking of his eyes had the force of law in the region; after studying him as a naturalist studies the effects of instinct in animals, everyone had learned to recognize the profound and silent wisdom of his slightest actions. "We're in for a hard winter," people would say; "Old Man Grandet has put on his fur-lined gloves: it's time to begin the harvest." Or, "Old Man Grandet is buying a lot of stave wood—there'll be plenty of wine this year."

Monsieur Grandet never bought any meat or bread. Each week his tenant farmers brought him, as part of their rent, a sufficient supply of capons, chickens, eggs, butter and wheat. He owned a mill whose tenant, in addition to paying his rent, had agreed to take a certain amount of grain and bring back the flour and bran. Although she was no longer young, Big Nanon, his only servant, personally baked the bread for the household every Saturday. Monsieur Grandet had arranged to keep himself supplied with vegetables by the vegetable farmers who rented his land. As for fruit, he harvested so much that he had a large part of it sold in the marketplace. His firewood was cut from his hedges or taken from the clumps of half-rotten trees which he cleared away from the edges of his fields; his tenant farmers carted it into town already cut, piled it up in his woodshed as a favor to him and received his thanks in exchange. His only known expenditures were for consecrated bread, clothing for his wife and daughter, the rent on their chairs in church, lighting, Big Nanon's wages, the tinning of his pots and pans, taxes, repairs on his buildings and the operating costs of his enterprises. He owned six hundred acres of woodland, recently purchased; he had it guarded by a neighbor's gamekeeper, to whom he had promised compensation. Only after this acquisition did he begin to eat game.

Monsieur Grandet's manners were extremely simple. He spoke little. He usually expressed his thoughts in short, aphoristic sentences uttered in a soft voice. Since the Revolution, when he first began to attract attention, he had always stuttered exasperatingly whenever he had to speak for any length of time or carry on a discussion. His stammer, the incoherence of his speech, the flood of words in which he drowned his thoughts, his apparent lack of logic—these things were attributed to his lack of education, but in reality they were deliberately assumed, and they will be sufficiently explained by certain events of this story. In any case, four sentences, as exact as algebraic formulas, usually served to embrace and resolve all the difficulties of his life and his business: "I don't know," "I can't," "I won't," and "We'll see about that."

He never said yes or no, and he never put anything in writing. When someone spoke to him he listened coldly, holding his chin in his right hand with his right elbow resting on the back of his left hand, and on all matters he reached conclusions from which he never departed. He deliberated for a long time over the smallest bargain. When, after a shrewd conversation, his opponent had revealed his secret aims, he would reply to him, "I can't decide about anything until I've talked it over with my wife." His wife, whom he had reduced to a state of complete serfdom, was his most useful screen in business.

He never went to anyone else's house, not wishing either to give or receive dinner invitations. He never made any noise; he seemed to economize everything, even movement. Filled with an ingrained respect for property rights, he never disturbed other people's belongings.

Despite the softness of his voice and the circumspection of his behavior, however, the speech and manners of a cooper often came through, especially when he was at home, where he relaxed more than anywhere else.

Physically, Grandet was a square, stocky man, five feet tall, with calves twelve inches in circumference, bony knees and broad shoulders. His face was round, suntanned and pockmarked. He had an angular chin, straight lips and white teeth. His eyes had the calm, voracious expression which legend ascribes to the basilisk. His heavily lined forehead was not without significant bumps. His yellowish, graying hair was described as silver and gold by several young people who did not realize the seriousness of a joke about Monsieur Grandet. His nose, thick at the tip, bore a veined wen. The common people, not without reason, said that this wen was full of malice. His face revealed dangerous cunning, cold integrity and the selfishness of a man accustomed to concentrating his feelings in the enjoyment of avarice and on the only person who really meant anything to him: his daughter Eugénie, his sole heiress. Attitude, manners, bearing—everything about him gave evidence of that self-assurance which comes from unvarying success in all one's undertakings.

Although seemingly good-natured and tolerant, Monsieur Grandet was actually as rigid as a poker.

His way of dressing never varied: it had been exactly the same ever since 1791. His heavy shoes were tied with leather thongs. In all weather he wore woolen stockings, short breeches made of coarse brown cloth and adorned with silver buckles, a velvet vest with yellow and brownish purple stripes, buttoned straight up the front, a loose brown coat with wide tails, a black cravat and a Quaker hat. Each pair of his gloves, as heavy as a gendarme's, lasted him for twenty months. To keep them clean, he methodically laid them on the brim of his hat, always in the same place.

The people of Saumur knew nothing more about Monsieur Grandet. Only six of them had the privilege of coming into his house. The most important of the first three was Monsieur Cruchot's nephew. Ever since his appointment as presiding magistrate of the civil court of Saumur, this young man had joined the name of Bonfons to that of Cruchot, and he was working hard to make Bonfons prevail over Cruchot. He was already signing his name as C. de Bonfons. Any litigant so ill-advised as to call him Monsieur Cruchot was soon made aware of his blunder in court. The magistrate was well disposed toward those who called him Your Honor, but he bestowed his most gracious smiles on the flatterers who called him Monsieur de Bonfons. He was thirty-three years old and the owner of the Bonfons *(Boni Fontis)* estate, which gave him an income of seven thousand francs a year. He expected to inherit from his uncle, the notary, and from another uncle, Abbé Cruchot, a dignitary of the chapter of Saint-Martin de Tours, both of whom were regarded as rather rich. These three Cruchots, backed up by a goodly number of cousins and allied with a score of families in the town, formed a faction, like the Medici in Florence long ago; and, like the Medici, the Cruchots had their Pazzi

Madame des Grassins, mother of a twenty-three-year-old son, assiduously came to play cards with Madame Grandet, hoping to marry her dear Adolphe to Mademoiselle Eugénie. Monsieur des Grassins, the banker, vigorously seconded his wife's maneuvers by constantly doing secret favors for the old miser, and he always arrived on the battlefield at the right time. These three des Grassins also had their supporters, cousins and faithful allies.

In the Cruchot camp, Abbé Cruchot, the Talleyrand of the family, ably backed up by his brother the notary, fought fiercely against the banker's wife, trying to reserve the rich inheritance for his nephew the judge.

The members of every social circle in Saumur were passionately interested in this undercover struggle between the Cruchots and the des Grassins, the prize of which was Eugénie Grandet's hand. Would Mademoiselle Grandet marry the judge or Monsieur Adolphe des Grassins? To this question, some people replied that Monsieur Grandet would not give his daughter to either one of them. The former cooper, they said, was consumed with ambition and was seeking as his son-in-law some Peer of France who would be willing, in exchange for an income of three hundred thousand francs a year, to accept all the Grandet barrels, past, present and future. Other people replied that Monsieur and Madame des Grassins were noble and extremely rich, that Adolphe was an attractive suitor and that, unless Grandet had a nephew of the pope up his sleeve, such a suitable match ought to satisfy a man who had begun life with nothing at all, whom everyone in Saumur had seen with a cooper's adze in his ⸻ who, furthermore, had once worn the red

The most sensible observers pointed out that Monsieur Cruchot de Bonfons was welcome in the house at any time, whereas his rival was received only on Sundays. Their opponents claimed that Madame des Grassins was on closer terms with the women of the Grandet family than the Cruchots were, and that she could therefore instill in their minds certain ideas which would sooner or later bring about her victory. To this it was replied that Abbé Cruchot was the most ingratiating man in the world and that, with a woman opposing a monk, the contest was equal. "They're running neck and neck," said one of the wits of Saumur.

Better informed, the older inhabitants of the region maintained that the Grandets were too shrewd to let the money go outside the family and that Mademoiselle Eugénie Grandet, of Saumur, would be married to the son of Monsieur Grandet, of Paris, a rich wholesale wine merchant. To this the Cruchotists and the Grassinians replied, "First of all, the two brothers haven't seen each other twice in the last thirty years. And then Monsieur Grandet, of Paris, has ambitious plans for his son. He's the mayor of an arrondisement, a deputy, a colonel in the National Guard and a magistrate of the court of commerce. He disowns the Grandets of Saumur and hopes to make an alliance with some family given a dukedom by Napoleon."

What wasn't said about an heiress who was a subject of conversation for twenty leagues around, and even in all the stagecoaches between Angers and Blois!

Early in 1818, the Cruchotists won a signal victory over the Grassinians. The estate of Froidfond, noted for its grounds, its admirable château, its farms, rivers, ponds and forests, and worth three million francs, was put up for sale by the young Marquis de Froidfond, who was forced to raise cash. Monsieur Cruchot the

notary, Judge Cruchot and Abbé Cruchot, aided by their
supporters, succeeded in preventing the sale of the property in small lots. The notary concluded an admirable
bargain with the young marquis by persuading him that
he would have to carry on endless lawsuits against the
purchasers before he could obtain the price of the lots
from them; it would be better to sell everything to
Monsieur Grandet, who was solvent and could pay
for the estate in cash. The illustrious marquisate of
Froidfond was therefore swallowed up by Monsieur
Grandet, who, to the great astonishment of everyone
in town, paid for it immediately, after the formalities,
with a discount for cash. This transaction created a stir
as far away as Nantes and Orléans.

Monsieur Grandet went to see his château in a cart
that happened to be returning there. After casting a pro-
prietary glance at his estate, he came back to Saumur,
convinced that he had invested his money at five per
cent and aglow with the magnificent idea of rounding
out the marquisate of Froidfond by concentrating all his
property in it. Then, to replenish his treasury, which was
now nearly empty, he decided to cut down all his woods
and forests and sell the poplars in his meadows.

It is now easy to understand the full meaning of
the term "the Grandet house," that pale, cold, silent
house standing in the upper part of town, sheltered by
the ruined ramparts.

The two pillars and the vaulted arch forming the
bay of the doorway were, like the rest of the house,
made of tufa, a kind of white stone peculiar to the banks
of the Loire and so soft that it rarely lasts more than
two hundred years. The many irregular holes which had
been strangely hollowed out by the harshness of the
climate gave the arch and pillars of the bay the appearance of the vermiculated stone often used in French

architecture and also made it look something like the entrance to a jail. Above the arch there was a long bas-relief of hard stone representing the four seasons; its figures were blackened and worn. This bas-relief was surmounted by a projecting plinth on which grew a number of plants whose seeds had been sown there by chance: yellow pellitory, bindweed, convolvus, plantain and a little cherry tree that was already quite tall.

The door, made of solid oak, brown, dried out and cracked in all directions, was frail in appearance but it was actually firmly held together by a network of bolts arranged in symmetrical patterns. In the middle of the second, smaller door there was a little square grating with rusted, closely set bars. It served as a motif, so to speak, for a knocker that was attached to it by a ring and struck against the grimacing head of an enormous nail. This knocker, oblong in shape and of the kind our ancestors used to call a Jack-o'-the-clock, looked like a large exclamation point; on examining it carefully, an antiquarian would have found a few traces of the essentially comical figure it had once represented, but which was now worn away by long use.

Through the little grating, designed to enable the occupants of the house to identify friends in time of civil war, the curious could perceive, at the end of a dark, greenish vault, a few dilapidated steps leading up to a garden picturesquely enclosed by thick, damp, oozing walls overgrown with tufts of sickly shrubs. These walls were those of the ramparts, on which rose the gardens of several neighboring houses.

On the first floor of the house, the largest room was the living room, whose entrance was under the vault of the carriage gate. Few people realize the importance of a living room in the small towns of Anjou, Touraine and Berry. It serves as an antechamber, drawing room, study, boudoir and dining room, all rolled into one. It is the center of family life, the common gathering place. There, the neighborhood barber came in twice a year to cut Monsieur Grandet's hair; there, the tenant farmers, the parish priest, the sub-prefect and the miller's helper came in to carry out their various missions. This room, whose two windows faced the street, had a plank floor; gray panels with ancient moldings covered the walls from top to bottom; the exposed beams of the ceiling were also painted gray and the spaces between them were filled in with plaster which had turned yellow.

An old copper clock, inlaid with tortoise-shell arabesques, adorned the badly carved white stone mantelpiece, on which there was a greenish mirror whose edges, beveled to show its thickness, reflected a thin strip of light along its damascened steel frame. The two gilded copper candelabrá which decorated the corners of the mantelpiece served a double purpose: by removing the roses which served as sockets, the main branch could be fitted into a bluish marble pedestal partially covered with old copper, and this pedestal formed a candlestick for everyday use.

The chairs, antique in form, were upholstered in tapestries representing the fables of La Fontaine, but it was necessary to know this in order to recognize the subjects, for the colors were so faded and the figures were so riddled with darns that it was difficult to make them out. In each corner of the room were cupboards, something like buffets, above which there were dirty shelves. An old card table, whose inlaid top formed a chessboard, stood between the two windows. Over this table there was an oval barometer with a black border embellished by strips of gilded wood on which the flies had frolicked with such abandon that the gilding had become a problem.

On the wall opposite the fireplace hung two pastel portraits which were supposed to represent Madame Grandet's grandfather, old Monsieur de la Bertellière, as a lieutenant in the French Guards, and the late Madame Gentillet, dressed as a shepherdess. Both windows were draped with curtains of Tours silk, held back with tasseled silk cords. This luxurious decoration, so little in keeping with Grandet's habits, had been included in the purchase of the house, along with the mirror, the clock, the tapestried chairs and the rosewood cupboards.

In front of the window nearest to the door was a straw-bottomed chair mounted on casters in order to raise Madame Grandet to a height which enabled her to see the people passing in the street. A work table of faded cherry wood filled the window recess, and Eugénie Grandet's little armchair was placed close beside it. For the past fifteen years, mother and daughter had peacefully spent their days in this spot, from April to November. On the first of November, they could take up their winter station beside the fireplace. Only on that day did Grandet allow a fire to be lighted in the room, and he had it put out on March 31, paying no heed to the cold weather of early spring or autumn. A footwarmer, filled with glowing embers from the kitchen fire which Big Nanon skillfully saved for them, helped Madame and Mademoiselle Grandet through the chilliest mornings and evenings of April and October.

The mother and daughter kept all the household linen in repair, and they spent their days so conscientiously in this menial work that if Eugénie wanted to embroider a collar for her mother, she was forced to shorten her hours of sleep, deceiving her father to obtain light. The miser had long since established the custom of handing out candles to his daughter and

Big Nanon, just as every morning he handed out the bread and provisions for the day's consumption.

Big Nanon was perhaps the only human being capable of accepting her master's tyranny. Everyone in town envied the Grandets for having her in their service. Big Nanon, so called because she was five feet eight inches tall, had been employed by Grandet for the past thirty-five years. Although her wages were only sixty francs a year, she was regarded as one of the richest servants in Saumur. Those sixty francs, piled up over a period of thirty-five years, had recently enabled her to invest four thousand francs in a lifetime annuity with Monsieur Cruchot. This fruit of her long and persistent thrift seemed enormous. Every other servant in town, seeing a poor woman in her sixties with an assured income for her old age, was jealous of her because of it, without considering the harsh servitude by which it had been acquired.

At the age of twenty-two, the poor girl had been unable to find a position anywhere because her face seemed so repulsive, although this feeling was quite unjust: her face would have been greatly admired on the shoulders of a grenadier of the Guards, but most people feel that there is a proper place for everything. She had worked on a farm, keeping the cows, but she was forced to leave it when it was ruined by fire. She came to Saumur to seek work as a servant, animated by that robust courage which stops at nothing.

Monsieur Grandet was then thinking of getting married and wanted to set up his household as soon as possible. His attention was caught by this girl, who was being turned away from one house after another. As a cooper, he was a good judge of physical strength, and he realized the advantages to be derived from a female built like a Hercules, planted on her feet like a sixty-year-old oak on its roots, with strong hips, a square back, hands like a wagon driver and an integrity as stalwart as her unstained virtue. He was not dismayed by the warts that adorned her martial face, her brick-red complexion, her muscular arms or her rags, even though he was still at an age when the heart constantly quivers. He clothed, shod and fed the poor girl, paid her wages and put her to work without treating her too harshly.

On seeing herself given this kind of reception, Big Nanon secretly wept for joy and became sincerely attached to the cooper, despite the feudal manner in which he exploited her. Nanon did everything: she did the cooking and heavy washing, she went off to wash the household linen in the Loire and carried it back on her shoulders, she got up at dawn and went to bed late, she prepared food for all the grape pickers during the harvest and kept an eye on the gleaners, she defended her master's property like a faithful watchdog, and finally, filled with blind confidence in him, she obeyed his most outlandish whims without a murmur.

In the famous year of 1811, when the harvest was incredibly laborious, Grandet decided to give his old watch to Nanon after twenty years of service. It was the only present she had ever received from him. Although he let her have his old shoes (they fitted her), this quarterly dividend of shoes cannot be regarded as a present because they were nearly worn out when she received them.

Necessity made the poor girl so miserly that Grandet finally came to love her as one loves a dog, and she let him put around her neck a spiked collar whose pricks she no longer felt. If he cut the bread a little too parsimoniously, she did not complain; she cheerfully shared in the hygienic advantages resulting from the austere diet of the household, in which no one was ever ill. And then Nanon was part of the family: she laughed when Grandet laughed, reflected his sadness and shivered from cold, warmed herself and worked with him. How many sweet compensations there were in that equality! Never had the master reproached the servant for the apricots, peaches, plums or nectarines eaten beneath the tree. "Go on, enjoy yourself, Nanon!" he would say to her in years when the branches were so heavy with fruit that the farmers had to feed it to the pigs.

For a country girl who, in her youth, had reaped nothing but harsh treatment, for a pauper charitably given a home, Old Man Grandet's equivocal laugh was a genuine ray of sunshine. Furthermore, Nanon's simple heart and narrow head could contain only one feeling and one idea. After thirty-five years with Grandet, she still saw herself arriving ragged and barefoot in his workshop; she could still hear the cooper saying to her, "What can I do for you, my dear?" and her gratitude was still young.

Sometimes Grandet would reflect that this poor creature had never heard the slightest word of flattery, that she knew nothing of all the tender feelings aroused by a woman, and that she could appear before God more chaste than the Virgin Mary herself. When these thoughts occurred to him, Grandet, seized with pity, would look at her and say, "Poor Nanon!" His exclamation was always followed by an indefinable glance from the old servant. These two words, repeated now and then, had for a long time formed an unbroken chain of friendship to which each exclamation added another link. There was something vaguely horrible about this pity, lodged in Grandet's heart and gratefully accepted by the old maid. This abominable miserly pity, which awakened countless pleasures in the old cooper's heart, was for Nanon the sum of all her happiness. Who wouldn't say "Poor Nanon!" God will recognize his angels by the inflection of their voices and by their mysterious sorrows.

There were in Saumur many households in which the servants were better treated, but in which the masters nevertheless received no satisfaction. Hence another common remark: "What do the Grandets do for their Big Nanon to make her so attached to them? She'd go through fire and brimstone for them!"

Her kitchen, whose barred windows faced the courtyard, was always clean, neat and cold, a real miser's kitchen in which nothing must be wasted. When she had washed the dishes, locked up the leftovers from dinner and put out her fire, she left her kitchen, which was separated from the living room by a hall, and went in to spin hemp beside her employers. The whole family got along with one candle for the evening. Nanon slept at the end of the hall in a little room lighted only by a barred window. Her robust health enabled her to live with impunity in that wretched hole, from which she could hear any sound that broke the deep silence which reigned in the house night and day. Like a watchdog, she was expected to sleep with one eye open, resting and keeping watch over the house at the same time.

The other parts of the house will be described when they become relevant to our narrative; but the sketch we have given of the living room, in which all the luxury of the household was displayed, may lead the reader to anticipate the barrenness of the upper stories.

Early one evening in the middle of November, 1819, Big Nanon lit the fire for the first time. The autumn had been mild. This particular day was a festive occasion well known to the Cruchotists and the Grassinians, so the six antagonists were preparing to come, fully equipped for battle, to Grandet's living room, where they would try to outdo one another in displays of friendship. That morning, everyone in Saumur had seen Madame and Mademoiselle Grandet, accompanied by Nanon, going to mass in the parish church, and everyone knew it was Mademoiselle Eugénie's birthday. Therefore, having calculated the hour when dinner would be over, Monsieur Cruchot, Abbé Cruchot and Monsieur C. de Bonfons were hurrying to arrive before the des Grassins to extend their best wishes to Mademoiselle Grandet. All three of them carried enormous bouquets they had picked in their little greenhouses. The stems of the flowers which the judge intended to present to her were ingeniously tied with a white satin ribbon with gold fringe.

That morning Grandet, in accordance with his custom on the memorable occasions of Eugénie's birthday and name day, had come to surprise her in her bed and solemnly handed her his paternal gift, consisting, as it had for the past thirteen years, of an unusual gold coin. Madame Grandet usually gave her daughter either a summer or a winter dress, depending on the season. These two dresses, plus the gold coins she acquired on New Year's Day and her father's name day, constituted a small income of about three hundred francs, which Grandet liked to see her accumulate. Was it not simply transferring his money from one strongbox to another and nourishing, so to speak, the avarice of his heiress? He occasionally asked her to give him an account of her savings, to which the la Bertellières had formerly contributed. "That will be your marriage dozen," he would remark.

The marriage dozen is an ancient custom which is still widespread and religiously preserved in several regions of central France. In Berry or Anjou, when a girl marries, her family or that of her husband must give her a purse containing, according to their means, a dozen, twelve dozen or twelve hundred gold or silver coins. The poorest shepherdess would not get married without her dozen, even if it is composed only of copper coins. In Issoudun, people still talk about a dozen consisting of a hundred and forty-four Portuguese gold pieces, which was given to a certain rich heiress. Pope Clement VII, uncle of Catherine de Medici, gave her a dozen ancient gold medals of great value, when she married Henri II.

During dinner Grandet, overjoyed to see his Eugénie more beautiful than ever in her new dress, cried out, "Since it's Eugénie's birthday, let's light a fire! It will bring good luck."

"Mademoiselle will be married before her next birthday, I'm sure of it!" said Big Nanon, carrying away the remains of a goose, the cooper's pheasant.

"I don't see anyone suitable for her in Saumur," said Madame Grandet, looking at her husband with a timid expression which, considering her age, revealed the complete conjugal servitude under which the poor woman suffered.

Grandet contemplated his daughter and said gaily, "The girl is twenty-three today—we'll have to arrange something for her before long!"

Eugénie and her mother silently exchanged a significant glance.

Madame Grandet was a thin, dried-out woman, yellow as a quince, awkward and slow, one of those women who seem born to be tyrannized. She had big bones, a big nose, a big forehead and big eyes. At first sight she reminded one of those spongy fruits which have lost their juice and their flavor. Her teeth were black and few, her mouth was wrinkled and she had a protruding chin. She was a good woman, a true la Bertellière. Abbé Cruchot managed to find occasional opportunities to tell her that she had once been rather attractive, and she believed him. An angelic sweetness, the resignation of an insect tormented by children, a rare piety, an unfailing equanimity and a kind heart made her universally pitied and respected.

Her husband never gave her more than six francs at a time for her minor expenses. Although ridiculous in appearance, this woman who, by her dowry and her inheritances, had given Monsieur Grandet more than three hundred thousand francs, had always felt so deeply humiliated by her dependency and the serfdom against which the gentleness of her soul forbade her to revolt that she had never asked for a single sou or made any comment on the documents which Monsieur Cruchot presented for her signature. Her conduct was dominated by her foolish secret pride and by her nobility of soul, which Grandet constantly ignored and wounded.

Madame Grandet invariably wore a dress of greenish levantine silk; she had become accustomed to making each one of them last for an entire year. She also wore a large white cotton shawl and a straw hat, and usually a black taffeta apron. Since she seldom left the house, she did not wear out many shoes. She never wanted anything for herself. Grandet, who was sometimes seized with remorse when he remembered how long it had been since the last time he had given his wife six francs, always demanded a small extra sum for her when he sold the year's harvest. The four or five louis presented by the Dutchman or the Belgian who bought the Grandet vintage formed the major part of her yearly income. But after she had received her five louis, her husband often said to her, as though their funds were held in common, "Can you lend me a few sous?" And the poor woman, happy to be able to do something for a man whom her confessor represented to her as her lord and master, always gave him back, in the course of the winter, a considerable part of her income.

When Grandet took from his pocket the five-franc coin he allotted to his daughter each month for her incidental expenses—needles, thread and toilet articles—he never failed to say to his wife, after buttoning his vest pocket, "And what about you, mother? Do you need anything?"

"We'll see about that later, my dear," Madame Grandet would reply, animated by a sense of maternal dignity.

What a waste of noble sentiment! Grandet considered himself extremely generous to his wife. When philosophers come across people like Nanon, Madame Grandet and Eugénie, are they not justified in concluding that Providence is basically ironical?

After this dinner, during which the question of Eugénie's marriage was mentioned for the first time, Nanon went to get a bottle of black currant brandy from Monsieur Grandet's bedroom and almost fell down the stairs on her way back.

"Clumsy fool!" said her master. "Are you going to start falling down the stairs too?"

"Monsieur, it's because of that loose step on your staircase."

"She's right," said Madame Grandet. "You should have had it repaired long ago. Eugénie almost sprained her ankle on it yesterday."

"Well," said Grandet to Nanon, seeing that she had turned pale, "since it's Eugénie's birthday, and since you almost fell down the stairs, you can have a little glass of brandy to make you feel better."

"I've certainly earned it!" said Nanon. "A lot of people would have broken the bottle if they'd been in my place, but I'd have broken my elbow to save it if I'd had to."

"Poor Nanon!" said Grandet, pouring a glass of brandy for her.

"Did you hurt yourself?" asked Eugénie, looking at her with concern.

"No, I broke my fall by leaning backward."

"Well, since it's Eugénie's birthday," said Grandet, "I'll fix your step for you. You women never remember to put your foot on the corner where it's still solid."

He took the candle, leaving his wife, his daughter and his servant with no light other than that of the brightly burning fire, and went off to get boards, nails and his tools.

"Do you need any help?" Nanon called out to him when she heard him hammering on the staircase.

"No, no—I'm an old hand at this!" replied the former cooper.

Just as Grandet was personally repairing the dilapidated staircase, whistling at the top of his lungs as he remembered the days of his youth, the three Cruchots knocked on the door.

"Is that you, Monsieur Cruchot?" asked Nanon, peering through the little grating.

"Yes," replied the judge.

Nanon opened the door, and the light of the fire, reflected under the arch of the doorway, enabled the three Cruchots to see the entrance to the living room.

"Ah, I see you're celebrating tonight!" said Nanon, smelling the flowers.

"Excuse me, gentlemen," shouted Grandet, recognizing the voices of his friends, "I'll be with you in a minute! I'm not uppity—I'm patching up my staircase myself."

"Go right ahead, Monsieur Grandet; a man's home is his castle," said the judge sententiously, laughing to himself at this allusion which no one else understood.

Madame and Mademoiselle Grandet stood up. The judge, taking advantage of the darkness, said to Eugénie, "Allow me, mademoiselle, on the occasion of your birthday, to wish you a long series of happy years and a continuation of the good health you now enjoy."

He presented her with a bouquet of flowers that were rare in Saumur, then, taking her by the elbows, he kissed her on both sides of the neck with a self-assurance that embarrassed her. The judge, who looked like a large rusty nail, felt that this was the way to woo her.

"Don't mind me," said Grandet, coming back into the living room. "You really let yourself go on holidays, judge!"

"But with mademoiselle," replied Abbé Cruchot, armed with his bouquet, "every day would be a holiday for my nephew." He then kissed Eugénie's hand. As for Monsieur Cruchot the notary, he straightforwardly kissed her on both cheeks and said, "How quickly they grow up! Twelve months in every year!"

As he put back the candle in front of the clock on the mantelpiece, Grandet, who never let go of a joke and repeated it over and over again when it seemed amusing to him, said, "Since it's Eugénie's birthday, let's light up the candelabra!" He carefully removed their branches, put a socket on each pedestal, took from Nanon a new candle wrapped in paper, placed it in the socket, tested it to make sure it was firmly in place, lit it and came back to sit down beside his wife, looking in turn at his friends, his daughter and the two candles.

Abbé Cruchot, a round, chubby little man with a flat red wig and the face of a playful old woman, stretched out his feet, which were well shod in heavy shoes with silver buckles, and said, "The des Grassins haven't come yet?"

"Not yet," said Grandet.

"They are coming, though, aren't they?" asked the old notary, screwing up his face, which was as full of holes as a skimming ladle.

"I think so," replied Madame Grandet.

"Are your grapes all picked now?" Judge de Bonfons asked Grandet.

"Yes, everywhere!" said the old winegrower, standing up to pace up and down the room and throwing out his chest in a gesture as proud as the word he had just spoken: "Everywhere!"

Through the door of the hall leading to the kitchen, he saw Big Nanon sitting in front of her fire with a candle, preparing to spin there in order not to intrude on the celebration. "Nanon," he said, stepping into the hall, "will you please put out your fire and your candle and come in with us? Good heavens, the living room is big enough for all of us!"

"But monsieur, you have guests . . ."

"Aren't you just as good as they are? They all come from Adam's rib, the same as you."

Grandet came back to the judge and asked him, "Have you sold your harvest yet?"

"No, I'm hanging on to it! If the wine is good now, it will be even better two years from now. As you know, the winegrowers have sworn to keep up the prices they've agreed on, and this year the Belgians won't get the best of us. If they go away, let them go— they'll be back!"

"Yes, but let's not do anything rash," said Grandet in a tone that made the judge shudder.

"Could he be making a deal with them?" wondered Cruchot.

Just then a knock on the door announced the des Grassins family, and their arrival interrupted a conversation begun between Madame Grandet and Abbé Cruchot.

Madame des Grassins was one of those plump, lively, pink and white little women who, thanks to the monastic routine of the provinces and the habits of a virtuous life, are still young at forty. They are like those last roses of autumn which are pleasant to look at, but whose petals have something cold about them and whose perfume is growing weak. She dressed rather well, having her clothes sent from Paris; she set the fashion in Saumur and gave parties.

Her husband, a former quartermaster in the Imperial Guards who had been seriously wounded at Austerlitz and was now retired, still had, in spite of his deference to Grandet, the apparent frankness of a soldier.

"Hello, Grandet," he said to the winegrower, holding out his hand to him and assuming the air of superiority with which he always crushed the Cruchots. "Mademoiselle," he said to Eugénie after greeting Madame Grandet, "you're still as beautiful and wise as ever, so I really don't know what more I can wish you." Then he presented her with a little box which his servant had brought and which contained heather from the Cape, a flower only recently introduced into Europe and still quite rare.

Madame des Grassins embraced Eugénie very affectionately, squeezed her hand and said to her, "Adolphe has asked me to let him give you my little present."

A tall, blond young man, pale and delicate-looking, with rather good manners, who seemed timid, but had just spent nine or ten thousand francs over and above the cost of his food and lodging in Paris, where he had gone to study law, stepped up to Eugénie, kissed her on both cheeks and handed her a sewing box in which all the implements were of silver gilt. It was a shoddy piece of merchandise in spite of the shield on which the initials E.G., rather well engraved in Gothic letters, might have given some people an impression of careful workmanship.

As she opened it, Eugénie felt one of those surges of perfect, unexpected delight which make a young girl blush, start and quiver with pleasure. She looked at her father, as though asking him if he would allow her to accept the gift. He said, "Take it, daughter!" in a tone that would have done credit to an actor.

The three Cruchots were dumbfounded when they saw the happy, excited glance which the heiress cast at Adolphe des Grassins. Such opulence seemed incredible to her. Monsieur des Grassins offered Grandet a pinch of snuff, took one himself, brushed off the grains which had fallen on the ribbon of the Legion of Honor attached to the buttonhole of his blue coat, then looked at the Cruchots with an expression that seemed to say, "Let's see you parry that thrust!"

Madame des Grassins glanced at the blue jars containing the bouquets brought by the Cruchots, seeking out their presents with the simulated good faith of a sarcastic woman. At this delicate juncture, Abbé Cruchot let the company sit down in a circle in front of the fire and walked off to the other end of the room with Grandet. When the two old men were in the window recess farthest away from the des Grassins, the priest said in the miser's ear, "Those people throw money out the window!"

"What's wrong with that if it falls into my cellar?" retorted the old winegrower.

"If you wanted to give your daughter a pair of gold scissors, you could afford it," said the priest.

"I've given her something better than scissors," replied Grandet.

"My nephew's an idiot," thought the priest, looking at the judge, whose tousled hair made his swarthy face still less attractive. "Why couldn't he think of some little bagatelle that would have made a good impression?"

"Shall we have a game of cards, Madame Grandet?" asked Madame des Grassins.

"Now that we're all together, we could have two tables . . ."

"Since it's Eugénie's birthday, why don't you all play lotto?" said Grandet. "The two children can join in." The former cooper, who never played games of any kind, pointed to his daughter and Adolphe. "Go ahead, Nanon, set up the tables."

"We'll help you, Mademoiselle Nanon," said Madame des Grassins gaily, delighted at the pleasure she had given Eugénie.

"I've never been so happy in my life!" the heiress said to her. "I've never seen anything so pretty anywhere!"

"It was Adolphe who picked it out and brought it back from Paris," Madame des Grassins whispered in her ear.

"Go right ahead, you damned schemer!" thought the judge. "If you or your husband ever have a lawsuit, you'll have a hard time winning it!"

The notary, sitting in a corner, looked at the priest calmly and thought, "No matter what the des Grassins do, the fact remains that my fortune, my brother's and my nephew's add up to a million one hundred thousand francs. The des Grassins have only half that much, at the very most, and they have a daughter, too! Let them give all the birthday presents they like—they'll all belong to us some day, along with the heiress!"

At half-past eight the tables were set up. The pretty Madame des Grassins had succeeded in placing her son beside Eugénie. The actors in this scene, which was apparently commonplace but actually extremely interesting, took up their multicolored numbered cards and blue glass chips. They seemed to be listening to the witticisms of the old notary, who never drew a number without making a remark, but in reality they were all thinking of Monsieur Grandet's millions.

The old cooper looked smugly at Madame des Grassins' pink feathers and immaculate clothes, at the banker's martial countenance, at Adolphe, the judge, the priest and the notary, and said to himself, "They're all after my money. They keep coming here, in spite of their boredom, because they want my daughter. Well, neither family will ever have her! I'm using all these people as harpoons to fish with!"

This family gaiety in the old gray room, dimly lighted by two candles, this laughter, accompanied by the sound of Big Nanon's spinning wheel and sincere only on the lips of Eugénie or her mother, this pettiness in connection with such high hopes, this young girl who, like those birds which are the unwitting victims of the high price put on them, was being hunted down and hemmed in by hypocritical demonstrations of friendship which deceived her—everything combined to give the scene a kind of ludicrous sadness. And was it not a scene common to all times and all places, but reduced to its simplest terms? Grandet's face, as he exploited the two families' false devotion and turned it to his own advantage, dominated the scene and made its meaning clear. Was it not all the power of Money, the only modern god that is truly worshiped, expressed in a single countenance?

The softer sentiments of life occupied only a secondary place here. They animated three pure hearts: those of Nanon, Eugénie and her mother. And even so, how much ignorance there was in their naïveté! Eugénie and her mother knew nothing of Grandet's fortune; they judged the things of this world only by the light of their own pale ideas, and they neither valued nor despised money, accustomed as they were to doing without it. Their emotions, frustrated without their knowledge yet still very much alive, and the isolation of their existence made them curious exceptions in this gathering of people whose lives were entirely materialistic. How terrible is man's condition! There is not one of his joys which is not based on some form of ignorance.

Just after Madame Grandet had won sixteen sous, the largest amount that had ever been bet in that living room, and while Big Nanon was still laughing delightedly to see her mistress pocketing this impressive sum, there was such a loud knock on the door that the women all started in their chairs.

"No one from Saumur would ever knock like that," said the notary.

"Why should anyone bang that way!" said Nanon. "Are they trying to break down our door?"

"Who the devil can it be?" exclaimed Grandet.

Nanon took one of the two candles and went toward the door, accompanied by Grandet.

"Grandet! Grandet!" cried his wife. Impelled by a vague feeling of alarm, she rushed to the door of the living room.

All the players looked at each other.

"Why don't we go too?" said Monsieur des Grassins. "There was something sinister about that knock."

Monsieur des Grassins scarcely had time to glimpse the face of a young man accompanied by the stage-coach porter, who was carrying two enormous boxes and dragging several traveling bags. Grandet turned brusquely to his wife and said, "Madame Grandet, go back to your lotto and let me talk to this gentleman." Then he quickly closed the door of the living room. The agitated players went back to their places, but they did not resume their game.

"Is it someone from Saumur, Monsieur des Grassins?" asked Madame des Grassins.

"No, he's a traveler."

"He could only have come from Paris."

"That's true," said the notary, taking out his old watch, which was as thick as two fingers and looked like a Dutch ship. "It's nine o'clock. No sir, the mail coach is never late!"

"Is it a young gentleman?" asked Abbé Cruchot.

"Yes," replied Monsieur des Grassins. "And he has baggage with him that must weigh at least six hundred pounds."

"Nanon hasn't come back yet," said Eugénie.

"It must be one of your relatives," said the judge.

"Let's place our bets," said Madame Grandet gently. "I could tell from Monsieur Grandet's voice that he was annoyed; perhaps he won't like it if he hears us talking about his affairs."

"Mademoiselle," said Adolphe to Eugénie, who was sitting beside him, "it's no doubt your cousin Grandet, a very handsome young man whom I saw at Monsieur de Nucingen's ball."

Adolphe stopped short: his mother had just stepped on his foot. Then, after she had asked him aloud to give her two sous for her bet, she whispered in his ear, "Shut up, you idiot!"

Just then Grandet came in without Big Nanon, whose footsteps, and those of the porter, could be heard on the stairs. He was followed by the traveler, who for the past few moments had aroused such curiosity and occupied everyone's imagination so intensely that his arrival in that house and his descent into the midst of that gathering might be compared to that of a snail in a beehive, or the introduction of a peacock into some obscure village barnyard.

"Sit down by the fire," Grandet said to him.

Before sitting down, the young stranger bowed very graciously to the assembled company. The men stood up to reply with a polite inclination and the ladies curtsied ceremoniously.

"You must be cold, monsieur," said Madame Grandet. "You've perhaps come from . . ."

"Just like a woman!" said the old winegrower, interrupting his perusal of a letter he was holding in his hand. "Let the young man rest a little!"

"But father," said Eugénie, "perhaps the gentleman needs something."

"He has a tongue," replied the winegrower sternly.

Only the stranger was surprised at this scene. The others were used to the old man's despotic ways. However, after the two women's remarks had been greeted with these replies, the stranger stood up, turned his back to the fire, raised one of his feet to warm the sole of his boot and said to Eugénie. "Thank you, cousin, but I had dinner at Tours. And," he added, looking at Grandet, "I don't need anything; I'm not even tired."

"Have you come from the capital, monsieur?" asked Madame des Grassins.

On hearing her address him, Charles Grandet, the son of Monsieur Grandet of Paris, picked up a monocle hanging from his neck by a chain and raised it to his right eye to examine the objects on the table and the people seated around it, stared most impertinently at Madame des Grassins and said to her, after he had seen everything, "Yes, madame. . . . I see you're playing lotto, aunt," he added. "Please go on with your game; it's too amusing to stop."

"I was sure he was the cousin," thought Madame des Grassins, glancing at him quickly from time to time.

"Forty-seven!" cried the old priest. "Mark it down, Madame des Grassins—isn't that your number?"

Monsieur des Grassins placed a chip on his wife's card while, filled with gloomy forebodings, she alternately studied the cousin from Paris and Eugénie, with no thought of lotto. The young heiress occasionally cast a furtive glance at her cousin, and the banker's wife could easily detect in her a rising tide of surprise or curiosity.

II

The Cousin from Paris

Monsieur Charles Grandet, a handsome young man of twenty-two, presented at that moment a strange contrast with the worthy provincials who, already rather deeply offended by his aristocratic manners, were all studying him in order to ridicule him. This requires an explanation.

At the age of twenty-two, young men are still close enough to childhood to lapse into childish behavior. Ninety-nine out of a hundred of them, perhaps, would therefore have behaved as Charles Grandet did. A few days before that evening, his father had told him to go and spend a few months with his uncle in Saumur. Perhaps Monsieur Grandet, of Paris, was thinking of Eugénie. Charles, who had just ventured into the provinces for the first time in his life, had decided to appear there with the superiority of a young man of fashion, to overawe the entire district with his opulence, to make his visit a memorable event and to import the refinements of Paris life. In short, he intended to spend more time polishing his nails in Saumur than he had ever done in Paris, and to affect that excessive care in dress which an elegant young man sometimes discards in favor of a casualness which is not without charm.

Charles therefore brought with him the handsomest hunting costume, the handsomest gun, the handsomest hunting knife and the handsomest sheath in Paris. He brought his collection of fancy vests: there were gray, white, black and scarab-colored ones; some contained glints of gold, some were spangled and others were mottled; there were double-breasted and single-breasted ones; some had rolled collars and some were buttoned all the way up with gold buttons. He brought every kind of collar and cravat in favor at that time. He brought two suits made by Buisson and his finest linen. He brought his magnificent set of gold toilet articles, a present from his mother. He brought all his elegant trinkets, including a beautiful little inkstand given to him by the most charming lady in the world, at least in his opinion, a great lady whom he called Annette, and who was now taking a conjugal, boring trip to Scotland, the victim of a few suspicions to which she had been forced to sacrifice her happiness temporarily; and he brought a great deal of attractive stationery on which to write her a letter every two weeks. He brought, in short, as complete a cargo of Parisian baubles as one could possibly assemble; from the riding crop used to provoke a duel to the beautifully chased pistols used to finish it, there were all the implements with which a young idler cultivates his life.

Since his father had told him to travel alone and modestly, he had come in a brougham reserved entirely for himself, pleased at not having been forced to ruin a magnificent traveling carriage which he had ordered so that he could go to meet his Annette, the great lady who . . . etc., and whom he was to join at Baden-Baden in June.

Charles expected to meet dozens of people in his uncle's house, to go hunting in his uncle's forests; in other words, to lead the kind of life one leads in a château. At first it had not occurred to him to try to find his uncle in Saumur, where he had merely asked the way to Froidfond; but when he learned that he was in town, he assumed that he would find him in a great mansion. In order to make a proper first impression in his uncle's house, whether in Saumur or Froidfond, he had put on his most attractive traveling clothes; they were elegant yet simple, truly "adorable," to use the word which, at that time, epitomized the particular perfection of any person or thing. He had just had a hairdresser in Tours recurl his handsome light brown hair; he had put on fresh linen and a black satin cravat, combined with a round collar to enhance the charm of his fair, smiling face. A traveling coat, half unbuttoned, fitted tightly around his waist and revealed a double-breasted cashmere vest, beneath which there was a second white vest. His watch, casually dropped into a pocket, was attached to one of his buttonholes by a short gold chain. His gray trousers were buttoned on the sides, and their seams were embellished with patterns in black silk embroidery. He gracefully handled a cane whose chased gold knob did not mar the freshness of his gray gloves. Finally, his cap was in excellent taste.

Only a Parisian, and a Parisian of the most exalted sphere, could array himself in this manner without appearing ridiculous, and at the same time give a certain foppish harmony to all that frippery, which, in this case, was backed up with an air of gallant courage, the air of a young man who has a brace of fine pistols, good aim, and Annette.

Now, if you wish to understand fully the mutual surprise of the Saumurians and the young Parisian, if you wish to visualize clearly the bright gleam which the stranger's elegance cast in the midst of the gray shadows of the living room and the faces which composed the domestic scene, try to picture the Cruchots to yourself. All three of them took snuff, and they had long since given up all effort to avoid the nose drippings and little black specks which dotted the fronts of their reddish-brown shirts, with their rumpled collars and yellowish pleats. Their soft cravats twisted into ropes as soon as they tied them around their necks. The enormous quantity of linen they owned enabled them to have it washed only twice a year and keep it piled up in the bottom of their dressers; it also enabled time to impregnate it with its gray, dingy hues. Inelegance and senility had achieved perfect harmony in these men. Their faces, as faded as their shabby clothes, as wrinkled as their trousers, seemed worn, callous and contorted.

The general negligence of the other costumes, all of which lacked finish and freshness, as is usual in the provinces, where people gradually cease dressing to please one another and begin to pay serious attention to the price of a pair of gloves, was in keeping with the slovenliness of the Cruchots. Contempt for fashion was the only point on which the Grassinians and the Cruchotists were in perfect agreement. Whenever the Parisian picked up his monocle to examine the singular furnishings of the room, the beams of the ceiling, the color of the woodwork or the dots which the flies had printed on it in sufficient number to punctuate the *Encyclopédie Méthodique* and the *Moniteur,* the lotto players immediately looked up and stared at him with as much curiosity as they would have shown for a giraffe. Monsieur des Grassins and his son, though not unfamiliar with the appearance of a man of the world, nevertheless shared the astonishment of those around them, whether because they felt the indefinable influence of a general emotion or because they seconded it by casting sarcastic glances which seemed to say, "That's what they're like in Paris!" Everyone, moreover, was able to observe Charles at leisure, without fear of displeasing the master of the house. Grandet was engrossed in the long letter he was holding, and to read it he had taken the only candle on the table, without consideration for his guests or their pleasure.

Eugénie, to whom such perfection of dress or person was entirely unknown, felt as though she were seeing in her cousin a creature descended from some celestial realm. She inhaled with delight the fragrance given off by that glossy hair so gracefully curled. She would have liked to touch the satiny leather of those fine gloves. She envied Charles for his small hands, his complexion, the freshness and delicacy of his features. In short—if it is possible to sum up in such a comparison the impressions which the elegant young man produced on an ignorant girl who was constantly occupied in mending stockings and patching up her father's wardrobe, and whose life had been spent beneath that dirty ceiling without seeing more than one person an hour pass by in the silent street—the sight of her cousin filled her with a feeling of delicate sensual pleasure like that aroused in a young man by the fanciful figures of women drawn by Westall in English albums and so deftly engraved by Finden that one scarcely dares to breathe on the paper, for fear of blowing away those celestial apparitions.

Charles took from his pocket a handkerchief embroidered by the great lady who was traveling in Scotland. When she saw this beautiful handiwork,

which had been made with love during hours lost to love,
Eugénie looked at her cousin to see if he was really going
to use it. His manners, his gestures, the way he picked up
his monocle, his affected impertinence, his contempt for
the sewing box which had just given such pleasure to the
rich heiress and which he obviously regarded as either
worthless or ridiculous—in short, everything about him
that offended the Cruchots and the des Grassins—filled
her with such delight that before going to sleep she had
to spend a long time dreaming about this paragon of
cousins.

The numbers were drawn very slowly, but the lotto
game soon ended. Big Nanon came in and said loudly,
"Madame, I'll have to have some sheets to make this
gentleman's bed with." Madame Grandet went out with
Nanon. Madame des Grassins then said softly, "Let's
keep our money and stop playing." Each player took
his two sous from the old chipped saucer in which he
had placed them; then the entire company, moving in
a body, wheeled around to face the fire.

"Is the game over?" asked Grandet, without looking up from his letter.

"Yes, yes," replied Madame des Grassins, going
over to sit down beside Charles.

Eugénie, moved by one of those impulses which
spring up in the heart of a young girl when a feeling has
lodged itself there for the first time, left the living room
to go and help her mother and Nanon. If she had been
questioned by a shrewd confessor, she would no doubt
have admitted to him that she was thinking of neither
her mother nor Nanon, but that she was agitated by a
keen desire to inspect her cousin's bedroom in the hope
that she might be able to do something for him, place
something there for him, remedy an oversight, provide
for everything in order to make the room as elegant and

comfortable as possible. She already regarded herself as the only one capable of understanding her cousin's tastes and ideas.

She arrived just in time to demonstrate to her mother and Nanon, who were coming back thinking that they had done everything, that everything still had to be done. She gave Big Nanon the idea of warming the sheets with embers from the fire; she herself covered the old table with a clean cloth and told Nanon she must be sure to change it every morning. She convinced her mother of the necessity of making a good fire in the fireplace and persuaded Nanon to bring up a large pile of firewood and leave it in the hall, without saying anything to her father. She hurried downstairs to take from one of the corner cupboards in the living room an old lacquered tray inherited from the late Monsieur de la Bertellière; she also took a hexagonal crystal goblet, a small decorated spoon and an ancient flask engraved with cupids. She then triumphantly placed all these things on one corner of the mantelpiece. More ideas had thronged into her mind in the past quarter of an hour than had ever occurred to her before in her life.

"Mama," she said, "my cousin will never be able to stand the smell of a tallow candle—why don't we buy some wax ones?" And, light as a bird, she went off to take from her purse the five-franc coin she had received for her monthly expenses. "Here, take this, Nanon," she said. "And hurry!"

"But what will your father say?" This terrible objection was put forward by Madame Grandet when she saw her daughter holding a sugar bowl of old Sèvres china which Grandet had brought back from Froidfond. "And where will you get the sugar?" she added. "Have you lost your mind?"

"Nanon can buy some sugar when she buys the wax candles, mama."

"But what about your father?"

"Would he want his nephew not even to be able to drink a glass of sugared water? And besides, he won't even notice."

"Your father sees everything," said Madame Grandet, shaking her head.

Nanon hesitated; she knew her master.

"Go on, Nanon—since it's my birthday!"

Nanon let out a loud laugh on hearing the first joke her young mistress had ever made, and she obeyed her.

While Eugénie and her mother were doing their best to embellish the bedroom which Monsieur Grandet had assigned to his nephew, Charles found himself the object of the attentions of Madame des Grassins, who was flirting with him.

"You're very brave, monsieur," she said to him, "to leave the pleasures of the capital in winter and come to live in Saumur. But if we don't frighten you too much, you'll see that people can enjoy themselves here too." And she gave him one of those flirtatious glances which one sees only in the provinces, where, out of habit, the women express so much coyness and prudence in their eyes that they radiate the dainty concupiscence peculiar to those ecclesiastics who regard any pleasure as either a deliberate theft or an unintentional lapse from virtue.

Charles felt so disoriented in that living room, so far away from the spacious château and luxurious existence he had attributed to his uncle, that in looking attentively at Madame des Grassins he finally began to see in her a faint resemblance to some of the faces he had left behind in Paris. He responded graciously to the tacit invitation that was being extended to him and there naturally followed a conversation in which Madame des Grassins gradually lowered her voice to bring it into harmony with the intimate nature of the things she was saying. She and Charles both felt a need to confide in someone; therefore, after a few moments of coquettish chatter and half-serious pleasantries, the adroit provincial was able to say to him, without fear of being overheard by the other people in the room, who were discussing the sale of wines, a subject with which everyone in Saumur was preoccupied at that time:

"Monsieur, if you'll do us the honor of coming to see us, I'm sure my husband will be as delighted as I am. Our drawing room is the only one in Saumur where you'll find both the nobility and the most important businessmen. We belong to both groups. Our house is the only place where they're willing to meet with each other, because they enjoy themselves there. My husband, I'm proud to say, is equally respected by both classes. So we'll try to relieve some of the boredom of your stay here. If you spent all your time in Monsieur Grandet's house, what would become of you? Your uncle is an old miser who thinks of nothing except his vines, your aunt is a pious soul who's incapable of putting two ideas together, and your cousin is an uneducated, commonplace little fool who has no dowry and spends all her time mending dishrags."

"She's not bad, this woman," thought Charles Grandet as he replied to Madame des Grassins' simpering advances.

"It seems to me, my dear, that you're trying to monopolize this young man," said the fat, self-important banker, laughing.

On hearing these words, the notary and the judge exchanged a few more or less malicious remarks; but the priest looked at them knowingly and summed up their thoughts as he took a pinch of snuff and passed his snuffbox around: "Who could give the young man a better welcome to Saumur than Madame des Grassins?"

"Just what do you mean by that, Abbé?" asked Monsieur des Grassins.

"I mean it, monsieur, in the best possible sense for you, for your wife, for the town of Saumur . . . and for this gentleman," added the wily old man, turning to Charles.

Without seeming to pay the slightest attention to them, Abbé Cruchot had managed to guess the nature of the conversation between Charles and Madame des Grassins.

"Monsieur," said Adolphe at length, addressing Charles in a manner intended to be casual, "I don't know if you remember me, but I once had the pleasure of sitting opposite you at a ball given by the Baron de Nucingen, and . . ."

"Of course, monsieur, of course!" replied Charles, surprised to find himself the object of everyone's attention. "Is this gentleman your son?" he asked Madame des Grassins.

The priest looked maliciously at her.

"Yes, monsieur," she said.

"Then you must have been quite young when you were in Paris," said Charles to Adolphe.

"Yes, we send them off to Babylon as soon as they're weaned," said the priest. Madame des Grassins questioned him with an amazingly penetrating glance. "You have to come to the provinces," he went on, "to find women in their thirties as youthful as Madame des Grassins here, with sons who are about to finish law school. I clearly remember the days when young men and ladies stood on chairs to watch you dancing at a ball, madame," he added, turning to his female adversary. "To me, it seems as though your triumphs took place only yesterday . . ."

"Oh, the old scoundrel!" thought Madame des Grassins. "Has he guessed what's been passing through my mind?"

"It looks as though I'm going to be quite successful in Saumur," thought Charles, unbuttoning his coat, putting his hand in his vest and looking off into the distance to imitate the pose given to Lord Byron by Chantrey.

Grandet's inattention, or rather his preoccupation with the letter he was reading, had escaped neither the notary nor the judge, who were trying to guess its contents by the almost imperceptible movements of the old man's face, which was brightly illuminated by the candle. The winegrower was having difficulty in maintaining the usual calm of his expression. It will be easy to imagine the look on his face as he read this fateful letter:

> *My dear brother,*
>
> *It has been almost twenty-three years since the last time we saw each other. My marriage was the occasion of our last meeting. We were both happy when we left each other then; I could hardly foresee that you would one day be the sole support of our family, whose prosperity made you so happy at the time. When you read this letter, I will no longer be alive. In my position I do not wish to live in the dishonor of bankruptcy. I have clung to the edge of the abyss until the last moment, always hoping that I would be able to regain a foothold. Now I must fall. The combined bankruptcies of my broker and of Roguin, my notary, have taken away my last resources and left me nothing. I*

have the sorrow of owing nearly four million francs, with assets totaling no more than a quarter of that amount. The wines I have in storage are now affected by the ruinous fall in prices caused by the abundance and quality of the harvest in your region. In three days Paris will say, "Monsieur Grandet was a swindler." And, in spite of all my integrity, I shall lie in a shroud of infamy.

I have deprived my son of both his name, which I have blemished, and his mother's fortune. He knows nothing of this, the poor boy whom I adore. We parted affectionately. He was not aware, fortunately, that my life was ebbing away in that last good-by. Will he not curse me some day? My brother, my dear brother, the curses of our children are terrible! They can appeal against ours, but theirs are irrevocable. Grandet, you are my elder brother, you owe me your protection: do what is necessary to keep Charles from speaking bitter words over my grave. My brother, if I were writing to you in my blood and my tears there would be less pain in this letter than I am now putting into it, for I would be weeping and bleeding, I would die, I would no longer suffer; but I am now suffering and I gaze on death with dry eyes. From now on you are Charles's father! He has no relatives on his mother's side, you know why. Why did I not conform to the prejudices of society? Why did I give in to love? Why did I marry the illegitimate daughter of a great nobleman? Charles no longer has a family. Oh, my unfortunate son! My son! . . .

*Listen to me, Grandet, I am not writing to
ask anything for myself; besides, your holdings
are perhaps not large enough to cover a mort-
gage of three million francs. But, for my son's
sake, I want you to know, my brother, that I
clasp my hands beseechingly when I think of
you. I am about to die, Grandet, and I confide
Charles to your care. At last I can look at my
pistols without pain, feeling sure that you will
be a father to him. Charles loved me; I was so
good to him, I never opposed his wishes; he
will not curse me. Besides, as you will see, he
has a gentle nature. He takes after his mother;
he will never cause you any trouble. Poor boy!
Accustomed to the enjoyment of luxury; he
knows nothing of the hardship to which you
and I were both condemned by the poverty of
our early years . . . And now he's ruined, and
all alone! Yes, all his friends will desert him,
and I will be the cause of his humiliation. Oh,
I wish I had the strength to send him straight
to heaven, where his mother is waiting for
him! But this is madness . . . I return to my
misfortune, to that of Charles.*

*I have sent him to you so that you can
gently break the news of my death to him and
tell him of the fate that lies in store for him.
Be a father to him, but a kind father. Do not
tear him away from his idle life too abruptly;
you would kill him. I beg him on my knees to
waive all claims which, as his mother's heir,
he may have against my estate. But this is
a superfluous plea; he is honorable and he
will realize that he must not become one of
my creditors. Persuade him to give up all his*

rights as my heir when the time comes. Reveal
to him the harsh conditions under which he
must live from now on because of me and,
if he still has any love for me, tell him in
my name that all is not lost for him. Yes,
work, which saved both of us, can give him
back the fortune I have taken away from him.
And if he is willing to listen to the voice of his
father, who for his sake would like to emerge
from the tomb for a moment, let him leave,
let him go to the Indies! My brother, Charles
is an honorable and courageous young man;
you will see to it that he has goods to trade
with, and he would rather die than fail to pay
back the money you will lend him. For you
will lend it to him, Grandet! Otherwise you
will suffer terrible remorse. If my son were to
find neither help nor kindness in you, I would
ask God for eternal vengeance against your
harshness!

If I had been able to save anything, I
would have had the right to give him a sum
of money from his mother's estate; but my last
monthly payments absorbed all my resources.
I would have preferred not to die in doubt
about my son's fate; I would have preferred
to feel your sacred promise in the warmth of
your hand, which would have reassured me.
But time is short. I am forced to draw up my
balance sheet while Charles is traveling. I am
trying to prove, by the good faith in which I
have conducted my affairs, that my disaster
has not been caused by any shortcoming or
dishonesty on my part. Is this not the best
thing I could do for Charles?

*Farewell, my brother. May all God's bless-
ings be yours for the generous guardianship I
am confiding to you, and which I did not doubt
that you will accept. There will always be a
voice praying for you in the world to which
we must all go some day, and to which I have
already gone.*

Victor-Ange-Guillaume Grandet

"What were you saying?" asked Old Man Grandet,
carefully folding the letter along its original creases and
putting it into his vest pocket. He gave his nephew a
humble, fearful look, beneath which he hid his emotions
and his calculations. "Have you warmed yourself up by
now?"

"Yes, I'm quite warm, uncle."

"Well, where have our women gone?" asked the
uncle, already forgetting that his nephew was going to
sleep in his house.

Just then Eugénie and Madame Grandet came in.

"Is everything ready upstairs?" asked the old man,
recovering his composure.

"Yes, father."

"Well, then, nephew, if you're tired, Nanon will
show you to your room. I'm afraid it's not the kind
of room a dandy would like, but I hope you'll forgive
a poor winegrower who never has an extra sou. Our
taxes eat up everything."

"We don't want to overstay our welcome, Grandet," said the banker. "You may have some things you
want to talk over with your nephew, so we'll tell you
good night now. We'll see you tomorrow."

At these words everyone stood up, and each bowed
according to his character. The old notary went to the
entrance hall for his lantern, came back to light it and

offered to accompany the des Grassins. Madame des Grassins had not foreseen the incident that was to end the evening prematurely, and her servant had not yet arrived.

"Will you do me the honor of taking my arm, madame?" said Abbé Cruchot to Madame des Grassins.

"Thank you, Abbé, but I have my son," she replied curtly.

"A lady runs no risk of compromising herself with me," said the priest.

"Go on, take Monsieur Cruchot's arm," said her husband.

The priest led the pretty lady swiftly enough to draw her a few paces in front of the procession.

"He's a very attractive young man, madame," he said to her, squeezing her arm. "I'm afraid everything is settled now. You'll have to say good-by to Mademoiselle Grandet; Eugénie will go to the Parisian. Unless this cousin of hers is infatuated with some Parisian woman, your son Adolphe will find him to be the most formidable rival . . ."

"Don't be ridiculous, Abbé. That young man won't take long to discover that Eugénie's a little fool, a girl with no freshness at all. Did you look at her closely? She was as yellow as a quince this evening."

"Did you by any chance point that out to her cousin?"

"I didn't mince words . . ."

"Always place yourself next to Eugénie, madame, and you won't have to say much to the young man against her—he himself will make comparisons that will . . ."

"First of all, he's promised to come to dinner day after tomorrow."

"Ah, madame, if you wanted to . . ."

"Just what do you think I'd want to do, Abbé? Are you trying to give me bad advice? I haven't reached the age of thirty-nine with a spotless reputation, thank God, only to compromise it, even for the empire of the Grand Mogul! You and I are both old enough to talk frankly about such things. For a priest, you have some very incongruous ideas. You ought to be ashamed of yourself—you're as bad as Faublas!"

"So you've read *Faublas*?"

"No, Abbé; I meant to say *Les Liaisons Dangereuses*."

"Oh, that's a much less immoral book!" said the priest, laughing. "But you're trying to make me sound as corrupt as the young men of today! I merely wanted to . . ."

"You can't deny that you were trying to give me bad ideas. It's quite obvious. If the young man—and he *is* attractive, I won't deny it—were to become interested in me, he'd forget about his cousin. I know there are good mothers in Paris who show that kind of devotion to the happiness and welfare of their children, but we're in the provinces, Abbé."

"That's true, madame."

"And," she went on, "I wouldn't want a hundred million francs bought at that price, and neither would Adolphe."

"I wasn't talking about a hundred million francs, madame. That temptation might be too strong for either of us. But I do think that an honorable woman can, in all innocence, indulge in a few harmless coquetries which are part of her social duties anyway, and which . . ."

"Do you really think so?"

"Shouldn't we all try to be pleasant to one another, madame? . . . Excuse me while I blow my nose . . . I assure you, madame, that the way he looked at you was a little more flattering than the way he looked at me; but I forgave him for preferring beauty to old age . . ."

"It's obvious," said the judge in his loud voice, "that Monsieur Grandet of Paris has sent his son to Saumur with extremely matrimonial intentions."

"But in that case the cousin wouldn't have dropped in suddenly like a bombshell," replied the notary.

"That doesn't mean anything," remarked Monsieur des Grassins. "You know how wily the old man is."

"Des Grassins, my dear, I've invited that young man to dinner. You'll have to go and invite Monsieur and Madame de Larsonnière and the du Hutoys, including their beautiful daughter, of course. I hope she'll be well dressed this time! Her mother makes her wear such ugly clothes, out of jealousy! I also hope you'll do us the honor of coming, gentlemen," she added, stopping the procession to turn around and face the two Cruchots.

"We're in front of your house now, madame," said the notary.

After taking leave of the three des Grassins, the three Cruchots headed for home, using their provincial genius for analysis to study every possible angle of the great event of the evening, which had altered the respective positions of the Cruchotists and the Grassinians. The admirable common sense which guided the actions of these shrewd schemers made them all feel the necessity of a temporary alliance against the common enemy. Must they not all pool their efforts to prevent Eugénie from falling in love with her cousin, and Charles from thinking of her? Would the Parisian be able to withstand the treacherous insinuations, the soft-spoken calumnies, the disparaging remarks enveloped in praise and the ingenuous denials that would be constantly uttered around him to deceive him?

When the four relatives were left alone in the living room, Monsieur Grandet said to his nephew, "It's time to go to bed now. It's too late to talk about the reasons for your visit; we'll find a good opportunity for that tomorrow. We have breakfast at eight o'clock here. At noon, we have a little fruit, a piece of bread and a glass of white wine. Then we have dinner, like the Parisians, at five o'clock. That's our schedule. If you want to take a look at the town or its surroundings, you're free as the air. I hope you'll excuse me if my business doesn't always allow me to accompany you. You'll probably hear everyone around here saying I'm rich. 'Monsieur Grandet this, Monsieur Grandet that!' I let them talk; their gossip doesn't do my credit any harm. But I don't have a sou to my name, and at my age I still work like a young journeyman whose entire fortune consists of a cheap drawknife and two strong arms. Soon you may discover for yourself what a franc is worth when you have to sweat for it . . . Come, Nanon, the candles!"

"I hope you'll find everything you need, nephew," said Madame Grandet, "but if there's anything you want, you can call Nanon."

"That's quite unlikely, my dear aunt: I believe I've brought everything with me. Allow me to wish you and my young cousin good night."

Nanon handed Charles a lighted wax candle. It was a candle from Anjou, quite yellow in hue, shopworn and so similar to a tallow candle in appearance that Monsieur Grandet, who had no reason even to suspect its presence in his house, did not notice this luxury.

"I'll show you the way," said the old man.

Instead of going out through the door of the living room which opened into the entrance hall, Grandet ceremoniously walked along the hall separating the living room from the kitchen. This hall was closed off from the staircase by a swinging door with a large oval pane of glass, in order to keep out some of the cold that poured into it. But in winter the north wind whistled through nevertheless and, in spite of the padding placed around the doors of the living room, the temperature was scarcely comfortable inside.

Nanon bolted the front door, closed up the living room and went out to the stable to untie a wolf dog whose voice was so hoarse that he sounded as though he had laryngitis. This animal, whose ferocity was notorious, recognized no one but Nanon. The two primitive creatures understood each other.

When Charles saw the yellowish, smoke-darkened walls and worm-eaten banister of the staircase, whose steps quivered beneath his uncle's heavy tread, his disillusionment began to grow at an accelerated pace. He felt as though he were in a chicken coop. His aunt and his cousin, toward whom he turned with a questioning look, were so thoroughly accustomed to this staircase that, not guessing the cause of his astonishment, they took his expression for one of friendliness and responded to it with a pleasant smile which increased his despair. "What the devil did my father send me here for?" he wondered.

When he reached the first landing he saw three doors painted red, without casings, imbedded in the dusty wall. They were fitted with exposed iron bands, bolted in place, whose ends were shaped to resemble flames, as were the long plates of the locks. The door at the top of the staircase, opening into the room above the kitchen, had obviously been walled up. Grandet used this room as his office; the only entrance to it was through his bedroom. The lone window which let light into it faced the courtyard and was protected by a heavy iron grating.

No one, not even Madame Grandet, was allowed to enter this room; the old man wanted to be alone there, like an alchemist at his furnace. There, no doubt, some hiding-place had been very skillfully contrived; there were stored the deeds to his property; there hung the scales for weighing his gold coins; there every night he secretly wrote out his receipts and vouchers and made his calculations, so that other businessmen always saw him ready for everything and might imagine that he had some fairy or demon at his command. There, no doubt, when Nanon was shaking the rafters with her snoring, when the wolf dog was yawning and keeping watch in the courtyard, when Madame and Mademoiselle Grandet were sound asleep, the old cooper came in to stroke, fondle, caress and gloat over his gold. The walls were thick, the shutters were discreet. He alone had the key to this laboratory, where, it was said, he pored over maps on which his fruit trees were marked and figured out the production of his land, down to the last vine and bundle of firewood.

The entrance to Eugénie's room was opposite this walled-up door. Then, at the other end of the landing, were the old couple's rooms, which occupied the whole front of the house. Madame Grandet had a room next to Eugénie's, which one could enter through a glazed door. The master's bedroom was separated from his wife's by a partition, and from the mysterious office by a thick wall.

Monsieur Grandet had lodged his nephew on the third floor in the high-ceilinged attic room above his bedroom, so that he could hear him if he should take it into his head to come and go.

When Eugénie and her mother reached the middle of the landing, they gave each other their usual good-night kiss; then, after taking leave of Charles with a few words which sounded cold on their lips but were undoubtedly warm in the daughter's heart, they went to their respective bedrooms.

"This is your room, nephew," said Old Man Grandet to Charles, opening the door for him. "If you need to go outside, call Nanon; without her, I'm sorry, but the dog would eat you up without a word! Sleep well. Good night. . . . Aha! I see the ladies have made a fire for you."

Just then Nanon appeared, carrying a warming pan.

"Well, here's something new!" said Monsieur Grandet. "Do you think my nephew is a woman in childbirth? Please take your embers away, Nanon!"

"But Monsieur, the sheets are damp, and this gentleman really is as delicate as a woman."

"All right, then, go ahead, since you've taken it into your head," said Grandet, pushing her on the shoulder. "But be careful you don't set the place on fire!" Then the miser went downstairs, muttering to himself.

Charles stood aghast in the midst of his bags. After glancing at the sloping walls covered with yellow flowered wallpaper of the kind usually found in country taverns, at the fluted limestone fireplace which made him feel cold just to look at it, at the yellow wooden chairs with glossy cane bottoms, which seemed to have more than four corners, at the open bedside cabinet that was big enough to hold a small infantry sergeant, and at the meager rag carpet lying at the foot of a canopied bed whose worm-eaten hangings quivered as though they were about to fall off, he looked gravely at Big Nanon and said to her, "Tell me, my dear girl, am I really in the house of Monsieur Grandet, former Mayor of Saumur, and the brother of Monsieur Grandet of Paris?"

"Yes, monsieur, you're in the house of a very kind, very gentle and very perfect gentleman. Shall I help you unpack?"

"Yes, I'll be grateful to you if you will, old trooper! Were you ever in the marines of the Imperial Guard?"

"Oh, oh, oh! What's that, the marines of the Guard? Are they salty? Do they go on the water?"

"Please get my dressing gown out of that suitcase. Here's the key."

Nanon was amazed at the sight of a green silk dressing gown with gold flowers and antique designs. "Are you going to wear that in bed?" she asked.

"Yes."

"Holy Virgin! What a beautiful altar front it would make for the parish! Give that to the Church, my handsome young man, and it will save your soul; otherwise, it will make you lose it. Oh, how nice you look like that! I'm going to call mademoiselle so she can see you."

"Come now, Nanon, since Nanon it is, will you keep quiet? Let me go to bed, I'll unpack my things tomorrow. And if you like my dressing gown so much, you can save your own soul with it. I'm too good a Christian not to give it to you when I leave, and you can do whatever you like with it."

Nanon stood rooted to the spot, staring at Charles, unable to believe what he had just said.

"Give me that beautiful robe?" she said as she turned to leave. "You must be dreaming already, monsieur. Good night."

"Good night, Nanon."

Just before he went to sleep, Charles said to himself, "What am I doing here? My father's no fool, so there must be a reason for this visit. Well, 'let us put off serious matters till tomorrow,' as some old Greek said."

"Oh, how nice my cousin is!" thought Eugénie, interrupting her prayers, which were not finished that night.

Madame Grandet had no thoughts at all as she went to bed. Through the door in the middle of the partition, she could hear the miser pacing up and down his room. Like all timid wives, she had studied the character of her lord and master. As the gull foresees the storm, she had sensed, from certain almost imperceptible signs, the inner tempest that was agitating Grandet and, to use her own expression, she was "playing dead."

Grandet looked at the door of his office, reinforced on the inside with sheet iron, and said to himself, "Whatever gave my brother the mad idea of bequeathing his son to me? A fine inheritance! I don't have fifty francs to give him. Anyway, what would fifty francs mean to that young fop, who stared at my barometer as though he wanted to toss it into the fire?" As he thought of the consequences of that tragic will, Grandet was perhaps even more upset than his brother had been while writing it.

"Am I really going to have that golden gown?" thought Nanon, who fell asleep arrayed in her altar front and dreamed of flowers, carpets and damask for the first time in her life, as Eugénie dreamed of love.

III

Love in the Provinces

In the pure and monotonous life of a young girl, there comes a delightful time when the sun shines its rays into her soul, when flowers express thoughts, when the throbbing of the heart communicates its warm fecundity to the brain and dissolves all ideas into a vague desire—a day of innocent melancholy and gentle pleasantries! When babies begin to see, they smile; when a girl first glimpses sentiment in nature, she smiles as she smiled when she was a baby. If light is the first love of life, is not love the light of the heart? The time to see clearly the things of this earth had come to Eugénie.

She got up early, like all provincial girls, said her prayers and began to dress, an occupation which would have meaning from now on. First she brushed her chestnut hair, then she twisted the thick braids on top of her head with great care, making sure no loose strands escaped and giving her coiffure a symmetry which enhanced the candor of her face, whose unsophisticated lines were in harmony with the simplicity of her accessories. As she washed her hands several times in pure water, which hardened and reddened her skin, she looked at her pretty round arms and wondered how her cousin managed to have such soft, white hands and neatly trimmed fingernails. She put on new stockings and her prettiest shoes. She laced herself straight, without skipping a single eyelet. Finally, wishing for the first time in her life to look her best, she felt the satisfaction of putting on a fresh, well-cut dress which made her attractive.

When she had finished dressing, she heard the parish clock begin to strike and was surprised to count only seven strokes. Her desire to have all the time necessary to dress herself well had made her get up too early. Ignorant of the art of rearranging one curl ten times and studying the effect each time, she simply crossed her arms, sat down in front of her window and began to contemplate the courtyard, the narrow garden and the terraces that rose high above it. It was a melancholy and limited view, but it was not devoid of the mysterious beauties peculiar to solitary spots and uncultivated nature.

Near the kitchen there was a well surrounded by a curb, with a pulley attached to a curved iron rod embraced by a vine whose leaves had been shriveled, reddened and blighted by the season; from there, the twisted stem of the vine extended to the wall, clung to it, ran along the house and ended on a woodshed in which the firewood was stacked as neatly as a bibliophile's books. The stony surface of the courtyard displayed those blackish hues produced in time by moss, weeds and lack of use. The thick walls presented their green coating, streaked with wavy brown lines. Finally, the eight steps which rose at the far end of the courtyard and led to the garden gate were disjointed and buried beneath tall plants, like the tomb of a knight interred by his window in the days of the crusades. Above a worn stone foundation rose a latticed gate made of rotten wood, half fallen with age, on which the creeping vines intertwined at will. On each side of this gate projected the twisted branches of two stunted apple trees. Three parallel lanes, graveled and separated by beds of earth held in place by boxwood borders, made up this garden, which ended at the bottom of the terrace with a clump of linden trees. At one end there were raspberry bushes; at the other, an enormous walnut tree whose branches drooped down to the cooper's office. A clear day and the beautiful autumn sunlight natural to the banks of the Loire were beginning to dissipate the glaze which the night had laid over the picturesque objects, the walls and the plants which adorned the garden and the courtyard.

Eugénie found new charm in the sight of all these things, which had formerly seemed so commonplace to her. A thousand confused thoughts sprang up in her mind and grew there as the sunlight grew brighter outside. She finally felt that surge of vague, inexplicable pleasure which envelops the soul as a cloud might envelop the body. Her reflections were in accord with the details of that singular landscape, and the harmonies of her heart echoed those of nature.

When the sunlight reached a section of the wall from which hung maidenhair ferns with thick leaves whose colors were constantly changing like those of a pigeon's breast, celestial rays of hope illuminated the future for Eugénie. From then on she took pleasure in looking at that section of wall, with its pale flowers, its bluebells, its withered grasses, with which were mingled memories as sweet as those of childhood. The sound that each leaf made as it fell from its branch into the

resonant courtyard gave an answer to the young girl's
secret questions. She could have stayed there all morning, unaware of the passing hours.

Then came tumultuous stirrings of the soul. She
stood up frequently, walked over to her mirror and
looked at herself in it, like an honest author who examines his work to criticize and chastise himself.

"I'm not beautiful enough for him!" Such was
Eugénie's thought, a humble thought which is a fertile
source of suffering. The poor girl was unjust to herself;
but modesty, or rather fear, is one of the chief virtues
of love. Eugénie was a robust girl of the kind one often
sees among the lower middle classes, and whose charms
seem rather coarse. But, while she resembled the Venus
de Milo, her form and features were ennobled by that
sweetness of Christian sentiment which purifies a woman
and gives her a distinction unknown to the sculptors of
antiquity. She had a very large head with the masculine
yet delicate forehead of the Jupiter of Phidias, and gray
eyes to which her chaste life, clearly reflected in them,
imparted a radiant light. The features of her round face,
once fresh and pink, had been coarsened by an attack of
smallpox which, while not severe enough to leave any
scars, had destroyed the velvety smoothness of her skin;
it was still so soft and fine, however, that her mother's
pure kiss left a momentary red mark on it. Her nose
was a little too large, but it was in harmony with her
bright red lips, whose countless little lines were full of
love and kindness. Her neck was perfectly round. Her
full bosom, carefully veiled, attracted the eye and gave
rise to pleasant thoughts; it may have lacked some of
the charm given by fashionable clothes, but, to the
connoisseur, the firmness of her stately figure had its
own charm. Eugénie, tall and buxom, had nothing of
the kind of prettiness that appeals to the masses, but

she had that beauty, so easy to recognize, of which only artists become enamored.

A painter who seeks in this world a model of the Virgin Mary's celestial purity, who examines all of womankind in an effort to find those modestly proud eyes glimpsed by Raphael, those virginal lines often due to the hazards of heredity, but which can be preserved or acquired only by a modest Christian life—such a painter, in love with his ideal model, would instantly have found in Eugénie's face that innate nobility that is unaware of itself; he would have seen a whole world of love beneath that calm brow and, in the shape of her eyes and the way she moved her eyelids, he would have felt a hint of something divine. Her features, the contours of her face, which had never been contorted or wearied by pleasure, resembled the lines of a horizon gently traced in the distance beyond tranquil lakes. This calm, rosy face, radiant as a full-blown flower, rested the soul, communicated the charm of the spirit reflected in it and held the attention.

Eugènie was still on the shore of life where childish illusions blossom, where one gathers daisies with a delight that is never recaptured later. As she looked at herself in the mirror, not yet knowing what love was, she said to herself, "I'm too ugly, he won't pay any attention to me!"

Then she opened the door of her room, which faced the staircase, and craned her neck to hear the noises of the household. "He's not up yet," she thought, hearing Nanon cough as she bustled to and fro, sweeping out the living room, lighting her fire, chaining up the watchdog and speaking to her animals in the stable.

Eugènie immediately went downstairs and ran to Nanon, who was milking the cow.

"Nanon, dear Nanon, please make some cream for my cousin's coffee!"

"You should have asked me that yesterday, mademoiselle," said Nanon, bursting into loud laughter. "I can't make cream. Your cousin's a darling, really a darling! You didn't see him in his silk and gold dressing gown, but I did. He wears linen as fine as a priest's surplice."

"Nanon, please make us a cake."

"And who'll give me the wood to bake it with, and the flour, and the butter?" said Nanon, who, in her capacity as Grandet's prime minister, sometimes took on an enormous importance in the eyes of Eugénie and her mother. "Do you want me to rob the man so I can feed your cousin fancy food? You ask him for butter, flour and wood—he's your father, so he can give it to you. . . . Here he is now, he's coming down to give out the provisions. . . ."

Eugénie ran out into the garden, filled with alarm, when she heard the staircase trembling beneath her father's footsteps. She was already feeling the effects of that profound modesty and that peculiar awareness of our happiness which makes us believe, not without reason, perhaps, that our thoughts are engraved on our foreheads and are instantly clear to everyone else. Conscious at last of the cold barrenness of her father's house, the poor girl felt a kind of rancor at not being able to make it harmonize with her cousin's elegance. She also felt a passionate need to do something for him. But what? She had no idea. Naïve and sincere, she gave her angelic nature free rein without mistrusting either her impressions or her feelings. The sight of her cousin had been enough to awaken in her the natural inclinations of a woman, and they asserted themselves all the more vigorously because, having reached her twenty-third year, her intelligence and her desires were fully developed.

For the first time, the sight of her father struck terror into her heart; she saw him as the master of her fate and she felt guilty over having concealed some of her thoughts from him. She began to walk swiftly, surprised to notice that the air she breathed seemed purer, that the sunshine seemed more invigorating and that it seemed to give her spiritual warmth and new life.

While she was trying to think of a stratagem to obtain the ingredients for the cake, one of those quarrels as rare as swallows in winter had broken out between Big Nanon and Grandet. Armed with his keys, the old man had come down to measure out the provisions necessary for the day's consumption.

"Is there any bread left from yesterday?" he asked Nanon.

"Not a crumb, monsieur."

Grandet picked up a large round loaf, well sprinkled with flour and molded in one of those flat baskets used in Anjou for baking. He was about to cut it when Nanon said to him, "There are five of us today, monsieur."

"That's true," replied Grandet, "but your loaf weighs six pounds; there'll be some left over. Besides, you'll see that these young men of Paris don't eat any bread."

"Do you mean to say they eat nothing but spread?"

In Anjou, the word "spread," in the language of the common people, refers to anything eaten on bread, from butter spread on a slice, a commonplace spread, to peach jam, the most distinguished of spreads; and all those who, in their childhood, have licked off the spread and left the bread will understand the meaning of this phrase.

"No," replied Grandet, "they eat neither spread nor bread. They're almost like marriageable daughters."

Finally, after parsimoniously ordaining the day's menu, the old man was about to go to his fruit storeroom, having first locked the pantry cupboards, when Nanon stopped him to ask, "Monsieur, would you please give me some flour and butter so I can make a cake for the children?"

"Do you want to pillage the whole house because of my nephew?"

"I wasn't thinking of your nephew any more than I was thinking of your dog, no more than you were thinking of him yourself. . . . Look, you've only given me six lumps of sugar—I need eight!"

"What's the matter with you, Nanon? I've never seen you like this before. What kind of ideas have you taken into your head? Do you think you're running this household? You'll have six lumps of sugar, and that's all!"

"Well then, what will your nephew sweeten his coffee with?"

"With two lumps of sugar; I'll do without."

"You'll do without sugar at your age? I'd rather buy it for you out of my own pocket!"

"Mind your own business!"

In spite of its lowered price, sugar was still, in the old cooper's eyes, the most expensive of all colonial products; to him it was still worth six francs a pound. The necessity to use it sparingly, which had impressed itself on his mind under the Empire, had become one of his most ineradicable habits.

All women, even the most simpleminded, know how to use cunning to achieve their ends; Nanon abandoned the question of sugar in order to obtain the cake. "Mademoiselle," she shouted through the window, "you want a cake, don't you?"

"No, no," replied Eugénie.

"All right, Nanon," said Grandet, hearing his daughter's voice, "here you are." He opened the bin in which he kept the flour, gave her a measure of it and added a few ounces of butter to the piece he had already cut.

"I'll need some wood to heat up the oven," said the implacable Nanon.

"All right, take as much as you need," replied Grandet sadly. "But I want you to make us a fruit tart, and you can cook the whole dinner in the oven— that way, you won't have to light two fires."

"Of course!" exclaimed Nanon. "You don't have to tell me that!"

Grandet cast an almost paternal glance at his faithful prime minister.

"Mademoiselle," she cried, "we're going to have a cake!"

Old Man Grandet came back laden with his fruit and laid out a first plateful of it on the kitchen table.

"Look what pretty boots your nephew has, Monsieur," said Nanon. "What leather! How good it smells! I wonder what you're supposed to clean it with. . . . Should I use some of your egg polish?"

"I think egg polish would spoil that kind of leather, Nanon. Anyway, tell him you don't know how to polish morocco. . . . Yes it's morocco. He'll buy something to polish his boots with in Saumur and bring it to you himself. I hear they put sugar in their polish to make it brighter."

"Then these must be good to eat!" said the servant, raising the boots to her nose. "Oh, they smell like madame's eau de Cologne! Isn't that funny?"

"Funny!" said her master. "Do you think it's funny to spend more money on boots than the man who wears them is worth?"

"Monsieur," she said to Grandet when he had come back after locking the fruit storeroom, "shouldn't I make a pot of soup once or twice a week, because of your . . ."

"Yes."

"Then I'll have to go to the butcher shop."

"Not at all. You can make us some chicken broth; the farmers will give you all the poultry you need. But I'm going to tell Cornoiller to kill me some crows. They make the best broth in the world."

"Is it true, Monsieur, that they eat dead bodies?"

"Don't be so silly, Nanon! They eat whatever they can get, like anyone else. And don't we live off the dead ourselves? What are inheritances, after all?"

Having no more orders to give, Grandet looked at his watch and, seeing that he still had half an hour before breakfast, he took his hat, went out to kiss his daughter and said to her, "Would you like to go for a walk in my meadows along the Loire? I've got something to do there."

Eugénie went inside to put on her straw hat, lined with pink taffeta; then the father and daughter walked along the winding street to the public square.

"Where are you headed for so early in the morning?" asked Monsieur Cruchot, the notary, when he met Grandet.

"I'm going to look at something," replied the old man, not deceived by his friend's early morning walk.

When Old Man Grandet went to look at something, the notary knew from experience that there was always something to be gained by going with him; he therefore accompanied him.

"Come along, Cruchot," Grandet said to the notary. "You're a friend of mine, so I'm going to show you how foolish it is to plant poplar trees on good land. . . ."

"But what about the sixty thousand francs you got for the ones in your meadows along the Loire?" said Cruchot, opening his eyes wide in amazement. "Do you regard that as nothing at all? What luck you had! Cutting your trees just when they ran short of softwood in Nantes and selling them at thirty francs!"

Eugénie listened without knowing that she was approaching the most solemn moment of her life, that the notary was about to make her father announce an all-important decision concerning her.

Grandêt had reached the magnificent meadows he owned on the banks of the Loire, where thirty workmen were busy clearing, filling in and leveling the ground where the poplars had stood.

"Look how much land a poplar tree takes up, Monsieur Cruchot," he said to the notary. "Jean," he shouted to one of the workmen, "m-m-measure with your ruler in b-b-both directions!"

"Four feet by eight," replied the workman when he had finished.

"Thirty-two square feet wasted," said Grandet to Cruchot. "I had three hundred poplars in this row, didn't I? Well, three h-h-hundred times thirty-two s-s-square feet t-t-took up f-f-five hundred in hay; add twice that much for the sides—fifteen hundred; and the same for the middle rows. Let's s-s-s-say it comes to a thousand bundles of hay."

"Well," said Cruchot, to help his friend out, "a thousand bundles of hay are worth about six hundred francs."

"S-s-s-say t-t-twelve hundred, counting the three or four hundred francs for the second growth. Now f-ffigure out how m-m-m-much t-t-twelve hundred francs a year f-f-for forty years w-w-w-will yield with c-c-c-compound interest."

"Something like sixty thousand francs," said the notary.

"Right, it would c-c-come to no m-m-more than sixty thousand francs. Well," continued the winegrower without stuttering, "two thousand poplar trees forty years old wouldn't bring in more than fifty thousand francs. It's a loss. I found that out," he said rancorously. "Jean," he called out, "fill in all the holes except the ones along the Loire. Bring the poplars I bought and plant them in those holes. By putting them next to the river, we'll let them nourish themselves at the expense of the government," he added, turning to Cruchot and twitching the wen on his nose in a way that was equivalent to the most ironical of smiles.

"Well, it's obvious that poplar trees should be planted only on poor land," said Cruchot, dazed by Grandet's calculations.

"That is perfectly correct," replied the cooper ironically.

Eugénie, who had been looking at the sublime scenery of the Loire without paying any attention to her father's calculations, soon began to listen to Cruchot's remarks when she heard him say to his client, "So you've brought in a son-in-law from Paris! Everyone in Saumur is talking about your nephew. I suppose you'll be wanting me to draw up a marriage contract before long, won't you, Papa Grandet?"

"You c-c-came out early to t-t-t-tell me that," said Grandet, accompanying this observation with a twitch of his wen. "Well, old f-f-friend, I'll be frank with you; I'll t-t-t-tell you what you want to know. The t-t-t-truth is that I'd rather throw m-m-my d-d-d-daughter in the

Loire than g-g-give her to her c-c-cousin. You c-c-can announce that. . . . But no; l-l-let p-p-p-people go on talking."

This reply made Eugénie feel faint. The dim hopes that had begun to spring up in her heart suddenly grew to maturity, took shape before her eyes and formed a cluster of flowers which she now saw cut down and lying on the ground. Since the night before, she had been attached to Charles by all the ties of happiness that unite one soul with another; from now on, her suffering would strengthen them. Is it not part of the noble destiny of a woman to be more deeply affected by the majesty of sorrow than by the splendor of good fortune? How had all paternal feeling been extinguished in her father's heart? What crime had Charles committed? Mysterious questions! Already her newborn love, itself a profound mystery, was being enveloped in other mysteries.

Her legs trembled as she walked back, and when she came to the dark old street, which had seemed so cheerful to her till then, it suddenly struck her as gloomy; she breathed in the melancholy which time and things had imparted to it. She was spared none of the teachings of love.

When she was a short distance from the house she walked ahead of her father and waited for him at the door after she had knocked. But Grandet, having noticed that the notary was carrying an unopened newspaper, had said to him, "How are government stocks doing today?"

"You won't listen to me, Grandet," replied Cruchot. "Buy some without delay. You can still make twenty percent in two years, plus a high rate of interest; five thousand francs a year on eighty thousand. Shares are selling for eighty francs and fifty centimes now."

"We'll see about that," said Grandet, rubbing his chin.

"Good God!" exclaimed the notary, who had opened his newspaper.

"What's the matter?" cried Grandet.

Cruchot pushed the paper under his nose and said, "Read this!"

> *Monsieur Grandet, one of the most highly respected businessmen in Paris, shot himself in the head yesterday, after having made his usual appearance at the Bourse. He had sent in his resignation to the president of the Chamber of Deputies, and he had also resigned from his position as a judge of the court of commerce. He had been ruined by the bankruptcies of Monsieur Rouguin and Monsieur Souchet, his broker and notary respectively. Monsieur Grandet's credit and the esteem in which he was held were so great, however, that he would no doubt have been able to obtain help from other Paris businessmen. It is to be regretted that this honorable man should have yielded to a moment of despair. . . .*

"I knew it," said the old winegrower to the notary.

These words made Monsieur Cruchot's blood run cold. Despite his professional impassivity, he felt a chill run down his spine when it occurred to him that Grandet of Paris had perhaps vainly begged to borrow some of the millions possessed by Grandet of Saumur.

"And his son, who was so happy yesterday . . ."

"He still knows nothing about it," said Grandet with the same calm.

"Good-by, Monsieur Grandet," said Cruchot. He understood everything now, and he went off to reassure Judge de Bonfons.

Grandet found breakfast on the table when he came in. Madame Grandet was already seated in her raised chair, knitting herself some sleeves for winter. Eugénie threw her arms around her neck and kissed her with the effusiveness that comes from secret sorrow.

"You can eat now," said Nanon as she came down the stairs four at a time. "The boy is sleeping like an angel. He looks so sweet with his eyes closed! I went in and called him—no answer!"

"Let him sleep," said Grandet. "He'll wake up soon enough to hear the bad news."

"What's the matter?" asked Eugénie as she dropped into her coffee two of the small lumps of sugar, weighing no one knew how many grams, which the old man amused himself by cutting up in his spare time. Madame Grandet, who had not dared to ask this question, looked at her husband.

"His father has shot himself."

"My uncle?" said Eugénie.

"Poor young man!" cried Madame Grandet.

"Poor is right!" said Grandet. "He doesn't have a sou to his name."

"But right now he's sleeping as though he were king of the whole world," said Nanon gently.

Eugénie stopped eating. Her heart contracted as the heart does when compassion, aroused by the unhappiness of the man she loves, flows through a woman's whole body for the first time. She began to weep.

"You didn't know your uncle, so why are you crying?" said her father, glancing at her with the expression of a hungry tiger; it was no doubt the same expression his face wore when he looked at his piles of gold.

"But monsieur," said the servant, "who couldn't help feeling sorry for the poor young man sleeping like a log up there, without knowing what's happened?"

"I'm not talking to you, Nanon! Hold your tongue."

Eugénie learned at that moment that a woman in love must always conceal her feelings. She said nothing.

"I hope you'll say nothing to him until I come back, Madame Grandet," continued the old man. "I have to go and straighten out the ditch of my fields along the road. I'll be back at noon for lunch; I'll talk over my nephew's affairs with him then. As for you, Mademoiselle Eugénie, if it's that young fop you're crying for, you'd better dry your tears, my child. He'll be off to the East Indies in no time at all. You'll never see him again. . . ."

He took his gloves from the brim of his hat, put them on with his usual calm, making them fit tightly by pushing the fingers of one hand between those of the other, and walked out.

"Oh mama, I'm suffocating!" cried Eugénie when she was alone with her mother. "I've never suffered like this before!"

Madame Grandet, seeing her daughter turn pale, opened the window and made her breathe some fresh air.

"I feel better now," said Eugénie a few moments later.

This nervous agitation, in a nature which had until then seemed calm and cold, reacted on Madame Grandet. Looking at her daughter with that sympathetic intuition with which a mother is endowed for the object of her love, she guessed everything. Furthermore, the lives of those celebrated Hungarian sisters who were joined together by an error of nature were no more intimately connected than those of Eugénie and her mother, who were always together in the window recess or in church, and always slept in the same air.

"My poor child!" said Madame Grandet, taking Eugénie's head to press it to her breast.

At these words, the young girl looked up, questioned her mother with her eyes, trying to read her secret thoughts, and said to her, "Why send him to the Indies? If he's unhappy, why shouldn't he stay here? Isn't he our closest relative?"

"Yes, my child, that would be quite natural; but your father has his reasons and we must respect them."

The mother and daughter sat down in silence, one in her raised chair, the other in her little armchair; then they both took up their work again. Overcome with gratitude for the admirable understanding her mother had shown for her, Eugénie kissed her hand and said, "How good you are, my dear mother!"

These words brought a glow of happiness to her mother's face, aged and withered by long years of sorrow.

"Do you like him?" asked Eugénie.

Madame Grandet replied only with a smile; then, after a moment of silence, she said softly, "Are you already in love with him? That would be wrong."

"Wrong?" said Eugénie. "Why? You like him, Nanon likes him, so why shouldn't I like him too? . . . Let's set the table for his breakfast, mama!"

She threw down her sewing; her mother followed suit and said, "You've gone mad!" But she took pleasure in justifying her daughter's madness by sharing it.

Eugénie called Nanon.

"What do you want now, mademoiselle?"

"Nanon, you'll have some cream for lunch, won't you?"

"Yes, for lunch," replied the old servant.

"Well, give him some good strong coffee; I've heard Monsieur des Grassins say they make coffee very strong in Paris. Put in a lot of it."

"And where do you expect me to get it?"

"Buy some."

"And what if your father sees me?"

"He's gone off to his fields."

"Then I'll leave right now. But Monsieur Fessard has already asked me if the Three Wise Men were staying with us, when he sold me the wax candles. Everybody in town will find out about our extravagance."

"If your father notices anything," said Madame Grandet, "he's quite capable of beating us."

"Then let him beat us; we'll take his blows on our knees."

Madame Grandet's only reply was to raise her eyes to heaven. Nanon put on her hat and left. Eugénie took out some clean table linen and went off to get a few of the bunches of grapes which she had amused herself by hanging on strings in the attic. She tiptoed along the hall to keep from waking up her cousin, but she could not resist stopping in front of his door to listen to his regular breathing. "Sorrow is awake while he sleeps," she thought.

She took the greenest leaves of the vine, arranged her grapes as attractively as an experienced chef could have done and triumphantly brought them back to the table. She pillaged the pears her father had counted out in the kitchen and piled them in a pyramid among the leaves. She hurried to and fro, running and skipping. She would have liked to sack her father's house completely, but he had the keys to everything.

Nanon came back with two fresh eggs. When she saw them, Eugénie felt like throwing her arms around her neck.

"The farmer from La Lande had some in his basket. I asked him for a couple of them and he gave them to me as a favor, the darling!"

After making careful preparations for two hours, during which she put down her sewing at least twenty times to go and watch the coffee boiling or listen to the sounds her cousin made as he got up, Eugénie succeeded in producing a lunch that was quite simple and inexpensive, but which represented a shocking departure from the established customs of the household. Lunch was always eaten standing. Each person took a little bread, a piece of fruit or some butter, and a glass of wine. When she saw the table placed in front of the fire, with one of the armchairs at her cousin's place, when she saw the two plates of fruit, the egg cup, the bottle of white wine, the bread and the sugar piled up in a saucer, Eugénie trembled in every limb as she thought, for the first time, of the look her father would give her if he were to come in at that moment. She therefore glanced frequently at the clock, trying to estimate whether her cousin would be able to finish his lunch before the old man's return.

"Don't worry, Eugénie: if your father comes in, I'll take all the blame," said Madame Grandet.

Eugénie could not hold back a tear. "Oh, my dear mother!" she cried. "I haven't loved you enough!"

After walking back and forth in his room an endless number of times, humming to himself, Charles finally came downstairs. Fortunately it was only eleven o'clock. The Parisian! He had dressed himself as elegantly as he would have done if he had been in the castle of the noble lady who was traveling in Scotland. He walked in with that air of smiling affability which is so becoming to youth; it made Eugénie feel sad and happy at the same time. He had taken the destruction of his castles in Anjou as a joke, and he greeted his aunt cheerfully.

"Did you sleep well last night, my dear aunt? And you, cousin?"

"I slept very well, Monsieur, but what about you?" said Madame Grandet.

"I slept perfectly."

"You must be hungry, cousin," said Eugénie. "Would you like to sit down at the table?"

"I never eat anything before noon, when I get up; but I ate so badly during my trip that this time I won't refuse. Besides . . ." He took from his pocket the most charming flat watch ever made by Bréguet. "Why, it's only eleven o'clock! I'm up early."

"Early?" said Madame Grandet.

"Yes, but I wanted to unpack. Well, I'll be glad to eat something, just a little snack: some kind of poultry; a partridge, perhaps."

"Holy Virgin!" exclaimed Nanon when she heard these words.

"A partridge . . ." thought Eugénie, who would have been willing to give all her savings for one.

"Come and sit down," said his aunt.

The dandy sank into the armchair in the same way that a pretty woman sits down on a sofa. Eugénie and her mother took chairs and sat down beside him in front of the fire.

"Do you live here all year round?" asked Charles, noticing that the living room looked even uglier in the daytime than it had by candlelight.

"All year round," replied Eugénie, looking at him, "except during the grape harvest. We go to help Nanon then, and we all live in the abbey of Noyers."

"Don't you ever go anywhere?"

"Sometimes on Sundays, after vespers, when the weather is good," said Madame Grandet, "we walk to the bridge, or go to watch the hay being cut."

"Do you ever go to the theater?"

"To the theater!" cried Madame Grandet. "To watch actors? But Monsieur, don't you know that's a mortal sin?"

"Here you are, Monsieur," said Nanon, bringing the eggs. "We'll give you your poultry in the shell."

"Oh! Fresh eggs!" said Charles, who, like those accustomed to luxury, had already forgotten about his partridge. "Why, they're delicious! Would you please bring me some butter, my dear girl?"

"Butter!" said the servant. "But then you won't have a cake!"

"Come, Nanon, bring in some butter!" cried Eugénie.

As her cousin cut his bread into strips to dip into his softboiled eggs, Eugénie watched him with as much pleasure as a young Paris working girl derives from seeing a melodrama in which virtue triumphs in the end. It is true that Charles, raised by a gracious mother and polished by a distinguished lady of fashion, had the winsome, refined and delicate movements of a coquette. The compassion and tenderness of a young girl exert a truly magnetic attraction. When Charles found himself the object of his cousin's and his aunt's attentions, he was unable to escape the influence of the feelings which flowed toward him and, so to speak, inundated him. He gave Eugénie a tender, caressing glance, a glance that seemed to smile. As he contemplated her he became aware of the exquisite harmony of the features of her pure face, of her innocent manner, of the magic clarity of her eyes, in which young thoughts of love were sparkling and desire knew nothing of sensuality.

"My dear cousin, if you were in a box at the opera, wearing an evening gown, I guarantee you that my aunt would be right: you'd make the men commit sins of envy and the women sins of jealousy."

This compliment touched Eugénie's heart and made it pound joyfully, even though she did not understand it.

"Oh, cousin," she said, "you're just making fun of a poor provincial girl."

"If you knew me better, cousin, you'd know that I despise sarcasm; it shrivels the heart, offends all the feelings. . . ." And he daintily swallowed a strip of buttered bread dipped in egg yolk. "No, I'm probably not clever enough to make fun of other people, and that defect has done me a great deal of harm. In Paris, it's possible to destroy a man by saying, 'He has a kind heart,' which really means, 'The poor fellow is as stupid as a rhinoceros.' But since I'm rich and known as a man who can hit the target at thirty paces with the first shot, using any kind of pistol, people think twice before making fun of me."

"What you've just said, nephew, shows that you have a kind heart."

"That's a very pretty ring you have on," said Eugénie. "Would you mind showing it to me?"

Charles held out his hand as he took off the ring and Eugénie blushed when she grazed his pink nails with her fingertips.

"Look at this beautiful workmanship, mother!"

"Oh, there's a lot of gold in that!" said Nanon, bringing in the coffee.

"What's that?" asked Charles, laughing and pointing to a dark, oblong earthenware pot, glazed on the outside and lined on the inside with china, with a ring of ashes around it. Grains of coffee were falling and rising to the surface of the boiling liquid it contained.

"It's boiled coffee," said Nanon.

"Ah, my dear aunt, I'll leave at least one pleasant trace of my stay here: you're very much behind the times, I'll teach you to make good coffee in a Chaptal pot." He tried to explain the working of the Chaptal coffeepot.

"If I had to do all that," said Nanon, "I wouldn't have time for anything else. I'll never make coffee in one of those things, you can be sure of that! Who would get the grass for our cow while I was making the coffee?"

"I'll make it," said Eugénie.

"Child!" said Madame Grandet, looking at her daughter.

At this word, which reminded them of the grief that was about to overwhelm the unfortunate young man, the three women became silent and looked at him with an expression of pity which rather startled him. "What's the matter, cousin?" he said to Eugénie.

Just as she was about to reply, her mother said, "Sh! You know your father said he was going to speak to monsieur . . ."

"Call me Charles," said young Grandet.

"Oh, is your first name Charles?" said Eugénie. "It's a beautiful name!"

Premonitions of disaster are nearly always justified. At this point, Nanon, Madame Grandet and Eugénie, who had been shuddering at the thought of the old cooper's return, heard the sound of a familiar knock on the door.

"There's papa!" said Eugénie.

She took away the saucer containing the sugar, leaving a few lumps of it on the tablecloth. Nanon took away the plate that had held the eggs. Madame Grandet started like a frightened doe. Charles was surprised by the panic he saw around him, but he could not account for it. "Why, what's the matter?" he asked.

"My father's coming!" said Eugénie.

"Well, what's wrong with that?"

Monsieur Grandet walked in, glanced sharply at the table and at Charles; he saw everything.

"Aha! I see you've prepared a real feast for your nephew!" he said, without stuttering. "That's good, very good, excellent! When the cat's away, the mice will play."

"A feast?" thought Charles, unable even to suspect the customs and standards of the household.

"Give me my glass, Nanon," said the old man.

Eugénie brought the glass. Grandet took a horn-handled knife with a broad blade from his vest pocket, cut a slice of bread, took a little butter, carefully spread it on the bread and began to eat, standing up. Just then Charles put some sugar into his coffee. Grandet noticed the lumps of sugar and stared at his wife, who turned pale and took three steps forward. He leaned toward the poor woman's ear and asked her, "Where did you get all that sugar?"

"Nanon went to buy it from Fessard; we didn't have any left."

It is impossible to imagine the profound interest the three women took in this mute scene. Nanon had left her kitchen and was now looking into the living room to see what would happen. Charles, having tasted his coffee and found it too bitter, looked around for the sugar, which Grandet had already put away.

"What do you want, nephew?" asked the old man.

"The sugar."

"Put some milk in your coffee," replied the master

of the house, "that will make it taste less bitter."

Eugénie brought back the saucer of sugar which Grandet had put away and set it on the table, looking at him calmly. The Parisian lady who holds a silken ladder with her frail arms to enable her lover to escape certainly shows no more courage than Eugénie did in putting the sugar back on the table. The lover will reward the Parisian lady when she proudly shows him the bruises on her pretty arms: each injured vein will be bathed in tears and kisses and healed by pleasure. But Charles would never know anything of the profound agitation that was breaking his cousin's heart as she cringed beneath the old cooper's gaze.

"Aren't you going to eat anything, my dear?" Grandet asked his wife.

The poor slave stepped forward, timorously cut a slice of bread and took a pear. Eugénie boldly offered her father some grapes, saying, "Try some of my dried grapes, papa. . . . You'll eat some of them, won't you, cousin? I brought these nice bunches especially for you."

"Oh! If no one stops them, they'll pillage the whole town of Saumur for you, nephew! When you've finished eating, we'll go out into the garden together; I have some rather unpleasant things to tell you, and I'm afraid they can't be sweetened with sugar."

Eugénie and her mother gave Charles a look whose meaning was impossible to interpret.

"What is it you want to tell me, uncle?" he asked. "Since the death of my poor mother" (at these last words his voice softened), "there can be no other misfortune for me. . . ."

"Nephew, who can know the afflictions by which God chooses to test us?" said his aunt.

"Come, come!" said Grandet. "Don't start that kind of nonsense again! Nephew, it pains me to see those pretty white hands of yours." He showed him the ham-like hands which nature had placed at the ends of his own arms. "There's a pair of hands made for raking in money! You've been brought up to put your feet in the kind of leather used to make wallets for us to carry our bills in. That's bad, very bad!"

"What do you mean, uncle? May the devil take me if I understand a word of what you're saying!"

"Come," said Grandet.

The miser snapped his knife shut, drank the rest of his white wine and opened the door.

"Be brave, cousin!"

Chilled by Eugénie's tone, Charles was filled with dread as he followed his terrifying uncle. Eugénie, her mother and Nanon went into the kitchen, impelled by an invincible curiosity to spy on the two actors of the scene that was about to take place in the damp little garden.

At first Grandet walked silently with his nephew. He was not upset by the prospect of informing Charles of his father's death, but he felt a kind of compassion at the thought that he was penniless, and he was trying to find words that would soften this harsh truth. It was easy to say, "You've lost your father"; fathers usually die before their children. But all the misfortunes in this world were summed up in the words, "You haven't a franc to your name!" And for the third time the old man walked along the middle lane with the gravel crunching beneath his feet.

At important moments in our lives, our souls become strongly attached to the places where joys or sorrows overwhelm us. Charles therefore examined with particular attention the box hedges of the little garden, the withered leaves falling to the ground, the dilapidated walls, the odd shapes of the fruit trees—picturesque details that were to remain engraved in his mind, forever mingled with the memory of that crucial moment, by a mnemonic device peculiar to the passions.

"It's very warm, the weather is fine today," said Grandet, taking a deep breath.

"Yes, uncle . . . But why . . ."

"Well, my boy," replied his uncle, "I have bad news for you. Your father is in very bad condition. . . ."

"Then why am I here?" said Charles. "Nanon," he shouted, "order some post horses for me! I'm sure I can find a carriage around here," he added, turning to his uncle, who remained motionless.

"There's no need for horses and a carriage," replied Grandet, looking at Charles, who stared silently into space. "Yes, poor boy, you've guessed it: he's dead. But that's nothing, there's something much worse: he shot himself . . ."

"My father?"

"Yes. But that's nothing. The newspapers are all gossiping about it, as though it were any concern of theirs! Here, read this."

Grandet, who had borrowed Cruchot's newspaper, placed the fateful article in front of Charles's eyes. At that moment the poor young man, who was still a boy, still at an age when the feelings well up spontaneously, burst into tears.

"Good, good," thought Grandet. "His eyes frightened me. He's crying now, so he'll be all right."

"That's still not the worst of it, my poor nephew," he said aloud, not knowing whether or not Charles was listening to him. "That's nothing; you'll get over it. But . . ."

"Never! Never! My father! My father!"

"He's ruined you. You have no money at all."

"What do I care about that? Where's my father? . . . My father!"

The sound of his weeping and sobbing was horribly magnified and echoed by the walls of the garden. The three women, overcome with pity, were also weeping: tears are often as contagious as laughter. Without listening to his uncle, Charles ran across the courtyard, found the staircase, went up to his room, threw himself on the bed and hid his face in the sheets to weep in peace away from his relatives.

"We'll have to let the first shower pass over," said Grandet on coming back into the living room, where Eugénie and her mother had hurriedly returned to their places and were working with trembling hands after having wiped their eyes. "But that young man is worthless. He's more concerned with the dead than he is with money."

Eugénie shuddered when she heard her father express himself in this way about the most sacred of all sorrows. From that moment she began to judge him.

Although muffled, Charles's sobs echoed through the resonant house, and his heartrending moans, which seemed to come from the depths of the earth, ceased only toward evening, after gradually growing weaker and weaker.

"Poor boy!" said Madame Grandet.

A fatal exclamation! Old Man Grandet looked at his wife, Eugénie and the sugar bowl; he remembered the extraordinary lunch that had been prepared for the unfortunate relative. He planted himself in the middle of the room and said, with his usual calm, "Well, Madame Grandet, I hope you're not going to continue your extravagance. I don't give you *my* money so that you can stuff that young fool with sugar."

"Mother had nothing to do with it," said Eugénie. "I was the one who . . ."

"Is it because you've come of age," interrupted

Grandet, "that you want to defy me? Remember, Eugénie . . ."

"Father, when your brother's son is in your house he shouldn't lack . . ."

"Ta, ta, ta, ta!" said the old cooper on four chromatic tones. "My brother's son this, my nephew that! Charles is nothing to me, he's completely penniless. His father went bankrupt. And when the young fop has cried his fill, he'll have to clear out of here; I won't have him turning my whole house upside down!"

"What does it mean to go bankrupt?" asked Eugénie.

"To go bankrupt," replied her father, "is to commit the most dishonorable of all the acts that can dishonor a man."

"Then it must be a very great sin," said Madame Grandet, "and our brother will be damned."

"There you go again with your litanies," he said to his wife, shrugging his shoulders. "Bankruptcy, Eugénie, is a kind of theft which is unfortunately protected by the law. People entrusted their property to Guillaume Grandet on the strength of his reputation for honor and integrity, then he took everything and left them only their eyes to weep with. A bankrupt is worse than a highway robber: the robber attacks you, you can defend yourself, he risks his life; but the bankrupt . . . In short, Eugénie, Charles is dishonored."

These words reverberated in the poor girl's heart and weighed heavily on it. As upright as a flower born in the heart of a forest is delicate, she knew nothing of the maxims of the world, its specious arguments or its sophisms; she therefore accepted the horrible explanation of bankruptcy which her father had purposely given her, without pointing out the distinction between an involuntary bankruptcy and a deliberate one.

"But father, couldn't you have done something to prevent the disaster?"

"My brother didn't consult me; besides, he had debts amounting to four million francs."

"How much is a million francs, father?" she asked, with the simplicity of a child who believes he can promptly get what he wants.

"A million francs?" said Grandet. "Why, it's a million twenty-sou coins, and it takes five of those to make five francs."

"Good heavens!" exclaimed Eugénie. "How could my uncle have had four million francs all to himself? Is there anyone else in France with that much money?"

Old Man Grandet stroked his chin and smiled, and his wen seemed to expand.

"But what will become of my cousin Charles?"

"He'll go off to the Indies, where, in accordance with his father's wishes, he'll try to make his fortune."

"But does he have enough money to go there?"

"I'll pay his fare . . . to . . . yes, to Nantes."

Eugénie threw her arms around his neck and cried out, "Oh, father, you're so kind!" she kissed him so warmly that he almost felt ashamed, for his conscience was bothering him a little. "Does it take long to make a million francs?" she asked.

"Well," said the cooper, "you know what a napoleon is: it takes fifty thousand of them to make a million francs."

"Mama, we'll have novenas said for him."

"I was just thinking of that," replied her mother.

"That's right, you can't think of anything except how to spend more money!" cried Grandet. "Do you think I'm made of money?"

Just then a hollow moan, more sorrowful than any

of the others, came down from the attic and struck terror into the hearts of Eugénie and her mother.

"Nanon, go up there and make sure he's not killing himself," said Grandet. "Now then," he went on, turning to his wife and daughter, who had turned pale at these words, "I don't want you two to do anything foolish. I'm going to leave you now. First I'm going to pay a visit to our Dutchmen, who are leaving today; then I'll go to see Cruchot and talk this over with him."

He left. When he had closed the door, Eugénie and her mother began to breathe more freely. Before that morning, Eugénie had never felt constrained in her father's presence, but for the past few hours her feelings and ideas had been constantly changing.

"Mama, how many louis do they pay for a barrel of wine?"

"Your father sells his for something between a hundred and a hundred and fifty francs, sometimes as much as two hundred, according to what I've been told."

"So when his harvest comes to fourteen hundred barrels . . ."

"Good heavens, child, I don't know how much that makes; your father never tells me anything about his business."

"But then father must be rich!"

"Perhaps. But Monsieur Cruchot told me he bought Froidfond two years ago. That may have taken most of his savings."

Eugénie, bewildered at this point by her father's wealth, carried her calculations no further.

"He didn't even know I was there, the poor darling!" said Nanon, coming back into the living room. "He's stretched out on his bed like a calf, crying like

Mary Magdalene! You have to see it to believe it! The poor boy's heart must be breaking!"

"Let's hurry upstairs and try to comfort him, mama; if there's a knock on the door, we'll come back downstairs."

Madame Grandet was unable to resist the sweetness of her daughter's voice. Eugénie was sublime; she was a woman.

With their hearts pounding, they both went up to Charles's room. The door was open. The young man neither saw nor heard anything. He uttered inarticulate cries as he gave free rein to his tears.

"How he loved his father!" said Eugénie softly.

It was impossible not to recognize, in the tone of these words, the hopes of a heart filled with a passion of which it was not yet aware. Madame Grandet looked at her daughter maternally and whispered in her ear, "Be careful or you may fall in love with him."

"Fall in love with him!" said Eugénie. "Oh, if you only knew what father said!"

Charles looked around and saw his aunt and cousin. "I've lost my father, my poor father!" he said. "If only he'd told me about his secret troubles, we'd have worked together to make things right again. Oh, God! My dear father! I was so sure I'd see him again that I'm afraid I kissed him good-by rather coldly . . ." His voice broke off in a sob.

"We'll pray for him," said Madame Grandet. "You must resign yourself to the will of God."

"Be brave, cousin," said Eugénie. "Your loss is irreparable; now you must think of saving your honor. . . ." With the intuition and subtlety of a woman who always keeps her presence of mind, even when she consoles, Eugénie was trying to distract her cousin from his grief by making him think of himself.

"My honor?" cried the young man, abruptly pushing back his hair. He sat up on the bed and crossed his arms. "Yes, that's true. . . . My uncle told me my father had gone bankrupt." He uttered a heartrending cry and hid his face in his hands. "Leave me, cousin, leave me! My God! Dear God, forgive my father, he must have suffered terribly!"

There was something horribly attractive in the sight of this youthful grief, so genuine, so spontaneous, so unselfish. It was a modest grief which the simple hearts of Eugénie and her mother understood when Charles motioned them to leave him alone. They went back downstairs, silently returned to their places near the window and worked for an hour or so without saying a word to each other. Eugénie had noticed, in the furtive glances she had cast at her cousin's belongings, the glance of a young girl who sees everything in the twinkling of an eye, the elegance of his toilet articles, the gold-embossed scissors and razors. This flash of luxury glimpsed through grief made Charles seem still more attractive to her, by contrast, perhaps. Never before had the imagination of those two women, constantly immersed in calm and solitude, been struck by such a solemn event, such a dramatic scene.

"Mama," said Eugénie, "we ought to wear mourning for my uncle."

"Your father will decide about that," replied Madame Grandet.

They lapsed into silence again. Eugénie drew her stitches with a regularity of movement which would have revealed to an observer the profusion of her thoughts. The adorable girl's first wish was to share her cousin's mourning.

Toward four o'clock a sudden knock on the door reverberated in Madame Grandet's heart. "What's the matter with your father?" she said to her daughter.

The winegrower came in with a joyful air. After taking off his gloves, he rubbed his hands together so vigorously that he would have taken the skin off them if it had not been tanned like Russia leather (although it lacked the odor of larchwood and incense). He paced up and down, glancing at the clock from time to time. Finally he could contain his secret no longer: "My dear," he said to his wife without stuttering, "I've outwitted them all. Our wine is sold! The Dutchmen and the Belgians were leaving this morning; I walked up and down in the square, in front of their inn, pretending I was just out for a stroll, with nothing special on my mind. What's-his-name, you know him, came up to me. The owners of all the good vineyards are holding on to their harvest; they want to wait, and I've done nothing to stop them. Our Belgian was desperate, I could see that. I came to terms with him: he's taking our wine for two hundred francs a barrel, half the amount in cash. I've been paid in gold. The papers are all signed. Here's six louis for you. In three months, the price of wine will fall."

These last words were spoken in a calm tone, but with such profound irony that the people of Saumur, who were at that moment standing in the public square, stunned by the news of the sale Grandet had just made, would have shuddered if they had heard them. A wave of panic would have made the price of wine fall fifty percent.

"You have a thousand barrels this year, haven't you, father?" asked Eugénie.

"That's right, sweetie." This term of endearment was the superlative expression of the old cooper's joy.

"That makes two hundred thousand twenty-sou coins, doesn't it?"

"Yes, Mademoiselle Grandet."

"Well then, father, you can easily save Charles from poverty."

The amazement, anger and stupefaction of Belshazzar on seeing the words *Mene, Mene, Tekel, Upharsin* could not even be compared to Grandet's cold rage when, having ceased to give any thought to his nephew, he suddenly found him lodged in his daughter's heart and calculations.

"What! Ever since that young fop set foot in my house, everything has gone wrong in it. You think you can buy delicacies and have feasts and parties. I won't have that in my house! At my age, I certainly know how to behave! Furthermore, I don't intend to take lessons from my daughter or anyone else. I'll treat my nephew the way he ought to be treated. You two don't have to stick your noses into it. As for you, Eugénie," he added, turning to her, "don't let me hear another word about this, or I'll send you to the abbey of Noyers with Nanon. I mean what I say; you'll be there no later than tomorrow if you're not careful. . . . Where is that boy? Has he come downstairs yet?"

"No, my dear," replied Madame Grandet.

"Well, what's he doing then?"

"He's weeping over his father's death," replied Eugénie.

Grandet looked at his daughter, unable to think of anything to say. *He* was a father too, after all. He paced up and down the living room a few times, then abruptly went up to his office to think over an investment in government stocks. The sale of all the trees on his two thousand acres of forest had brought him six hundred thousand francs; by adding to this amount the money he had received for his poplars, plus his income from the preceding year and the current year, aside from the two hundred thousand francs he had made from the sale he had just concluded, he could bring together a sum of nine hundred thousand francs. He was tempted by the twenty percent to be made within a short time on government stocks, which were now selling for seventy francs a share. He figured out his profits on the newspaper in which his brother's death was announced, hearing his nephew's moans but paying no attention to them.

Nanon came up and knocked on the wall to invite her master to come downstairs: dinner was served. When he reached the archway at the bottom of the stairs, Grandet said to himself, "Since the stocks will pay me eight percent interest, I'll buy them. In two years I'll have a million and a half francs, which I'll withdraw from Paris in gold. . . ."

"Where's my nephew?" he asked.

"He says he doesn't want to eat," replied Nanon. "It's not healthy."

"Well, at least we'll save on his food," said Grandet.

"That's true."

"Anyway, he won't go on crying forever. Hunger drives the wolf out of the woods."

The family was strangely silent at dinner.

"My dear," said Madame Grandet when the tablecloth had been taken away, "we must put on mourning."

"Really, Madame Grandet, all you can do is think up ways of spending money. Mourning is in the heart, not in the clothes."

"But you must wear mourning for a brother; the Church requires us . . ."

"Buy your mourning clothes out of your six louis. You can give me a piece of crêpe, that will be enough for me."

Eugénie raised her eyes to heaven without saying a word. For the first time in her life her generous instincts, formerly repressed and dormant but now suddenly awakened, were being outraged at every moment.

That evening was outwardly indistinguishable from a thousand other evenings of their monotonous existence, but it was actually the most horrible one they had ever spent. Eugénie worked without raising her eyes; she did not use the sewing box which Charles had scorned the night before. Madame Grandet knitted her sleeves. Grandet twiddled his thumbs for four hours, engrossed in calculations whose results were to amaze everyone in Saumur the next day.

No one came to visit the family that evening. At that moment the whole town was buzzing with the news of Grandet's masterful bargain, his brother's bankruptcy and his nephew's arrival. Impelled by their need to talk over their common interests, all the vineyard owners of the upper and middle classes of Saumur society had gathered in Monsieur des Grassins' house, where terrible imprecations were being hurled against the former mayor.

Nanon was spinning; the sound of her wheel was the only voice to be heard beneath the dingy beams of the living room ceiling.

"We're not wearing out our tongues," she remarked, showing her teeth, which were as large and as white as peeled almonds.

"We shouldn't wear anything out," replied Grandet, rousing himself from his meditations. He had before his eyes the prospect of eight million francs within three years, and he was sailing across that vast sea of gold. "Let's go to bed. I'll go tell my nephew good night for all of us and see if he wants anything to eat."

Madame Grandet stood on the second-floor landing to hear the conversation that was about to take place between Charles and the old man. Eugénie, bolder than her mother, went up two steps.

"Well, nephew, I see you're grief-stricken. Yes, weep, that's only natural. A father is a father. But we must bear our grief with patience. While you weep, I'm thinking of your future. I'm a good uncle, you see. Come, be brave. Would you like a little glass of wine?"

Wine costs nothing in Saumur; a glass of wine is offered as freely there as a cup of tea in India.

"But you have no light in here!" continued Grandet. "That's bad, very bad! You must be able to see what you're doing." He walked over to the mantelpiece. "Well, well, here's a wax candle!" he exclaimed. "Where the devil did they get hold of a wax candle? Those wenches would rip up the floor of my house to make a fire to boil the boy's eggs!"

When they heard these words, the mother and daughter went back to their rooms and slipped into bed with the speed of frightened mice scurrying back to their holes.

"Madame Grandet, do you have a secret treasure hidden away somewhere?" said the old man as he walked into his wife's room.

"I'm saying my prayers, dear; wait a moment," replied the poor mother in a faltering voice.

"The devil take your God!" grumbled Grandet.

Misers do not believe in a future life; the present is everything to them. This observation throws a horrible light on the present period, when, more than at any other time, money dominates the law, politics and morals. Institutions, books, men and doctrines—everything conspires to undermine the belief in a future life, a belief on which our social edifice has rested for the past eighteen hundred years. The grave is now a transition that inspires little fear. The future which formerly awaited us beyond the Requiem has been transferred to the present. To attain, *per fas et nefas,* the earthly paradise of luxury and selfish pleasure, to petrify the heart and macerate the body for the sake of fleeting possessions, as people once suffered the martyrdom of life for the sake of eternal reward—such is the thought uppermost in most minds today! And it is a thought that is written everywhere, even in the laws, which ask the legislator "What do you pay?" instead of "What do you think?" When this doctrine has passed from the bourgeoisie to the working class, what will become of the country?

"Are you through praying, Madame Grandet?" asked the old cooper.

"I'm praying for you, my dear."

"Thank you very much! Good night. We'll have a little talk tomorrow."

The poor woman went to sleep like a schoolboy who, not having learned his lessons, is afraid he may encounter the angry face of his master when he wakes up. Just as, out of fear, she was wrapping the sheets around herself in order not to hear anything, Eugénie slipped into the room, barefooted and in her nightgown, and kissed her on the forehead.

"Oh, mother dear," she said, "tomorrow I'll tell him it was my fault!"

"No; he'd send you to Noyers. Let me take care of everything, he won't eat me."

"Do you hear, mother?"

"What?"

"Listen: he's still crying."

"Go back to bed, daughter. You'll catch a cold, barefooted like that; the floor is damp."

Thus passed the fateful day which was to weigh heavily on the whole life of the rich yet poor heiress, whose sleep was no longer as deep and innocent as it had been till then.

It happens rather often that certain actions in human life appear to be implausible from a literary point of view, even though they are actually true. But is this not because we nearly always fail to cast the light of psychology on our spontaneous decisions in order to explain the mysteriously conceived reasons which have impelled us to make them? Perhaps Eugénie's profound passion ought to be analyzed down to its most delicate fibers, for it became a disease, as some cynics would say, and influenced her entire life. Many people prefer to deny the outcome rather than measure the strength of the bonds, knots and connections which link one fact to another in the moral realm. At this point, therefore, Eugénie's past life will serve as a guarantee, to observers of human nature, of her irreflective naïveté and the spontaneity of the emotions that welled up in her heart. Because her life had been so tranquil, feminine pity, the most ingenuous of all emotions, developed all the more forcefully in her soul.

Troubled by the events of the day, she woke up several times to listen for a sound from her cousin's room, thinking she had heard his sighs, which had been reverberating in her heart ever since the day before. Sometimes she pictured him dying of sorrow, sometimes she dreamed that he was starving. Toward morning, she clearly heard a terrible cry. She immediately dressed herself and ran softly, in the light of dawn, to her cousin, who had left his door open. The wax candle had burned down to the socket of the candlestick. Charles, overcome by nature, was sleeping fully dressed in an armchair, with his head resting on the bed. He was dreaming as people usually do when they go to sleep with an empty stomach. Eugénie was able to weep undisturbed; she was able to admire his handsome young face, mottled by grief, and his tear-swollen eyes which seemed to be shedding still more tears even though he was asleep. Charles instinctively sensed Eugénie's presence; he opened his eyes and saw her looking at him with compassion.

"Excuse me, cousin," he said, obviously unaware of the hour or of where he was.

"There are hearts that feel for you here, cousin; we thought you might be needing something. You ought to go to bed: you'll be exhausted if you stay like that."

"That's true."

"Well, good-by."

She hurried away, ashamed but still glad that she had come. Only innocence is capable of such boldness. When it is enlightened, virtue calculates as well as vice. Eugénie, who had not trembled before her cousin, was scarcely able to stand by the time she reached her room. Her life of ignorance had suddenly ceased; she reasoned about what she had done and reproached herself a thousand times. "What will he think of me? He'll think I'm in love with him!" This was precisely what she most wanted him to think. Sincere love has its own kind of foresight; it knows that love arouses love. What an event it was in the solitary young girl's life to have gone furtively into a young man's bedroom! Are there not certain thoughts and actions which, in love, are equivalent for certain souls to the most sacred vows of betrothal?

An hour later, she went into her mother's room and helped her get dressed as usual. Then the two women took up their places in front of the window and waited for Grandet with that anxiety which chills or warms the heart, contracts or dilates it, according to one's character, when one is dreading a scene or a punishment; this feeling is so natural that domestic animals experience it strongly enough to cry out when they are punished even slightly, whereas they remain silent when they injure themselves accidentally. The old man came downstairs. But he spoke absentmindedly to his wife, kissed Eugénie and sat down at the table without appearing to remember his threats of the night before.

"What's happened to my nephew? The boy certainly doesn't get in our way."

"He's still asleep, monsieur," replied Nanon.

"Good—he doesn't need a wax candle," said Grandet sarcastically.

Madame Grandet was amazed by this unexpected clemency, this caustic gaiety. She looked at her husband attentively. The goodman . . . (It may be well to point out here that in Touraine, Anjou, Poitou and Brittany, the word "goodman," frequently used to designate Grandet, is applied to the cruelest of men as well as to the kindliest, as soon as they have reached middle age. It is a title which gives no indication of the individual's goodness.) The goodman took his hat and gloves and said, "I'm going to take a stroll around the square—I want to meet our Cruchots."

"Eugénie, your father definitely has something on his mind."

Grandet, who slept little, spent half of his nights making the preliminary calculations which gave his views, observations and plans their astonishing accuracy and assured them of that unfailing success which amazed the people of Saumur. All human power is a compound of patience and time. The powerful will and watch. The life of a miser is a constant exercise of human power in the service of egotism. He relies on two qualities only: self-love and self-interest. But since self-interest is, in a sense, merely a kind of firm, conscious self-love, the continuous affirmation of a genuine superiority, self-love and self-interest are two parts of the same whole: egotism. Hence, perhaps, the enormous curiosity aroused by the skillful portrayal of a miser. Everyone has some kinship with these personages who outrage all human sentiments by combining them into one passion. Where is the man without desire, and what social desire can be satisfied without money?

Grandet really did have something on his mind, as his wife put it. There was in him, as in all misers, a persistent need to compete with other men, to win their money from them by any legal means. Is it not an act of power to squeeze money from one's fellow man? Does it not confirm one's right to despise those who are so weak that they let themselves be devoured in this world? Oh, who has really understood the lamb lying peacefully at the feet of God, the most touching symbol of all earthly victims and their future, the symbol of the glorification of suffering and weakness? The miser allows this lamb to grow fat, he pens it in, kills it, cooks it, eats it and despises it. The miser's nourishment is composed of money and disdain.

During the night the old man's ideas had taken another course, hence his clemency. He had hatched a plot to make fools of the Parisians, to outwit, swindle and trick them, to make them scurry to and fro, sweat, hope and turn pale, to amuse himself at their expense, he, a former cooper, ensconced in his dingy living room or climbing the worm-eaten staircase of his house in Saumur. He had been thinking about his nephew. He wanted to save his dead brother's honor without its costing either him or his nephew a single franc. His funds were about to be invested for the next three years; he would have nothing to do except manage his property, so he needed some new outlet for his malicious energy. His brother's bankruptcy had provided him with one. Having nothing to squeeze between his paws, he had decided to crush the Parisians for Charles's profit and present himself to the world as an excellent brother at little cost to himself.

Family honor counted so little in his scheme that his good intentions must be compared to the need gamblers feel to see a game well played even if they have no stake in it. The Cruchots were necessary to him; not wishing to go after them, he had decided to make them come to his house and begin to act out that very evening the comedy whose plot he had just conceived, in order to become an object of admiration to the whole town the next day, without having to spend a single franc.

IV

A Miser's Promises, Vows of Love

D uring her father's absence, Eugénie had the happiness of being able to devote herself openly to her beloved cousin, to lavish on him without fear the treasures of her compassion, one of woman's sublime superiorities, the only one she wants to make a man aware of, the only one she forgives him for letting her assume.

Three or four times Eugénie went to listen to the sound of her cousin's breathing, to find out if he was awake or asleep. Then, when he got up, she gave special care to everything involved in his breakfast: the cream, coffee, eggs, fruit, plates and glasses. She ran lightly up the old staircase to listen to the sounds he was making. Was he getting dressed? Was he still weeping? She went up to his door and called out, "Cousin!"

"Yes, cousin?"

"Do you want to have breakfast downstairs or in your room?"

"It makes no difference."

"How are you feeling?"

"My dear cousin, I'm ashamed to say it, but I'm hungry." For Eugénie, this conversation through the door was like an episode from a novel.

"Well, then, we'll bring your breakfast to your room, so that we won't annoy my father."

She ran down to the kitchen with the lightness of a bird.

"Nanon, go straighten up his room!"

The stairway, so often ascended and descended, in which the slightest sound reverberated, seemed to Eugénie to have lost its dilapidated aspect; she saw it as luminous, it spoke to her, it was as young as she, as young as her love, which it was serving. Finally her mother, her kind, indulgent mother, agreed to take part in the whims of her daughter's love. As soon as Charles's room had been cleaned, they both went up to keep the unhappy young man company—did not Christian charity require them to console him? The two women drew from their religion a goodly number of little sophisms to justify their improper conduct.

Charles Grandet found himself the object of the most tender and affectionate care. His grief-stricken heart keenly felt the sweetness of the gentle friendliness and exquisite sympathy which the two women, who lived under almost constant constraint, were able to express when they found themselves free for a moment in the realm of suffering, their natural sphere. Authorized by kinship, Eugénie began to put away the linen and toilet articles her cousin had brought with him, and she had time to marvel at each luxurious trifle, at the chased gold and silver trinkets she came across, and which she held in her hand for a long time on the pretext of examining them. Charles was deeply touched by the selfless interest shown in him by his aunt and

cousin; he knew Paris society well enough to realize
that, in his present situation, he would have found only
cold or indifferent hearts there. Eugénie appeared to
him in all the splendor of her special beauty; from then
on he admired the innocence of the character and way
of life which he had laughed at only the day before.
Therefore, when Eugénie took from Nanon the china
bowl full of coffee and cream to serve it to him with
all the ingenuousness of guileless emotion, casting an
affectionate glance at him, the Parisian's eyes filled with
tears; he took her hand and kissed it.

"Well, what's wrong now?" she asked.

"Oh, these are tears of gratitude!" he replied.

Eugénie abruptly turned toward the mantelpiece to
take the candlesticks. "Here, Nanon," she said, "take
these away."

When she looked at her cousin she was still blush-
ing quite noticeably, but at least her glance was able to
lie, to conceal the excessive joy that was flooding her
heart. Their eyes, however, expressed a single feeling,
just as their souls were mingled in a single thought:
the future was theirs. This tender emotion was all the
sweeter to Charles in the midst of his enormous sorrow
because it was so unexpected.

A knock on the door brought the two women back
to their places. They were fortunately able to go downstairs quickly enough to be back at their work when
Grandet entered. If he had met them under the archway,
it would have been enough to arouse his suspicion.

After lunch, which the old man ate hastily, the
gamekeeper, who had not yet received the compensation that had been promised to him, arrived from
Froidfond with a hare, some partridges that had been
killed in the park, some eels and two pike owed by the
millers.

"Well, well, good old Cornoiller has come in the nick of time! Is that good to eat?"

"Yes, my dear generous sir, they were killed two days ago."

"Come, Nanon, get a move on!" said the old man. "Take this, we'll have it for dinner; I'm entertaining two Cruchots."

Nanon opened her eyes wide in bewilderment and looked at everyone. "But where am I supposed to get lard and spices?"

"Give Nanon six francs, my dear," said Grandet to his wife, "and remind me to go down to the cellar to get some good wine."

"And now, Monsieur Grandet," began the game-keeper, who had prepared a speech to settle the question of his wages, "Monsieur Grandet . . ."

"Ta, ta, ta, ta! I know what you want to say," said Grandet. "You're a good fellow; we'll see about that tomorrow, I'm too busy today. Give him five francs, my dear," he said to his wife.

He hurried away. The poor woman was only too happy to buy peace for eleven francs. She knew that Grandet always kept quiet for two weeks after having thus taken back, bit by bit, the money he had given her.

"Here, Cornoiller," she said, slipping ten francs into his hand. "Some day we'll reward you for your services."

Cornoiller had nothing to say. He left.

"Madame," said Nanon, who had put on her black hat and picked up her basket, "I'll only need three francs. Keep the rest; don't worry, I'll manage."

"Make a good dinner, Nanon," said Eugénie. "My cousin will come down to eat with us."

"There's something unusual going on, I'm sure of it," said Madame Grandet. "This is only the third time since our marriage that your father has invited anyone to dinner."

Toward four o'clock, just as Eugénie and her mother had finished setting the table for six people and the head of the household had brought up a few bottles of those exquisite wines which provincials lovingly keep in reserve, Charles came into the living room. He was pale. There was a winsome sadness in his gestures, his countenance and the sound of his voice. His sorrow was unfeigned, he was really suffering; and the veil which grief had cast over his features gave him that interesting air so attractive to women. Eugénie loved him all the more for it. Also, perhaps, his unhappiness had made her feel closer to him. He was no longer the rich, handsome young man living in a world that was inaccessible to her, but a relative who had been plunged into frightful misery. Misery begets equality. Women and angels have this in common: all suffering creatures belong to them.

Charles and Eugénie understood each other and spoke only with their eyes, for the poor ruined dandy, the orphan, withdrew to a corner and remained there in calm, proud silence; but from time to time his cousin's gentle, caressing glance shone on him, forcing him to abandon his sad thoughts, to go off with her into the realm of hope and the future, where she wanted to be with him.

At that moment the people of Saumur were more excited by the dinner to which Grandet had invited the Cruchots than they had been the day before by the sale of his vintage, which constituted an act of high treason against the wine industry. If the crafty winegrower had given his dinner with the same idea that cost Alcibiades' dog its tail, he might have been a great man; but, feeling too superior to a town which he was constantly mocking, he cared nothing about Saumur. The des Grassins soon learned of the violent death and probable bankruptcy of Charles's father; they decided to go to see their client that very evening, in order to sympathize with him in his misfortune and show their friendship for him, while at the same time trying to discover the motives that had led him to invite the Cruchots to dinner in such circumstances.

At exactly five o'clock, Judge C. de Bonfons and his uncle, the notary, arrived in their Sunday best. The guests sat down to table and began to eat heartily. Grandet was solemn, Charles was taciturn, Eugénie was silent and Madame Grandet spoke no more than usual, so the dinner had a markedly funereal atmosphere.

When they all rose from table, Charles said to his aunt and uncle, "Please allow me to retire. I must begin a long and sad correspondence."

"Certainly, nephew."

After Charles was gone and the old man could safely assume that he was engrossed in his letter-writing and could hear nothing, he looked slyly at his wife and said, "Madame Grandet, what we're going to talk about would be Greek to you. It's seven-thirty, time for you to go off to bed. Good night, daughter." He kissed Eugénie and the two women left the room.

Now began the scene in which Old Man Grandet, more than at any other time in his life, made use of the skill he had acquired in his dealings with his fellow man, a skill which had often earned him the nickname of "the old shark" among those whom he had bitten a little too painfully. If the former Mayor of Saumur had had loftier ambitions, if fortunate circumstances had brought him to the upper levels of society and sent him to the gatherings in which the affairs of nations were treated, and if he had there made use of the genius with which his self-interest had endowed him, he would undoubtedly have been gloriously useful to France. But it is perhaps equally probable that, outside of Saumur, the old man would have cut a sorry figure. Perhaps there are minds that resemble those animals which cannot reproduce when they are taken out of their native climates.

"J-j-j-judge, you were s-s-s-saying that b-b-b-bankruptcy . . ."

The stuttering which the old man had affected for so long and which, like the deafness he complained of in rainy weather, was accepted as genuine, became on this occasion so tiresome to the two Cruchots that as they listened to him they unconsciously began to grimace, making strained efforts as though trying to help him finish the words in which he was deliberately entangling himself.

At this point it may be advisable to give the history of Grandet's stuttering and deafness. No one in the whole region could hear better or pronounce Anjou French more distinctly than the crafty winegrower. In spite of all his shrewdness, however, he had once been taken in by an Israelite who, in the course of the discussion, cupped his hand to his ear, supposedly to enable himself to hear better, and stammered so incoherently in his search for words that Grandet, a victim of his own humanity, felt obliged to suggest to the cunning Jew the words and ideas he was seeking, to complete his arguments for him, to say the things he ought to have said; in short, to become the Jew instead of Grandet. The cooper came out of this strange encounter having concluded the only bargain of which he had reason to complain during his entire business career. But while he lost financially, morally he gained a good lesson from which he later reaped many benefits. Finally, therefore, the old man blessed the Jew who had taught him the art of exhausting the patience of his business adversary and making him constantly lose sight of his own ideas as he tried to express Grandet's for him.

No other affair had ever required more urgently than this one the use of his deafness, his stuttering and the incomprehensible circumlocutions in which he enveloped his ideas. First of all, he did not want to take responsibility for his ideas; and also he wanted to be able to control his speech carefully, leaving his true intentions in doubt.

"M-m-Monsieur de B-b-b-Bonfons . . ." (This was the second time in the past three years that Grandet had addressed Judge Cruchot as Monsieur de Bonfons; this gave the judge reason to believe that the wily old man had chosen him as his son-in-law.) "Y-y-you were s-s-saying that in certain c-c-c-cases b-b-bankruptcies can b-b-be p-p-prevented b-b-b-by . . ."

"By the courts of commerce themselves. It happens every day," said Monsieur C. de Bonfons, pursuing Grandet's idea, or thinking he had guessed it, and wishing to explain it to him affectionately. "Listen . . ."

"I'm l-l-l-listening," replied the old man humbly, taking on the malicious expression of a child who is laughing up his sleeve at his teacher, while seeming to pay close attention.

"When an important and highly respected man like, for example, your late brother in Paris . . ."

"M-m-my b-b-b-brother, yes."

"Is threatened with insolvency . . ."

"That's c-c-called insolvency?"

"Yes. When his bankruptcy is imminent, the court of commerce, which has jurisdiction over him (follow this closely), has the power to issue a decree assigning liquidators to his firm. Liquidation is not bankruptcy, you see. If a man goes bankrupt, he's dishonored; if his firm is liquidated, he remains an honorable man."

"That's v-v-very d-d-different, if it d-d-d-doesn't c-cost any more," said Grandet.

"But a firm can be liquidated even without the help of the court. For," said the judge, taking a pinch of snuff, "how is a bankruptcy declared?"

"Yes, I n-n-never thought of that," replied Grandet.

"First," said the magistrate, "by filing a petition in bankruptcy with the record office of the court; this may be done by either the merchant himself or his duly registered agent. Secondly, at the request of the creditors. Now, if the merchant doesn't file a petition in bankruptcy and if no creditor asks the court for a judgment declaring the merchant in bankruptcy, what happens?"

"Y-y-yes, what d-d-d-does happen?"

"Then the family of the deceased, his representatives, his heirs, or the merchant himself, if he's not dead, or his friends, if he's in hiding, liquidate the firm. Perhaps you'd like to liquidate your brother's business?" asked the judge.

"Ah, Grandet!" exclaimed the notary. "That would be a noble thing to do! There's honor in the depths of our provinces. If you were to save your name, for it *is* your name, you'd be . . ."

"Sublime!" said the judge, interrupting his uncle.

"Of c-c-course," replied the old winegrower, "m-my b-b-brother's name was Grandet, the s-s-s-same as m-m-mine. There's n-no d-d-doubt about that. I d-d-don't d-d-deny it. And anyway, this l-l-liquidation m-might b-b-be advantageous in m-m-many ways to m-m-my n-n-nephew, whom I'm v-v-very fond of. B-b-but I'll have to look into it first. I d-d-don't know the shrewd scoundrels of Paris. I l-l-live in Saumur, y-y-you know! My v-v-vines, my d-d-drainage d-ditches, and all my other b-b-business to look after. . . . I've never g-g-given anyone a note. What is a note? I've received a l-l-lot of them, but I've never s-s-signed one. They c-c-can be c-cashed and d-d-discounted, but that's all I know about them. I've heard that you c-c-can b-buy up n-n-notes . . ."

"That's right," said the judge. "Notes can be bought in the market at a certain discount. Do you understand?"

Grandet cupped his hand, put it to his ear and the judge repeated his sentence.

"But," replied the winegrower, "is there anything to g-g-gain f-f-from that? At m-m-my age, I d-d-don't know anything about s-s-s-such things. I m-m-must stay here to l-l-look after my vines. The g-g-grapes pile up, and that's what b-b-brings in the money. . . . The h-h-harvest comes first. I have some important and p-p-profitable business to t-t-take care of at Froidfond. I c-c-can't abandon my land and g-g-go off to get m-mixed up in some c-c-complicated mess that I d-d-don't understand at all. You s-s-say I ought to be in Paris to l-l-liquidate, to stop the d-d-d-declaration of b-b-bankruptcy, but you c-c-can't b-be in two p-p-places at once, unless you're a little b-b-bird, and . . ."

"I understand!" cried the notary. "Well, old friend, you have friends, old friends, who are willing to show how devoted they are to you."

"Come on, make up your mind!" thought the winegrower.

"And if someone went to Paris, looked up your brother Guillaume's biggest creditor and said to him . . ."

"J-j-just a minute!" interrupted the old man. "Said what to him? Something like this: 'Monsieur Grandet of

Saumur th-th-this, Monsieur Grandet of S-Saumur that. He loves his b-b-brother, he loves his n-n-nephew. He's a g-g-good relative, he had v-v-very good intentions. He g-g-got a good price f-f-for his wine this year. Don't f-f-file a d-d-declaration of b-b-bankruptcy; c-c-call a meeting and ap-ap-appoint liquidators. Then Grandet will s-s-see what he can d-d-do. You'll g-g-get a lot m-m-more of your money b-b-back by liquidating than by letting the l-l-law stick its n-nose into the c-c-case.' Eh? Isn't that right?"

"Exactly!" said the judge.

"As you know, Monsieur de B-Bonfons, a man ought to examine the f-f-facts before m-m-making up his mind. If you c-c-can't, you c-c-can't. In every important b-b-business matter, you must know the assets and liabilities if you d-d-don't want to be ruined. Isn't that right?"

"Certainly," said the judge. "In my opinion, the debts can be bought up within several months, and then an arrangement can be made to pay them in full. Yes indeed, you can lead a dog a long way if you hold a piece of meat in front of him. If there's been no declaration of bankruptcy and you hold the proofs of indebtedness, you become as white as snow."

"As s-s-snow?" repeated Grandet, cupping his hand again. "I d-d-don't understand this snow you're t-t-talking about."

"Then why don't you listen to what I'm saying!" cried the judge.

"I'm l-l-listening."

"A note is a piece of merchandise whose price may fluctuate. That's a deduction from Jeremy Bentham's theory of usury. Bentham was an economist who proved that the prejudice against usurers was foolish."

"I see!" said the old man.

"Considering the fact that in principle, according to Bentham, money is merchandise, and that anything representing money also becomes merchandise," continued the judge; "considering, furthermore, that it is well known that, subject to the usual variations that govern commercial matters, the note as merchandise, bearing this or that signature, becomes, like any other commodity, plentiful or scarce, valuable or worthless, it is the verdict of this court . . . (Oh, how stupid of me! Excuse me.) In my opinion, you could buy up your brother's debts at twenty-five percent."

"You c-c-call him J-J-Jeremy Ben . . ."

"Bentham, an Englishman."

"There's a Jeremiah who'll help us avoid a lot of lamentations in business," said the notary, laughing.

"Those Englishmen s-s-sometimes show g-g-good sense," said Grandet. "So, according to B-Bentham, if my b-b-brother's notes are worth . . . n-n-not worth anything . . . That's right, isn't it? It s-s-seems clear to me . . . The creditors would be . . . no, they wouldn't be . . . I-I-I know what I'm t-t-trying to say, but . . ."

"Let me explain the whole thing to you," said the judge. "In law, if you hold the titles to all the debts of the Grandet firm, your brothers and his heirs owe nothing to anyone. Good."

"Good," repeated the old man.

"In equity, if your brother's notes are negotiated (negotiated, do you understand the term?) on the market at a reduction of a certain percent, and if one of your friends comes along and buys them up, without any pressure having been put on the creditors to sell them, the estate of the late Monsieur Grandet of Paris will be honorably cleared."

"That's true, b-b-business is b-business," said the cooper. "There's no d-d-denying it. . . . Just the s-s-same, though, it's d-d-difficult, you can understand that. I have n-n-no m-money, and I d-d-don't have the t-t-time, neither the t-t-time n-nor . . .

"Yes, I know: you can't leave Saumur. Well, I'm willing to go to Paris for you (you'll pay my expenses—they won't amount to much). I'll go to see the creditors. I'll talk to them and get them to grant an extension of time, then you can settle everything by adding a certain amount of cash to the assets in order to take over all title to the debts."

"B-b-but we'll have to wait and s-s-see about that. I c-c-can't, I won't c-c-commit myself without . . . You c-can't get b-b-blood from a t-t-turnip. You understand?"

"Yes, that's quite true."

"My head is s-s-spinning f-f-from all the things you've t-t-told me. This is the f-f-first t-time in my life that I've ever b-b-been forced to think about . . ."

"Yes, I know: you're not a lawyer."

"I'm a p-p-poor winegrower and I d-d-don't know anything about what you've j-j-just s-said. I'll h-h-have to think it all over."

"Well . . ." began the judge, preparing to resume the discussion.

"Nephew!" interrupted the notary reproachfully.

"Yes, uncle?"

"Let Monsieur Grandet explain his intentions to you. We've been discussing an important mission. Our dear friend ought to define it clearly . . ."

A knock on the door announced the arrival of the des Grassins family; their entrance and their greetings prevented Cruchot from finishing his sentence. The notary was glad of this interruption: Grandet was already beginning to scowl at him and his wen gave evidence of an inner storm. But, above all, the prudent notary regarded it as improper for a judge of the civil

court to go to Paris to make creditors come to terms
and involve himself in a dubious maneuver which vio-
lated the standards of strict integrity. Furthermore, not
having heard Grandet express the slightest willingness
to pay anything at all, he was instinctively afraid to see
his nephew commit himself in the matter. He therefore
took advantage of the moment when the des Grassins
entered to take the judge by the arm and draw him into
a window recess.

"You've shown enough good will now, nephew;
don't carry your devotion any further. Your desire for
his daughter is blinding you. My God, you don't have
to charge into this thing like a wild boar! Let me steer
the ship now; you can help me out when I need you.
Do you think it's proper for you to compromise your
dignity as a magistrate in such a . . ."

He did not finish; he heard Monsieur des Grassins
saying to the old cooper as he held out his hand to
him, "Grandet, we've heard about the terrible misfortune that's come to your family, the bankruptcy of the
house of Guillaume Grandet and your brother's death.
We've come to tell you how much we sympathize with
you on this sad occasion."

"The only misfortune," said the notary, interrupting the banker, "is the death of the younger Monsieur
Grandet. And he wouldn't have killed himself if he'd
thought of asking his brother to help him. Our old
friend here, who's a man of honor to his fingertips,
intends to liquidate the debts of the house of Grandet
in Paris. In order to spare him the trouble of going
through legal proceedings, my nephew, the judge, has
offered to leave for Paris immediately to negotiate with
the creditors and give them proper satisfaction."

These words, confirmed by Grandet's attitude as
he stroked his chin, completely disconcerted the three

des Grassins, who, on their way to Grandet's house, had thoroughly cursed his avarice and all but accused him of fratricide.

"Ah, I knew it!" cried the banker, looking at his wife. "Do you remember what I told you on the way here, Madame des Grassins? Grandet is the most honorable man in the world: he won't tolerate the slightest stain on his name! Money without honor is a disease. There's honor in our provinces! It's a noble thing to do, Grandet, very noble. I'm an old soldier and I can't disguise my thoughts, so I'll say it bluntly: it's sublime, by God!"

"Yes, b-b-but the s-s-sublime is v-v-very expensive," said the old man as the banker warmly shook his hand.

"But this, my dear Grandet, with all due respect to the judge here," said Monsieur des Grassins, "is a purely commercial matter and it ought to be handled by an expert businessman who's thoroughly familiar with creditors, disbursements and the computation of interest. I have to go to Paris on some business of my own, and I could take charge of . . ."

"We'll t-t-talk things over and t-t-t-try to s-s-see what c-c-can be d-d-done without c-c-committing me to anything I wouldn't want to d-d-do," stammered Grandet, "because, you see, the judge naturally asked me to pay his traveling expenses." He spoke these last words without stuttering.

"But it's a pleasure to be in Paris!" said Madame des Grassins. "I'd gladly pay to go there!" She made a gesture to her husband as though to encourage him to snatch this mission away from their adversaries at any cost; then she looked very ironically at the two Cruchots, whose faces had taken on a pitiful expression.

Grandet seized the banker by one of the buttons of

his coat, drew him into a corner and said to him, "I'd have much more confidence in you than in the judge. And besides, there's something else involved," he added, twitching his wen. "I want to buy some government stock. I have several thousand francs to invest, and I don't want to pay more than eighty francs a share. I'm told the price always goes down at the end of each month. You know all about those things, don't you?"

"I should say I do! Well, then, you want me to invest a few thousand francs for you?"

"Not much to begin with. But don't breathe a word about this! I don't want anyone to know I'm playing that game. Buy some shares for me at the end of the month, but don't say anything about it to the Cruchots; they'd be annoyed if they knew. Since you're going to Paris anyway, you can also find out how things stand for my poor nephew."

"You can count on me. I'll take the stagecoach tomorrow," said des Grassins loudly. "I'll come by to get your final instructions at . . . What time should I come?"

"At five o'clock, before dinner," said the winegrower, rubbing his hands together.

The two factions stood facing each other for a few moments, then, after a pause, des Grassins tapped Grandet on the shoulder and said, "It's good to have such good relatives . . ."

"Yes," replied Grandet, "it may not show, b-b-but I'm a g-good relative. I loved my brother and I'll b-b-be glad to p-prove it if . . . if it doesn't cost . . ."

"We'll leave you now, Grandet," said the banker, fortunately interrupting him before he had finished his sentence. "Since I'm going to Paris sooner than I'd planned, I must take care of some business matters right away."

"Very well. As for m-m-me, with regard t-t-t-to what we were j-j-just talking about, I'm going to retire to m-m-my room to d-d-d-deliberate, as Judge Cruchot would s-s-say."

"I'm no longer Monsieur de Bonfons, damn it!" thought the magistrate sadly; his face took on the expression of a judge who is bored by a lawyer's speech.

The heads of the two rival families went off together. They had all ceased to give any thought to the way Grandet had betrayed the whole winegrowing community that morning; they vainly sounded each other out, each trying to discover what the other thought about the old man's real intentions in this new affair.

"Are you coming to Madame d'Orsonval's house with us?" des Grassins asked the notary.

"We'll go there later," replied the judge. "I've promised to stop by Madame de Gribeaucourt's house for a short time this evening, so, with my uncle's permission, we'll go there first."

"Good-by for a while then, gentlemen," said Madame des Grassins.

And when the des Grassins were a few paces away from the two Cruchots, Adolphe said to his father, "They're hopping mad, aren't they?"

"Be quiet, son," replied his mother, "they may still be able to hear us. Besides, the expression you just used isn't in good taste; it sounds like something you picked up in law school."

"Well, uncle," exclaimed the judge when he saw that the des Grassins were out of earshot, "I began by being Judge de Bonfons and ended up as a mere Cruchot!"

"I saw how much that annoyed you; but the wind was favoring the des Grassins. Sometimes you're terribly foolish, in spite of all your intelligence! Let them sail off

on Old Man Grandet's 'We'll see' and just sit tight, my
boy; you'll marry Eugénie just the same."

In a few moments the news of Grandet's magnani-
mous decision was simultaneously announced in three
different houses, and soon the whole town was talking
of nothing but this proof of fraternal devotion. Grandet
was forgiven for the sale he had made in violation of
the agreement which all the winegrowers had sworn
to respect. Everyone admired his sense of honor and
praised his generosity, of which no one had believed
him capable. It is typical of the French character to
become enthusiastic, angry or impassioned over the
meteor of the present, the passing fancies of the moment.
Can it be that collective beings, peoples, have no
memory?

When Grandet had locked his door he called Nanon
and said to her, "Don't untie the watchdog and don't
go to sleep: we have work to do together. At eleven
o'clock, Cornoiller should be in front of the house with
the carriage from Froidfond. Listen for him so you can
stop him from knocking on the door, and tell him to
come right in. It's against police regulations to make
noise at night. Besides, the neighborhood doesn't need
to know I'm going to take a trip."

Having said this, Grandet went up to his study,
where Nanon heard him moving things, rummaging and
pacing back and forth, but with caution. He obviously
did not want to wake up his wife and daughter, and
above all he did not want to attract the attention of
his nephew, whom he had begun to curse when he saw
that there was a light in his room.

In the middle of the night, Eugénie, preoccupied
with her cousin, thought she heard the moan of a dying
man, and for her this dying man had to be Charles:
she had left him so pale, so desperate! Perhaps he

had killed himself. She quickly wrapped herself in a hooded coat and was about to leave her room when she saw such a bright light coming in through the cracks around her door that she was afraid a fire had broken out in the house; but she was soon reassured when she heard Nanon's heavy footsteps and the sound of her voice mingled with the neighing of several horses.

"Can father be taking my cousin away?" she wondered as she opened her door carefully to keep it from creaking, but wide enough to enable her to see what was going on in the hall.

Suddenly her eyes met those of her father; although his gaze was vague and distracted, it struck terror into her heart. He and Nanon were yoked together by a thick pole whose ends rested on their right shoulders; from it hung a rope to which was attached a small keg of the kind Grandet amused himself by making in the bakehouse in his spare time.

"Holy Virgin!" exclaimed Nanon softly. "It's so heavy!"

"What a shame it's only full of copper coins!" replied the old man. "Be careful not to bump against the candlestick."

The scene was illuminated by a single candle placed between two of the posts supporting the railing of the staircase.

"Cornoiller," said Grandet to his honorary gamekeeper, "have you brought your pistols?"

"Why, no—what's there to be afraid of with your copper coins?"

"Oh, nothing," said Old Man Grandet.

"Besides, we'll go fast," continued the gamekeeper. "Your farmers have picked out their best horses for you."

"Good, good. . . . Did you tell them where I was going?"

"I didn't know."

"Good. Is the carriage strong?"

"Strong, monsieur? It's strong enough to carry three thousand pounds! How much do those little barrels of yours weigh?"

"I ought to know that!" said Nanon. "They must weigh nearly eighteen hundred pounds."

"Will you keep quiet, Nanon! Tell my wife I've gone to the country. I'll be back in time for dinner. . . . Drive fast, Cornoiller: we must be in Angers before nine o'clock."

The carriage set off. Nanon bolted the big door, untied the dog and went to bed with a bruised shoulder. No one in the neighborhood knew anything of Grandet's departure or the object of his journey. The old man's precautions were perfectly effective. No one ever saw a sou in that house full of gold. Having learned that morning, from gossip along the waterfront, that the price of gold had doubled because a large number of ships were being fitted out in Nantes and that some speculators had arrived in Angers to buy it, the old winegrower, by simply borrowing some horses from his tenant farmers, had enabled himself to go to Angers to sell his gold and bring back in the form of treasury notes the sum necessary for the purchase of his government stocks, having increased it by the favorable rate of exchange.

"Father's going away," thought Eugénie, who had heard everything from the top of the stairs.

Silence had settled over the house again, and the distant rumble of the carriage, which had gradually faded away, no longer reverberated through the sleeping town. Just then Eugénie heard in her heart, before listening to it with her ears, a moan which pierced the walls, coming from the direction of her cousin's room. A strip of light, as thin as the edge of a saber, shone through the crack of the door and cut horizontally across the banisters of the old staircase. "He's suffering," she said as she climbed two of the steps.

A second moan brought her to the landing outside his room. The door was ajar. She pushed it open. Charles was sleeping with his head hanging outside the old armchair; his hand, from which a pen had fallen, was nearly touching the floor. Eugénie was frightened by the irregular breathing necessitated by his position; she quickly entered the room.

"He must be very tired," she thought as she looked at ten or twelve sealed letters. She read the addresses: "Farry, Breilman & Co., Carriage Makers," "Monsieur Buisson, Tailor," etc.

"He's no doubt settled all his affairs so that he can leave France soon," she thought. Then her eyes fell on two open letters. She suddenly felt faint when she read the words with which one of them began: "My dearest Annette . . ." Her heart began to pound and she felt as though she were rooted to the floor.

"His dearest Annette! He's in love, and he's loved in return! There's no more hope! . . . What has he written to her?" These thoughts flashed through her mind and her heart. She could see the words everywhere, even on the floor, in letters of fire. "I have to give up already! No, I won't read that letter. I must go away. . . . But what if I did read it?"

She looked at Charles, gently took hold of his head and placed it on the back of the armchair; he made no resistance, like a child who recognizes his mother even in his sleep and receives her care and kisses without awakening. Like a mother, Eugénie raised the hanging hand and, like a mother, she gently kissed his hair. "Dearest Annette!" A demon kept shrieking these two words in her ear.

"I know I'm probably doing wrong, but I'm going to read that letter anyway," she thought. Then she turned her head away, for her noble sense of honor had just begun to cry out in protest. For the first time in her life, right and wrong were opposing each other in her heart. Until then, she had never had to blush for anything she had done. Passion and curiosity won out. The pressure inside her heart increased with each phrase, and the keen ardor that swept over her as she read this letter made the pleasures of first love seem still more delightful to her:

> *My dearest Annette,*
> *Nothing could have separated us except the great misfortune which has now over-whelmed me and which could not have been foreseen by any human wisdom. My father has killed himself. His fortune and mine are entirely lost. I have become an orphan at an age when, because of the nature of my upbringing, I may still be regarded as a child, and yet I must rise up like a man from the abyss into which I have fallen. I have just spent part of this night in taking stock of my situation. If I want to leave France as an honorable man, and there is no question in my mind about that, I cannot bring together a hundred francs of my own to go off and try my luck in the Indies or America. Yes, my poor Anna, I am going to seek my fortune in the deadliest of climates. I have been told that in such places a man is sure to make a fortune within a short time. As for remaining*

*in Paris, I could not do it. Neither my soul
nor my face would be able to put up with
the insults, the coldness and the disdain which
await the ruined man, the son of a bankrupt!
My God! Two million francs in debt! I would
be killed in a duel the first week. Therefore I
will not return. Your love, the most tender and
devoted love that ever ennobled a man's heart,
cannot draw me back. Alas, my beloved, I do
not have enough money to go where you are,
to give and receive one last kiss, a kiss that
would give me the strength necessary for my
enterprise. . . .*

"Poor Charles, I was right to read his letter!"
thought Eugénie. "I have some gold—I'll give it to him."
She wiped away her tears and went on reading:

*I had never given any thought to the mis-
eries of poverty. If I have the hundred louis
needed for the journey, I will not have one sou
with which to buy merchandise for trading.
But no, I will not know how much money
I have left until my debts in Paris have been
settled. If I have nothing, I will calmly go to
Nantes and ship out as a common seaman. I
will begin over there as other energetic young
men have begun, young men who set out penniless and were rich when they returned from
the Indies.*
*Ever since this morning I have been coldly
contemplating my future. It is more horrible
for me than for anyone else, I who was pam-
pered by a mother who adored me and cherished by the kindest of fathers, I who found*

Anna's love as soon as I entered society! I had known only the flowers of life; such happiness could not last. Nevertheless, my dear Annette, I have more courage than one might expect a thoughtless young man to have, especially a young man accustomed to the affectionate indulgence of the most charming woman in Paris, cradled in the joys of family life, on whom everything smiled at home, and whose wishes were commands to his father. . . . Oh, my father, Annette! He is dead. . . .

Well, I have thought over my situation, and yours too. I have aged a great deal in twenty-four hours. If, in order to keep me with you in Paris, Anna darling, you were to sacrifice all the pleasures of luxury, your fine clothes, your box at the opera, we would still not have enough for my frivolous way of life; furthermore, I could not accept such sacrifices. So today marks the beginning of our eternal separation.

"He's leaving her! Dear God, how happy I am!" Eugénie leapt for joy. Charles stirred and she felt a chill of terror; fortunately for her, however, he did not wake up. She went on reading:

When will I return? I do not know. The climate of the Indies quickly ages a European, especially a European who works. Let us look ten years ahead. Ten years from now your daughter will be eighteen; she will be your companion, your spy. The world will be cruel to you, your daughter will be perhaps even crueler. We have seen examples of such social

judgments and ungrateful young daughters; let
us take warning from them. Keep in the depths
of your soul, as I will keep it in mine, the
memory of those four years of happiness, and
be faithful, if you can, to your poor friend.
I cannot demand this, however, because you
see, my dear Annette, I must adapt myself to
my situation, I must take a middle-class view of
life and calculate things on the basis of their real
value. I must therefore think of marriage, which
has become one of the necessities of my new life;
and I must admit that I have found, here in my
uncle's house in Saumur, a cousin whose man-
ners, face, mind and heart would please you,
and who, furthermore, seems to me to have . . .

"He must have been very tired to have stopped
writing to her," thought Eugénie, seeing that the letter
had stopped in the middle of this sentence.

She was justifying him! Was it not impossible for the
innocent girl to sense the coldness with which the letter
was impregnated? To a pure, unsophisticated young girl
who has been given a religious upbringing, everything is
love as soon as she sets foot in the enchanted regions
of love. She walks there surrounded by the celestial
light which emanates from her soul and casts its rays
on the man she loves; she colors him with the flames
of her own feelings and imputes her most beautiful
thoughts to him. A woman's mistakes almost always
arise from her belief in the good, or her confidence in
the true. The words "My dearest Annette, my beloved"
echoed in Eugénie's heart as the sweetest language of
love and caressed her soul as the divine notes of the
Venite Adoremus, repeated by the organ, had caressed
her ear when she was a child. Furthermore, the tears in

which Charles's eyes were still bathed gave evidence of all those noble qualities of heart which ought to win a young girl's love.

How could she know that if Charles loved his father so much and mourned his loss so sincerely, this tenderness came less from the goodness of his heart than from his father's indulgence? By always gratifying their son's whims and giving him all the pleasures of wealth, Monsieur and Madame Guillaume Grandet had prevented him from making those horrible calculations of which most children are more or less capable in Paris when, faced with the delights of Paris life, they develop desires and form plans which, to their chagrin, must be constantly postponed and delayed because their parents are still alive. The father's prodigality had therefore sown in his son's heart a genuine filial love, free of ulterior motives.

But Charles was nonetheless a child of Paris; having been taught by Parisian morality, and by Annette herself, to calculate everything, he was already an old man beneath his youthful mask. He had received the frightful education of that society in which, in the course of an evening, more crimes are committed in thought and word than are punished in the law courts, in which the greatest ideas are destroyed by witticisms, in which a person is considered strong only insofar as he sees things clearly—and there, to see things clearly means to believe in nothing, neither in feelings nor in men, nor even in events, for false events are fabricated there. There, to see things clearly, you must weigh a friend's purse every morning, you must be an expert in the art of placing yourself above whatever happens, you must never show spontaneous admiration for anything, whether it be a work of art or a noble deed, and you must give self-interest as the motive for every action.

After a thousand follies, the great lady, the beautiful Annette, forced Charles to think seriously; she spoke to him of his future as she ran a perfumed hand through his hair; while rearranging a curl, she taught him to see life in terms of cold reason: she made him effeminate and materialistic. It was a double corruption, but it was elegant, refined and in good taste.

"You're so foolish, Charles!" she had said to him. "I'll have a hard time teaching you the ways of the world. You treated Monsieur des Lupeaulx very badly. I know he's not a very honorable man, but wait till he's lost his power, then you can despise him all you like. Do you know what Madame Campan used to say to us? 'Children, as long as a man holds a position in the government, worship him; if he falls, help to drag him to the refuse heap. When he's in power he's a kind of god; after he's been pushed aside he's lower than Marat in his sewer, because he's still alive and Marat was dead. Life is a series of schemes and combinations; you must keep abreast of them and study them if you want to succeed in always keeping yourself in a good position.' "

Charles was too much a man of fashion, he had been too consistently happy with his parents, too much admired by the world, to have any noble sentiments. The grain of gold which his mother had dropped into his heart had been passed through the Parisian drawplate until it became a fragile filament; he had made frivolous use of it and it was about to be worn through by friction. But he was then only twenty-one. At that age, the freshness of youth seems inseparable from candor of soul. The voice, the expression of the eyes and the whole face seem to be in harmony with the feelings. It is for this reason that the sternest judges, the most skeptical lawyers, the most exacting moneylenders hesitate to believe in the premature aging of the heart or the corruption of self-interest when the eyes are still bathed in a pure fluid and there are no wrinkles on the forehead. Charles had never had occasion to apply the maxims of Parisian morality, and so far he still had the radiance of inexperience. But, unknown to himself, he had been inoculated with selfishness. The germs of political economy as it is practiced in Paris were latent in his heart and would soon begin to flourish when he ceased to be an idle spectator and became an actor in the drama of real life.

Nearly all young girls succumb to the sweet promises made by such outer appearances; but even if Eugénie had been as shrewd and observant as some provincial girls are, could she have mistrusted her cousin when his manner, speech and actions were still in harmony with the aspirations of his heart? Chance had decreed, unfortunately for her, that she was to observe the last effusions of genuine sensibility remaining in the young man's heart and hear the dying gasps of his conscience.

She put aside the letter which was, to her, so full of love and began to contemplate her sleeping cousin with satisfaction; the youthful illusions of life were still visible to her on his face. She swore to herself that she would always love him, then she glanced at another letter without attaching much importance to this further indiscretion. She began to read it, but only in order to obtain new proof of the noble qualities which, like all women, she attributed to the man of her choice.

> *Dear Alphonse,*
> *When you read this letter I will no longer have any friends; but I admit that, while mistrusting those fashionable people who use the word so lavishly, I have never doubted your friendship. I am therefore asking you to*

put my affairs in order, and I count on you to get as much as possible out of my possessions. You must know what my situation is by now. I have lost everything and I intend to go to the Indies. I have just written to everyone to whom I believe I owe money. I am enclosing the list, which is as accurate as it is possible for me to make it from memory. I think that my library, furniture, carriages, horses, etc., will bring in enough to pay off my debts. I will keep nothing for myself except a few worthless trifles which may serve to begin my stock of trading goods. I will send you from here, my dear Alphonse, an official power of attorney for the sale in case anything should be contested. Please send me all my weapons. Keep Briton for yourself. No one would be willing to pay what the noble animal is really worth, so I prefer to give him to you like the customary ring which a dying man bequeaths to the executor of his will. I have had a very comfortable traveling carriage built for me by Farry, Breilman & Co., but they have not delivered it yet. Try to persuade them to keep it without asking me for any payment; if they refuse, avoid doing anything that might reflect on my integrity in my present circumstances. I owe the islander six louis which I lost in a card game; be sure to pay . . .

"Dear cousin!" thought Eugénie, putting down the letter and hurrying off to her room with one of the lighted candles. With a surge of keen pleasure she opened one of the drawers of an old oaken dresser, a fine example of Renaissance craftsmanship on which the famous royal salamander, though half effaced, was still visible. She took out a large red velvet purse adorned with gold tassels and edged with worn gold braid, an inheritance from her grandmother. She proudly felt its weight, then happily set about determining the forgotten amount of her little hoard.

She began by separating twenty unused Portuguese gold pieces which had been minted in 1725, during the reign of John V. At the current rate of exchange they were worth five lisbonines or 168.4 francs each, according to her father, but their conventional value was 180 francs, because of their rarity, beauty and sunlike brilliance.

Item: 5 genovines, or 100-lire pieces from Genoa, another rare coin, worth 87 francs at the current rate of exchange, but 100 francs to collectors. She had inherited them from old Monsieur de la Bertellière.

Item: 3 Spanish gold quadruples from the time of Philip V, minted in 1729 and given to her by Madame Gentillet, who always repeated the same remarks each time she gave her one: "This little canary, this little yellow flower, is worth ninety-eight francs! Take good care of it, my dear: it will be the pride of your treasure!"

Item: 100 Dutch ducats, minted in 1756 and worth nearly 13 francs each. (These were the coins her father valued most highly, because the gold in them was 23 carats and a fraction.)

Item: A great curiosity! Two kinds of medals precious to misers: 3 rupees bearing the sign of the Scales and 5 rupees bearing the sign of the Virgin, all of pure 24-carat gold, the magnificent currency of the Great Mogul, each one worth 37.40 francs by weight, but at least 50 francs to connoisseurs who love to handle gold.

Item: the 40-franc napoleon received two days earlier, which she had casually dropped into her red purse.

This treasure contained unused, virgin coins, real works of art. Old Man Grandet asked about them occasionally and liked to take them out and look at them, so that he could point out to his daughter their intrinsic merits, such as the beauty of their milled edges, the brightness of their flat surfaces or the richness of their raised letters, whose sharp edges had not yet been notched. But she was not thinking of these rarieties, or of her father's mania, or of the danger involved in parting with a treasure that was so dear to him; no, she was thinking of her cousin, and she finally calculated, after making a few mistakes, that she possessed gold coins worth about 5800 francs at the current rate of exchange, but which could be sold to collectors for nearly 6000 francs.

At the sight of all her wealth she began to clap her hands, like a child forced to express its overflowing joy in spontaneous physical movement. Thus the father and his daughter had both counted their respective fortunes: he to go and sell his gold, she to cast it into a sea of affection.

She put the coins back into the old purse, picked it up and went downstairs without hesitation. Her cousin's secret distress made her oblivious to propriety and the lateness of the hour; and she was strengthened by her conscience, her devotion and her happiness.

Just as she appeared on the threshold of the door, holding the candle in one hand and her purse in the other, Charles woke up, saw her and sat gaping in surprise. She stepped forward, set the candlestick down on the table and said in a quavering voice, "Cousin, I must ask you to forgive me for a great wrong I've done you; God will forgive the sin if you'll wipe it away."

"What is it?" asked Charles, rubbing his eyes.

"I read those two letters."

Charles blushed.

"How did it happen?" she went on. "Why did I come up here? I really couldn't say now. But I'm tempted not to feel too repentant over having read those letters, because they've revealed to me your heart, your soul and . . ."

"And what?" asked Charles.

"And your plans, your need to have a sum . . ."

"My dear cousin . . ."

"Sh! Not so loud, cousin—don't wake anyone up. Here," she said, opening her purse, "are the savings of a poor girl who doesn't need anything. Take it, Charles. This morning I didn't know what money was, but now you've taught me: it's only a means, that's all. A cousin is almost a brother; you certainly have a right to borrow your sister's purse." Eugénie, as much a woman as a young girl, had not foreseen the possibility of a refusal, but her cousin remained silent. "Oh! You're not refusing, are you?" she asked. The beating of her heart seemed to reverberate in the profound silence. Her cousin's hesitation humiliated her, but the necessity that was weighing down on him presented itself more vividly to her mind and she bent her knee. "I won't get up till you've taken this gold!" she said. "I beg you, cousin, give me an answer! I must know if you respect me, if you're generous, if . . ."

When he heard this cry of noble despair, Charles's tears fell on his cousin's hand, which he had seized to stop her from kneeling. On feeling these warm tears, Eugénie snatched up her purse and emptied it out on the table.

"You *will* take it, won't you?" she said, weeping for joy. "Don't worry, cousin, you'll be rich. This gold will bring you good luck; some day you'll pay it back to me. Besides, we'll be partners. I'll accept any conditions you make. But you shouldn't attach so much importance to this gift."

Charles was finally able to express his feelings: "Yes, Eugénie, I'd have a very petty soul if I didn't accept. However, I don't want you to give me something for nothing, and I want to show as much confidence in you as you've shown in me."

"What do you want me to do?" she asked anxiously.

"Listen, my dear cousin, I have here . . ." He interrupted himself to point to a square box in a leather case standing on the dresser. "I have here something I value with my life. That box was a present from my mother. Since this morning I've been thinking that if she could rise from her grave she herself would sell the gold that her love made her put into that set of toilet articles; but if I were to do it, it would seem to me a sacrilege."

Eugénie gripped his hand convulsively when she heard these last words.

"No," he went on after a slight pause during which they exchanged a tender glance, "no, I don't want to destroy it or risk losing it during my travels. Dear Eugénie, I'm going to leave it with you. Never has one friend entrusted another with anything more sacred. Judge for yourself."

He went over and took the box out of its leather case, opened it and sadly showed his amazed cousin a set of toilet articles, whose workmanship gave the gold they contained a value far above its weight.

"What you're admiring now is nothing," he said, pressing a spring which opened a secret compartment. "These are worth more to me than all the gold in the world." He took out two portraits, two masterpieces by Madame de Mirbel, richly set in pearls.

"Oh, what a beautiful woman! That's the lady you were writing to, isn't . . ."

"No," he said, smiling. "This woman is my mother, and this is my father: they're your aunt and uncle. Eugénie, I ought to beg you on my knees to take care of this treasure for me. If I should perish after losing your little fortune, this gold would repay you; and you're the only person I could leave these portraits with, you're worthy of keeping them. But destroy them, if necessary, to keep anyone else from having them after you . . ." Eugénie said nothing. "You *will* take it, won't you?" he added engagingly.

On hearing her cousin repeat her own words to her, she gave him, for the first time, the look of a woman in love, one of those looks in which there is almost as much coquettishness as profundity. He took her hand and kissed it.

"Angel of purity! Money will never count for anything between us, will it? The feelings that make it mean something will be everything for us from now on."

"You look like your mother. Was her voice as soft as yours?"

"Oh, much softer!"

"Yes, for you," she said, looking down. "Come, Charles, you must go to bed now. I'm sure you're tired. I'll see you tomorrow."

She gently withdrew her hand from his. He accompanied her to her room, lighting her way with a candle. When they were both on the threshold of her door he said, "Oh, why am I penniless!"

"Well, my father is rich, I'm sure of that," she replied.

"Poor girl," said Charles, advancing one foot into

her room and leaning against the wall, "if he were, he wouldn't have let my father die, he wouldn't leave you in this poverty—his whole life would be different."

"But he owns Froidfond."

"And how much is Froidfond worth?"

"I don't know; but he owns Noyers, too."

"Some worthless farm!"

"He has vineyards and meadows . . ."

"They don't amount to anything," said Charles disdainfully. "If your father had as much as twenty-four thousand francs a year, would you live in this cold, barren room?" he added, advancing his left foot. "That's where you'll keep my treasures," he said, pointing to the old dresser in order to hide his thoughts.

"Go to bed now," she said, stopping him from entering her disorderly bedroom.

Charles withdrew and they bade each other good night with a smile.

They both went to sleep with the same dream, and from then on Charles began to scatter a few roses over his sorrow.

The next morning Madame Grandet found her daughter taking a stroll with Charles before breakfast. He was still sad, as was to be expected of an unfortunate young man who had just sunk, so to speak, to the bottom of his despair, and who, on measuring the depth of the abyss into which he had fallen, had felt the full weight of his future life.

"Father won't be back till dinner time," said Eugénie when she saw the look of anxiety on her mother's face.

It was easy to see from Eugénie's manner and expression, and from the extraordinary sweetness that softened her voice, that she and her cousin shared the same thoughts. Their souls had ardently united, perhaps even before they had felt the full strength of the sentiments that had brought them together. Charles stayed in the living room and his melancholy was respected there. Each of the three women had something to keep her busy. Since Grandet had forgotten to look after his affairs, a rather large number of people came to the house: the roofer, the plumber, the mason, the laborers, the carpenter, the crofters and the farmers. Some came to discuss terms for repairs that had to be made, others to pay their rent or collect money. Madame Grandet and Eugénie were therefore obliged to hurry back and forth, to reply to the endless speeches of the workmen and farmers. In her kitchen, Nanon took in the farm products delivered as payment of rent. She always waited for her master to tell her what was to be kept for the house and what was to be sold in the marketplace. Like many country gentlemen, the old man usually drank his bad wine and ate his spoiled fruit.

Toward five o'clock in the afternoon, Grandet returned from Angers. He had received fourteen thousand francs for his gold and in his wallet he had treasury notes that would bear interest until it was time for him to pay for his government stocks. He had left Cornoiller in Angers to take care of the horses, which were almost foundered, and bring them back slowly after giving them a good rest.

"I've just come back from Angers," he said to his wife. "I'm hungry."

"Haven't you eaten anything since yesterday?" shouted Nanon from the kitchen.

"Nothing," replied the old man.

Nanon brought in the soup. Des Grassins came to receive his client's instructions just as the family sat down to dinner. Grandet had paid no attention to his nephew.

"Don't let me interrupt you," said the banker, "we can talk while you're eating. Do you know how much gold is worth in Angers now? They've come to buy it up for Nantes. I'm going to send some there."

"Don't," said the old man. "They already have enough. You're a good friend and I wouldn't want you to waste your time."

"But gold is worth thirteen and a half francs there!"

"You mean it *was* worth that much."

"Where the devil did it come from?"

"I went to Angers last night," replied Grandet in a low voice.

The banker started in surprise. Then the two men began to speak to each other in whispers, glancing at Charles from time to time. Finally des Grassins let slip a second gesture of surprise, no doubt when the former cooper instructed him to invest for him a sum that would bring in an income of a hundred thousand francs a year.

"Monsieur Grandet," said the banker to Charles, "I'm going to Paris. If there's anything you'd like me to do for you there . . ."

"No, monsieur, there's nothing, thank you," replied Charles.

"Thank him better than that, nephew. This gentleman is going to settle the affairs of the house of Guillaume Grandet."

"Does that mean there's still some hope?" asked Charles.

"Why, aren't you my nephew?" cried the cooper with a convincing show of pride. "Your honor is ours. Aren't you a Grandet?"

Charles stood up, seized Old Man Grandet, embraced him, turned pale and left the room. Eugénie stared at her father in admiration.

"Well, good-by and good luck, my dear des Grassins. I hope you wrap those people around your little finger!"

The two diplomats shook hands. The former cooper showed the banker to the door, then, after locking it, he came back, sank into his armchair and said to Nanon, "Bring me some black currant brandy." But, too agitated to stay in one place, he stood up, looked at the portrait of Monsieur de la Bertellière and began to sing, doing what Nanon described as dance steps:

> *In the French Guards*
> *I had a good father . . .*

Nanon, Madame Grandet and Eugénie looked at one another in silence. The winegrower's joy always alarmed them when it reached its height.

The evening was soon over, first of all because Old Man Grandet chose to go to bed early, and when he went to bed everyone else in his house had to sleep, just as when Augustus drank, Poland was drunk; and then Nanon, Charles and Eugénie were just as tired as the head of the household. As for Madame Grandet, she slept, ate, drank and walked in accordance with her husband's wishes. However, during the two hours devoted to digestion, the cooper, more facetious than he had ever been before, muttered many of his favorite maxims; one sample will indicate the quality of his wit. When he had finished his brandy he looked at the glass and said, "You no sooner put your lips to a glass than it's empty! That's our whole story right there. You can't have your cake and eat it too. Money can't circulate and stay in your pocket at the same time, otherwise life would be too beautiful."

He was jovial and benevolent. When Nanon came

in with her spinning wheel he said to her, "You must be tired—put away your hemp."

"My goodness, I wouldn't know what to do with myself!" replied the servant.

"Poor Nanon! Would you like some brandy?"

"Well now, when it comes to brandy I won't say no! Madame makes it a lot better than the apothecaries do. The kind they sell is no good."

"They put too much sugar in it—it doesn't have any taste," said the old man.

The next morning the family, gathered at eight o'clock for breakfast, presented for the first time a picture of genuine intimacy. Misfortune had swiftly brought Madame Grandet, Eugénie and Charles close together, and even Nanon was in sympathy with them without realizing it. The four of them were beginning to form a family of their own. As for the old winegrower, his gratified avarice, and the certainty that he would soon be rid of the young fop without having to pay him anything except his fare to Nantes, made him almost indifferent to his nephew's presence in the house. He left the two children, as he called Charles and Eugénie, free to do as they pleased under the eye of Madame Grandet, whom he trusted without reserve in matters of social and religious morality. His time was completely taken up by the laying out of his meadows and ditches along the road, the planting of his poplar trees on the banks of the Loire and the winter work in his fields at Froidfond.

The springtime of love now began for Eugénie. Since the nocturnal scene in which she gave her treasure to her cousin, her heart had followed the treasure. Accomplices in the same secret, they looked at each other with an expression of mutual understanding which deepened their feelings and made them more completely shared, more intimate, by placing the two of them outside the realm of ordinary life. Did not the fact that they were cousins authorize a certain softness in the voice, a certain tenderness in the eyes? Thus Eugénie took pleasure in soothing her cousin's grief with the childlike joys of a newborn love.

Are there not charming similarities between the beginnings of love and those of life? Do we not lull a child with sweet songs and tender looks? Do we not tell him marvelous stories which gild the future for him? Does not hope constantly spread her radiant wings for him? Does he not shed tears of sorrow and tears of joy in rapid succession? Does he not quarrel over trifles: over pebbles with which he tries to build a flimsy palace, or flowers that are forgotten as soon as they are plucked? Is he not eager to seize time by the forelock, to press forward in life? Love is our second transformation.

Childhood and love were the same thing between Eugénie and Charles: it was first love, with all its childish ways, and it was all the sweeter to their hearts because they were wrapped in melancholy. And because their love had to struggle against the gloom of mourning from the moment it was born, it was all the more in harmony with the provincial austerity of the dilapidated house in which it had been conceived. When he exchanged a few words with his cousin beside the well in the silent courtyard or sat with her on a mossy bench in the little garden until sundown, when they were occupied in saying sweet nothings to each other or thoughtfully enjoying the calm that reigned between the ramparts and the house, as one does beneath the arches of a church, Charles understood the sanctity of love, for his great lady, his dear Annette, had revealed only its stormy agitation to him. He was now abandoning Parisian passion, which is coquettish, vain and sparkling, in favor of pure, true love.

He now liked his uncle's house, whose customs no longer seemed so ridiculous to him. He went downstairs early each morning so that he could talk with Eugénie for a few moments before Grandet came in to hand out the provisions; and when he heard the old man's footsteps on the stairs he hurried out into the garden. The little crime of the morning meeting, which was kept secret even from Eugénie's mother and which Nanon pretended not to notice, gave the most innocent love in the world the excitement of forbidden pleasures. Then after breakfast, when Grandet had gone off to see to his properties and enterprises, Charles would remain with the mother and daughter, experiencing unknown delights as he helped them unwind the thread, watched them work or listened to them chatter. The simplicity of that almost monastic life, which revealed to him the beauty of those souls to which the world was unknown, touched him deeply. He had thought such a way of life impossible in France; he had accepted its existence only in Germany, and even then only in stories and in the novels of Auguste Lafontaine. Soon Eugénie came to represent for him the ideal of Goethe's Marguerite, minus her sin.

And day by day his glances and words enchanted the poor girl, who blissfully abandoned herself to the current of love; she held tight to her happiness as a swimmer clutches a willow branch to pull himself out of the river and rest on the bank. Were not the most joyful hours of those fleeting days already saddened by the sorrow of a coming separation? Each day some little incident reminded them that this separation was not far off. Thus, three days after des Grassins' departure, Charles was taken by Grandet to the civil court, with all the solemnity that provincial people attach to such actions, to sign a document whereby he relinquished all claim to his father's estate. A terrible repudiation! A kind of domestic apostasy! He went to Monsieur Cruchot, the notary, to draw up two powers of attorney: one for des Grassins, the other for the friend entrusted with the sale of his belongings. Then he had to go through all the formalities for obtaining a passport. Finally, when he had received the simple mourning clothes he had requested from Paris, he called in a local tailor and sold him his useless wardrobe. Old Man Grandet was particularly pleased by this action. "Ah, now you look like a man who's ready to sail away, determined to make his fortune," he said to Charles when he saw him wearing a coat made of coarse black cloth. "That's good, very good!"

"I hope you'll believe me when I tell you, monsieur," replied Charles, "that I'll always know what's proper to my situation."

"What's that?" asked the old man, his eyes lighting up at the sight of a handful of gold which Charles had just shown him.

"Monsieur, I've gathered together all the buttons, rings and other useless trifles I own which may have some value; but since I don't know anyone in Saumur, I wanted to ask you this morning to . . ."

"To buy them from you?" interrupted Grandet.

"No, uncle, I wanted you to recommend some honest man who . . ."

"Give them to me, nephew—I'll go upstairs and estimate their value, then I'll come back and tell you within a centime what they're worth. That's jeweler's gold," he said, examining a long chain, "eighteen or nineteen carats."

The old man put out his broad hand and walked away with the mass of gold.

"Cousin," said Charles, "allow me to give you these two buttons, which you can use to fasten ribbons to your wrists. It makes a kind of bracelet that's quite fashionable nowadays."

"I accept them without hesitation, cousin," replied Eugénie, with an understanding glance.

"Aunt, this is my mother's thimble; I've always kept it carefully in my traveling kit," said Charles, presenting a pretty gold thimble to Madame Grandet, who had been wanting one for the past ten years.

"I couldn't possibly thank you enough, nephew," said the old mother, her eyes filling with tears. "Morning and night, in my prayers, I'll add the one that's the most important for you: the prayer for travelers. If I die, Eugénie will keep this little gem for you."

"They're worth nine hundred eighty-nine francs and seventy-five centimes, nephew," said Grandet, opening the door. "But, to save you the trouble of selling them, I'll pay you the money myself . . . in *livres*."

Along the banks of the Loire, the expression "in *livres*" means that six-*livre* coins must be accepted as six francs without deduction.

"I didn't dare suggest it to you," replied Charles, "but I was repelled by the idea of peddling my jewelry in the town where you live. As Napoleon used to say, people ought to wash their dirty linen at home. I thank you for your kindness."

Grandet scratched his ear and there was a moment of silence.

"My dear uncle," continued Charles, looking at him anxiously, as though afraid of hurting his feelings, "my cousin and my aunt have been good enough to accept a trifling remembrance of me; I hope you'll also accept these cuff links, which are no longer of any use to me. They'll remind you of a poor boy who'll be far away, and who'll often think of those who are now his only family."

"You mustn't give away everything you own, my dear boy. . . . What have you got, my dear?" he asked, eagerly turning to his wife. "Ah! A gold thimble! . . . And what about you, sweetie? Well, well! Diamond clasps! . . . All right, my boy, I'll accept your cuff links," he said, pressing Charles's hand. "But you must allow me to . . . to pay . . . your, yes . . . your fare to the Indies. Yes, I want to pay your fare; especially since, you see, my boy, in estimating the value of your jewelry I counted only the weight of the gold—the workmanship may increase the value. So that's settled. I'll give you fifteen hundred francs . . . in *livres*. I'll have to borrow it from Cruchot because I don't have a single franc here, unless Perrotet, whose rent is overdue, should pay me. That reminds me: I'll have to go see him right now."

He took his hat, put on his gloves and walked out.

"Then you're really going to leave us?" said Eugénie, looking at him with mingled sadness and admiration.

"I must," he replied, bowing his head.

For the past few days, Charles's bearing, manner and speech had been those of a man who is profoundly afflicted, but who feels enormous obligations weighing down on him and draws new courage from his misfortune. He no longer sighed; he had become a man. Eugénie had therefore never had a higher opinion of his character than when she saw him coming downstairs in clothes of coarse black cloth, which went well with his pale face and somber expression. On that day the two women put on mourning and went with Charles

to a requiem mass celebrated for the soul of the late
Guillaume Grandet.

At lunch Charles received some letters from Paris
and read them.

"Well, cousin, are you satisfied with the way your
affairs are going?" asked Eugénie in a low voice.

"You should never ask questions like that, daughter," remarked Grandet. "What the devil! I don't tell
you about my affairs, so why are you trying to stick
your nose into your cousin's? Leave the boy alone."

"Oh, I have no secrets!" said Charles.

"Ta, ta, ta, ta, nephew! You'll find out that in business you have to keep a checkrein on your tongue."

When the two lovers were alone in the garden,
Charles drew Eugénie over to the old bench beneath
the walnut tree, made her sit down beside him and
said to her, "I was right about Alphonse: he's been
doing wonderfully. He's handled my affairs prudently
and honorably. I have no debts in Paris now. He's sold
all my belongings for a good price and he tells me that
he's followed the advice of a sea captain and used the
three thousand francs left over to buy me a stock of
European curiosities that can be traded advantageously
in the Indies. He's sent my baggage to Nantes, where
there's a ship loading for Java. In five days, Eugénie,
we'll have to tell each other good-by—perhaps forever,
but certainly for a long time. My stock of merchandise
and the ten thousand francs that two friends of mine
are sending me will make a very small beginning. I
can't hope to come back for several years. My dear
cousin, don't attach your life to mine; I may perish,
and perhaps a good match may turn up for you. . . ."

"Do you love me?" she asked.

"Oh yes, very much!" he replied in a tone that
revealed the depth of his feeling.

"I'll wait, Charles . . . Good heavens, my father is at his window!" She said, pushing her cousin away as he leaned forward to kiss her.

She ran off to the archway and Charles followed her. When she saw him, she retreated to the foot of the stairs and pushed open the swinging door; then, without realizing too clearly where she was going, she found herself near Nanon's little room, in the darkest part of the hall. There Charles, who had gone with her, took her hand, pressed it to his heart, put his arm around her waist and drew her gently toward him. Eugénie no longer resisted; she received and gave the purest, the sweetest, and yet the most wholehearted of all kisses.

"Eugénie darling, a cousin is better than a brother: he can marry you," said Charles.

"So be it!" cried Nanon, opening the door of her wretched little room.

Frightened, the two lovers fled into the living room, where Eugénie went back to her sewing and Charles began to read the litanies of the Virgin in Madame Grandet's prayer book.

"Well, well!" said Nanon. "We're all saying our prayers now!"

As soon as Charles had announced his departure, Grandet began to do everything he could to make him believe he had his interests very much at heart. He was generous with everything that cost nothing, found a packer for him, then, having declared that the man wanted too much for his cases, he insisted on making them himself, using old lumber. He got up at dawn to plane, square off, polish and nail his planks, from which he made some fine packing cases. He put all of Charles's belongings into them and gave himself the task of having them sent down the Loire by boat, insuring them and making sure they got to Nantes at the right time.

After the kiss in the hall, the hours flew by for Eugénie with alarming speed. Sometimes she wanted to go with her cousin. Her torment will be understood by anyone who has known the most engaging of passions, the one whose duration is shortened every day by age, time, mortal illness or some of the other vicissitudes of human life. She often wept as she walked in the garden, which, like the courtyard, the house and the town, had now become too narrow for her: she had begun to project herself in advance over the vast expanses of the sea.

Finally the day before Charles's departure arrived. That morning, while Grandet and Nanon were absent, the precious box containing the two portraits was solemnly placed in the only drawer of the dresser which had a lock, and in which the now empty purse was already lying. The hiding of this treasure was accompanied by a great many kisses and tears. When Eugénie put the key in her bosom, she did not have the courage to forbid Charles to kiss the spot.

"It will always be there, my darling."

"And so will my heart."

"Oh, Charles, you mustn't!" she said scoldingly.

"But aren't we married?" he replied. "I have your promise; take mine."

They both said, "I'm yours forever! Forever!"

No promise made on this earth was ever purer; Eugénie's innocent confidence had momentarily sanctified Charles's love.

Breakfast was sad the next morning. In spite of the gold-embroidered dressing gown and the little gold cross which Charles gave her, even Nanon, free to express her feelings, had tears in her eyes.

"That poor, sweet young man is going off to sea. . . . May God protect him!"

At half-past ten the whole family left to accompany Charles to the stagecoach for Nantes. After untying the dog and locking the door, Nanon insisted on carrying Charles's traveling bag for him. All the tradesmen of the old street were standing in the doorways of their shops to watch the procession go by. Monsieur Cruchot, the notary, joined it when it reached the public square.

"Be sure not to cry, Eugénie," said her mother.

"Nephew," said Grandet at the door of the inn, kissing Charles on both cheeks, "leave poor and come back rich. You'll find your father's honor safe; I, Grandet, guarantee you that, because then, if you want to . . ."

"Oh uncle, you've sweetened the bitterness of my departure! That's the most wonderful present you could give me!"

Not understanding what the old cooper had been about to say, Charles shed tears of gratitude on his uncle's weather-beaten face while Eugénie pressed her cousin's hand and her father's with all her strength. Only the notary smiled in admiration of Grandet's cunning, for he alone had understood him.

The four Saumurians, surrounded by several other people, stood beside the stagecoach until it left; then, when it had disappeared over the bridge and could only be heard in the distance, Grandet said, "Pleasant journey!" Fortunately Monsieur Cruchot was the only one who understood this exclamation. Eugénie and her mother had gone to a place on the quay from where they could still see the stagecoach. They waved their white handkerchiefs and Charles waved his in reply.

"Mother, I wish I could have God's power for a moment," said Eugénie when she could no longer see Charles's handkerchief.

* * *

In order not to interrupt the course of events which took place within the Grandet family, we must now glance ahead at the operations which the old man carried out in Paris by means of the des Grassins. A month after the banker's departure, Grandet was in possession of a certificate for enough government stock, purchased at eighty francs a share, to yield him an income of a hundred thousand francs a year. The information given after his death by the inventory of his property never threw the slightest light on the means which his wary mind conceived to exchange the price of the certificate for the certificate itself. Monsieur Cruchot believed that Nanon had unwittingly been the trusty instrument by which the money was delivered. It was at about that time that she went away for five days on the pretext of putting something in order at Froidfond, as though the old man were capable of leaving anything in disorder!

With regard to the affairs of the house of Guillaume Grandet, all the old cooper's expectations were realized. As is well known, the Bank of France has precise information on all the large fortunes of Paris and the provinces. The names of des Grassins and Félix Grandet of Saumur were well known there and enjoyed the respect granted to all noted financial figures whose wealth is based on enormous holdings of unmortgaged land. The arrival of the banker from Saumur, who was said to be under orders to liquidate, for the sake of honor, the house of Grandet in Paris, was therefore enough to spare the deceased merchant's memory the shame of protested notes. The seals were broken in the presence of the creditors and the family notary began to make an official inventory of the estate. Des Grassins soon called a meeting of the creditors, who unanimously elected him and François Keller, head of a rich firm and one of the principal creditors, as joint liquidators and gave them all the powers necessary to save the honor of the family and give satisfaction to the creditors. The transactions were facilitated by the credit of Grandet of Saumur and the hope which, through des Grassins, he instilled in the hearts of the creditors; not one of them was recalcitrant. No one thought of transferring his claims to his profit-and-loss account, and everyone said to himself, "Grandet of Saumur will pay."

Six months went by. The Parisians had retired the bills in circulation and were now keeping them at the bottom of their wallets. This was the first result the cooper had wished to obtain.

Nine months after the first meeting, the two liquidators distributed forty-seven percent to each creditor. This sum was obtained by selling the securities, properties, goods and minor personal effects belonging to the late Guillaume Grandet, and the sale was made with scrupulous honesty.

The liquidation was carried out with the strictest integrity. The creditors were pleased to acknowledge the admirable and incontestable honor of the Grandets. When these praises had circulated for a suitable length of time, the creditors asked for the rest of their money. They had to write a collective letter to Grandet.

"Now they're beginning," said the old cooper as he threw the letter into the fire. "Be patient, my dear friends."

In reply to the proposals contained in this letter, Grandet of Saumur asked that all claims against his brother's estate be deposited with a notary, along with receipts for payments already made. The reason he gave was that he wanted to audit the accounts and obtain a precise statement of the assets and liabilities of the estate. This request gave rise to countless difficulties.

In general, a creditor is a kind of maniac. Ready to make a settlement one day, the next day he is filled with thoughts of fire and blood; and later he becomes the soul of compliancy. Today his wife is in a good humor, his latest child has cut his teeth, everything is going well at home and he does not want to lose a single sou; the next day it is raining, he cannot go out, he is melancholy and he says yes to any proposal capable of bringing the matter to a close; on the following day he must have guarantees; at the end of the month he is determined to seize all your property, the monster! The creditor is like the sparrow on whose tail little children are urged to place a grain of salt; but the creditor applies this image to his claim, which he can never lay his hands on.

Grandet had studied the atmospheric variations in creditors, and his brother's fulfilled all his predictions. Some of them became angry and flatly refused to deposit their claims with a notary. "Good! Things are going just the way I want them to!" thought Grandet, rubbing his hands together as he read the letters which des Grassins wrote to him on the subject. Others consented only on condition that their rights be clearly acknowledged, that they should not have to renounce any of them and that they should even be allowed the right to declare bankruptcy. This brought on further correspondence, after which Grandet of Saumur agreed to all the conditions requested. By means of this concession the more indulgent creditors were able to make the more stubborn ones listen to reason. The claims were deposited, though not without protest on the part of some of the creditors. "That old man is making fools of us all, including you," they said to des Grassins.

Twenty-three months after the death of Guillaume Grandet, many of the creditors, swept along by the stream of business in Paris, had forgotten about the money owed to them by the Grandet firm, or if they gave the matter any thought it was only to say to themselves, "I'm beginning to think the forty-seven percent is all I'm ever going to get."

The cooper had counted on the power of Time, who, as he put it, was a nice fellow. At the end of the third year, des Grassins wrote to him that, by paying out ten percent of the two million four hundred thousand francs still owed by the house of Grandet, he had persuaded the creditors to hand over their claims to him.

Grandet replied that the notary and the broker whose shocking bankruptcies had caused his brother's death were still alive, that they might have become solvent again in the meantime, and that they ought to be sued in order to get something out of them and reduce the deficit.

At the end of the fourth year the deficit was duly established at one million two hundred thousand francs. There were negotiations that lasted for six months between the liquidators and the creditors, between Grandet and the liquidators. In short, under pressure to pay up, Grandet of Saumur replied to the two liquidators, toward the ninth month of that year, that his nephew, who had made a fortune in the Indies, had stated his intention to pay his father's debts in full; Grandet could therefore not take it upon himself to settle them surreptitiously without consulting him, and he was awaiting a reply from him.

Halfway through the fifth year, the creditors were still held in check by the words "in full," which the sublime cooper uttered from time to time, laughing up his sleeve; and he always accompanied the words "Those Parisians!" with a sly smile and an oath. But the creditors were reserved for a fate without precedent in the annals of commerce. When the events of this story require them to reappear, they will be found in the same position in which Grandet had maintained them.

When government stocks reached a hundred and fifteen, Old Man Grandet sold his and withdrew from Paris about two million four hundred thousand francs in gold, which joined, in his little kegs, the six hundred thousand francs which his certificates had yielded him in compound interest. Des Grassins remained in Paris, for the following reasons: first of all, he was made a deputy; and secondly, father of a family but bored by the boring life of Saumur, he became infatuated with Florine, one of the prettiest actresses of Théâtre de Madame, and there was recrudescence of the quartermaster in the banker. It would be useless to speak of his conduct; in Saumur it was judged to be profoundly immoral. His wife was fortunate in having her property in her own name and in being intelligent enough to manage the Saumur banking firm; she carried on the business in her name, in order to repair the breaches made in her fortune by her husband's follies. The Cruchotists made the semi-widow's false position so much worse that she made a very bad match for her daughter and had to give up all hope for a marriage between her son and Eugénie Grandet. Adolphe joined his father in Paris and it was said that he became a worthless scoundrel there. The Cruchots exulted.

"Your husband doesn't have good sense," said Grandet as he lent Madame des Grassins a sum of money, with collateral. "I feel very sorry for you, you're a good little woman."

"Oh, monsieur," replied the poor lady, "who would have believed that on the day he left your house to go to Paris he was rushing headlong into ruin?"

"Heaven is my witness, madame, that up till the last moment I did everything I could to keep him from going. Judge Cruchot was eager to replace him, but he was determined to go; now we know why."

V

Family Sorrows

In any situation, a woman has more cause for sorrow than a man, and she suffers more. A man has his strength and the exercise of his power: he acts, moves, plans, thinks, embraces the future and finds consolation in it. This was true of Charles. But a woman stays behind, she remains face to face with her grief, from which nothing distracts her; she descends to the bottom of the abyss he has opened up, measures it and often fills it with her longings and tears. This was true of Eugénie. She was becoming initiated into her destiny. Feeling, loving, suffering and devotion will always be the basis of a woman's life. Eugénie was to experience every aspect of a woman's fate, except its consolations. Her happiness, gathered together like the nails scattered along a wall, to use Bossuet's sublime expression, would never even fill the hollow of her hand. Sorrows are never long in coming, and for her they came soon. The day after Charles's departure, the Grandet house resumed its usual aspect for everyone except Eugénie, who suddenly found it terribly empty. Unknown to her father, she insisted that Charles's room remain as he had left it. Madame Grandet and Nanon were willing accomplices in the maintenance of this status quo.

"Who knows, he may come back sooner than we think," said Eugénie.

"Oh, I wish he were here now!" replied Nanon. "I liked having him in the house. He was a very nice young man, a perfect gentleman; and he was almost as pretty as a girl, with that curly hair of his." Eugénie looked at her. "Good heavens, mademoiselle, your eyes look as though you'd just lost your soul! You shouldn't look at people like that."

From that day onward, Mademoiselle Grandet's beauty took on a new character. The solemn thoughts of love which slowly flowed into her soul, the dignity of a woman who is loved, gave her features that kind of radiance which painters render by a halo. Before the coming of her cousin, Eugénie might have been compared to the Virgin before the Conception; when he was gone she was like the Virgin Mother: she had conceived love. These two Marys, so different and so well depicted by certain Spanish painters, form one of the most brilliant of the inspiring figures in which Christianity abounds. On her way back from church on the day after Charles's departure (she had made a vow to go to mass every day), she bought a map of the world from the town bookseller. She tacked it on the wall beside her mirror so that she could follow her cousin's route to the Indies, so that every morning and every evening she could, in spirit, be aboard the ship that was carrying him there, see him, ask him a thousand questions, say to him, "Are you well? Are you suffering? Do you really think of me when you see that star whose beauty and use you taught me to know?"

And every morning she sat pensively beneath the walnut tree on the worm-eaten wooden bench covered with gray moss, the same bench on which they had said so many wonderful and foolish things to each other and woven such lovely dreams of the life they would share. She thought of the future as she looked up at the little patch of sky which the walls allowed her to see, then at the section of the old wall and the roof above Charles's room. In short, she was imbued with solitary love, the true, enduring kind of love which permeates every thought and becomes the substance, or, as our forefathers would have said, the very stuff of life.

When Grandet's "friends" came to play cards in the evening she was gay, she dissimulated her feelings; but all morning long she talked about Charles with her mother and Nanon. Nanon had realized that she could sympathize with her young mistress's suffering without failing in her duty toward her old master, and she sometimes said to Eugénie, "If I'd ever had a man of my own, I'd have . . . I'd have followed him into hell. I'd have . . . Well, I'd have been willing to die for him. But . . . well, it just never happened. I'll die without ever knowing what life is like. Would you believe it, mam'selle, that old Cornoiller, who's really a good man in his way, is always making eyes at me because of my money, just like the men that come here to court you and sniff your father's gold at the same time! Well, mam'selle, I have to admit I like it, even though it's not love."

Two months went by in this manner. The domestic life which had once been so monotonous was now enlivened by the enormous interest of the secret that bound the three women more closely together than ever. For them, Charles still lived and moved beneath the gray rafters of the living room. Morning and night, Eugénie opened the precious box and looked at the portrait of her aunt. One Sunday morning her mother came in unexpectedly as she was absorbed in trying to find Charles's features in those of the portrait. Madame Grandet was then initiated into the terrible secret that Charles had given Eugénie this gift in exchange for her treasure.

"You gave it all to him!" cried the horrified mother. "What will you tell your father on New Year's Day, when he wants to see your gold?"

Eugénie's eyes grew fixed, and the two women were in the grip of mortal terror through half the morning. They were so upset that they missed high mass and had to go to low mass instead.

In three days the year 1819 would be over. In three days a terrible drama would begin, a bourgeois tragedy without poison, dagger or bloodshed; but, for the actors in it, it would be crueler then all the tragedies enacted in the famous family of the Atridae.

"What will become of us?" said Madame Grandet to her daughter, letting her knitting lie in her lap. The poor woman had been so distraught for the past two months that she had not yet finished the woolen sleeves she needed for winter. This domestic detail, insignificant in appearance, had sad results for her. Because she was not wearing sleeves, she caught a severe chill when she broke into a sweat during one of her husband's frightful outbursts of rage.

"I was thinking, my poor child, that if you'd told me your secret sooner, we'd have had time to write to Monsieur des Grassins in Paris. He could have sent us more gold coins like the ones you had and, even though Grandet knows them well, perhaps . . ."

"But where could we have gotten so much money?"

"I'd have pawned my own property. Besides, Monsieur des Grassins would have . . ."

"It's too late now," interrupted Eugénie in a hollow, broken voice. "Don't we have to go to his room tomorrow morning to wish him a happy New Year?"

"But daughter, why couldn't I go to see the Cruchots?"

"No, no, that would be handing me over to them and putting us both in their power. Anyway, I've made up my mind. I did the right thing and I'm not sorry for it. God will protect me. May His holy will be done. Oh, if you'd read his letter, mother, you'd have thought only of him!"

On the following morning—January 1, 1820—the wild terror which had taken possession of the mother and daughter suggested to them the most natural excuse for not paying a solemn visit to Grandet in his room. The winter of 1819–20 was one of the harshest of the period. The snow was piled deep on the roofs. As soon as Madame Grandet heard her husband moving around in his room she said to him, "Grandet, tell Nanon to make a little fire in my room; it's so cold that I'm freezing under my blankets. I've reached an age when I need to take care of myself a little. . . . Besides," she went on after a slight pause, "Eugénie will come in here to dress. The poor girl might fall ill from dressing in her room in weather like this. Then we'll come down to wish you a happy New Year beside the fire in the living room."

"Ta, ta, ta, ta, what a tongue! What a way to begin the new year, Madame Grandet! I've never heard you talk so much before. And yet I don't think you've been eating bread soaked in wine. . . ." There was a moment of silence. "All right," continued the old man, to whom it had no doubt occurred that his wife's request would suit his purposes, "I'll do as you wish, Madame Grandet. You're really a good wife and I wouldn't want anything to happen to you at this stage of your life, although the la Bertellières are usually made of iron. . . . Isn't that right?" he cried, after a pause. "Anyway, we inherited from them, so I forgive them." And he coughed.

"You're quite gay this morning, monsieur," said the poor woman gravely.

"Why, I'm always gay . . .

> *Gay, cooper, be gay,*
> *Mend your washtub today,*"

he added, coming into his wife's room fully dressed. "Yes, by God, it's cold today, no doubt about that! We'll have a good breakfast, my dear. Des Grassins has sent me a pâté de foie gras with truffles! I'm going to pick it up at the stagecoach office. . . . des Grassins probably enclosed a double napoleon for Eugénie, too," he whispered in his wife's ear. "I have no more gold, my dear. I still had a few old coins left, I can tell you that, but I had to let them go for business expenses." And, to celebrate New Year's Day, he kissed her on the forehead.

"Eugénie," cried the good mother, "I don't know which side of the bed your father got up on, but he's in a cheerful mood this morning! Don't worry, we'll manage all right."

"What's got into the master?" asked Nanon as she came into her mistress's room to make a fire. "First of all he said to me, 'Good morning and happy New Year, Nanon, old girl! Go make a fire in my wife's room, she's cold.' And then I was dumbfounded to see him holding out his hand to give me a six-franc coin that's hardly been clipped at all! Here, madame, take a look at it! Oh, what a good man! He really is a fine man, no two ways about it. Some people get harder as they get older, but he's getting as mellow as your black currant brandy; he improves with age. He's a good, kindhearted man. . . ."

The secret of Grandet's cheerfulness lay in the complete success of his speculation. After deducting the amount which Grandet owed him for the discount on a hundred and fifty thousand francs in Dutch notes, and for the surplus which he had advanced him in order to make up the sum necessary for the purchase of enough government stocks to yield an income of a hundred thousand francs a year, Monsieur des Grassins had just sent him, by stagecoach, thirty thousand francs in silver coins, the balance of the first half-year's interest, along with a letter informing him that government stocks had gone up. They were then selling for eighty-nine, and by the end of January the leading capitalists were buying them for ninety-two. For the past two months, Grandet had been making twelve percent on his capital. He had checked over his accounts, and from now on he would receive fifty thousand francs twice a year without having to pay anything for taxes or overhead. He saw at last the advantages of owning stock, a kind of investment of which people in the provinces are extremely wary, and he could see himself in possession, within five years, of a capital of six million francs which would have been increased without much trouble and which, added to the value of his land, would compose a colossal fortune. The six-franc coin he had given to Nanon was perhaps her reward for an immense service which she had unwittingly rendered him.

"Oh, oh, where's Old Man Grandet going so early in the morning, running as though his house were on fire?" asked the tradesmen as they opened their shops. Then, when they saw him coming back from the waterfront followed by a porter from the stagecoach office pushing a wheelbarrow laden with full sacks, one of them said, "Water always flows toward the river: the old man was going after his money."

"It comes in to him from Paris, Froidfond and Holland," said another.

"He'll end up by buying the whole town of Saumur!" cried a third.

"He doesn't even notice the cold, his mind is always on his business," said a wife to her husband.

"Look, Monsieur Grandet, if those bags are too heavy for you, I'll be glad to take them off your hands," said a clothier, his nearest neighbor.

"Oh, there's nothing but copper coins in them," said the winegrower.

"He means silver," said the porter in a low voice.

"If you want me to treat you right, you'd better learn to keep your mouth shut," the old man said to the porter as he opened his front door.

"Oh, the old fox!" thought the porter. "I thought he was hard of hearing. There doesn't seem to be anything wrong with his ears when it's cold."

"Here's twenty sous as a New Year's present, and hold your tongue," said Grandet. "You can leave now, Nanon will bring back the wheelbarrow. . . . Nanon, have the two little birds gone off to mass?"

"Yes, monsieur."

"Come, get a move on! Let's go to work!" he cried, loading her up with bags. A few moments later the money had been carried up to his room, where he locked himself in. "Knock on the wall when breakfast is ready. Take the wheelbarrow back to the stagecoach office."

The family did not have breakfast until ten o'clock.

"Your father won't ask to see your gold here, and you can pretend to be very cold," said Madame Grandet to her daughter when they returned from mass. "Then we'll have time to replace your treasure before your birthday. . . ."

As Grandet came down the stairs he was planning to turn his Parisian silver coins into good, solid gold without delay and thinking of his admirable speculation in government stocks. He had decided to invest his income in them until they rose to one hundred. His meditations were to have disastrous consequences for Eugénie.

As soon as he came in the two women wished him a happy New Year, his daughter by affectionately hugging him, his wife gravely and with dignity.

"Listen, my child," he said as he kissed his daughter on both cheeks, "I'm working for you . . . I want you to be happy. It takes money to be happy. Without money, you might as well give up. Look, here's a brand-new napoleon I sent for from Paris. I swear I don't have one ounce of gold! You're the only one that has any. Show me your gold, sweetie."

"Oh, it's too cold; let's have breakfast," replied Eugénie.

"After breakfast, then, all right? It will help us digest better. . . . Look what good old des Grassins sent us! Go on, eat, children, it's free. Des Grassins is doing well and I'm satisfied with him; he's a shrewd man. He's doing a lot of good for Charles, and that's free too. He's straightening out the poor deceased Grandet's affairs very well. . . . Oh! This is good!" he said with his mouth full, after a pause. "Eat some of it, my dear! It will keep you fed for at least two days."

"I'm not hungry. I'm not feeling well, you know that."

"Come, come! You can stuff yourself all you like and nothing will go wrong with you. You're a la Bertellière, a solid woman. Your skin is a bit yellow, it's true, but I like yellow."

A condemned man awaiting an ignominious and public death feels less horror, perhaps, than Madame Grandet and her daughter felt as they awaited the events that were to follow this family breakfast. The more cheerfully the old winegrower talked as he ate, the heavier grew the hearts of the two women. But Eugénie had something to support her in this crisis: she drew strength from her love. "For him, for him," she said to herself, "I'd suffer a thousand deaths." At this thought she looked at her mother with courage flashing from her eyes.

"Take all this away," Grandet said to Nanon when breakfast was over, toward eleven o'clock, "but leave us the table. We'll be able to look at your little treasure more comfortably," he said, looking at Eugénie. "Little? What am I saying? You have gold worth five thousand nine hundred and fifty-nine francs by weight, plus forty more this morning: that makes you just one franc short of six thousand. Well, I'll give you the franc you need to make an even six thousand, because you see, sweetie . . . Well? Why are you listening to us, Nanon? Get out of here, get back to your work!"

Nanon disappeared.

"Listen, Eugénie, you must give me your gold. You won't refuse your old daddy, will you, sweetie?" The two women were silent. "I have no more gold. I had some, but it's gone. I'll give you six thousand francs in *livres* and tell you how to invest it. You must forget about your marriage dozen. When you marry, which will be soon, I'll find you a husband who'll give you the finest dozen anyone ever heard of in the whole province, so listen to me, sweetie, here's a wonderful opportunity for you: you can invest your six thousand francs with the government and every six months you'll get nearly two hundred francs in interest, with no worry about taxes, repairs, hail, frost or any of the other things that plague property owners. Perhaps you don't like the idea of parting with your gold, eh, sweetie? Bring it to me just the same. I'll collect more gold for you—Dutch and Portuguese coins, Mogul rupees, genovines—and, with the coins I'll give you for your birthdays and name days, within three years you'll have made up half of your pretty little golden treasure again. What do you say to that, sweetie? Come on, look up at me. Go get your precious little treasure. You ought to kiss me on the eyes for telling you these secrets and mysteries of the life and death of money. Really, coins live and move like people; they come and go, they sweat, they produce. . . ."

Eugénie stood up, but after taking several steps toward the door she abruptly turned around, looked at her father and said, "I no longer have *my* gold."

"You no longer have your gold?" cried Grandet, starting up like a horse which has heard a cannon fired ten paces away.

"No, I no longer have it."

"You're mistaken, Eugénie."

"No."

"By my father's pruning knife!"

When the cooper uttered this oath the rafters trembled.

"Good God and all the saints in heaven!" cried Nanon. "Look how pale madame is!"

"Grandet, your anger will kill me," said the poor woman.

"Nonsense! People in your family live forever! Eugénie, what have you done with your gold coins?" he shouted, rushing toward her.

"Monsieur," she said, falling at Madame Grandet's knees, "my mother is suffering terribly. . . . Look at her. . . . Don't kill her. . . ."

Grandet was alarmed by the pallor spread over his wife's face, which was usually so yellow.

"Nanon, help me go upstairs to bed," she said weakly. "I'm dying."

Nanon immediately gave her arm to her mistress; Eugénie did the same, and it was only with great difficulty that they succeeded in getting her up to her room, for she fainted at every step. Grandet was left alone. Nevertheless, he walked up seven or eight steps a few moments later and called out, "Eugénie, come downstairs as soon as your mother's in bed."

"Yes, father."

She came down a short time later, after reassuring her mother.

"Daughter," said Grandet, "you are going to tell me where your treasure is."

"Father, if you give me presents that aren't entirely at my disposal, you can take them back," replied Eugénie coldly, taking the napoleon from the mantelpiece and handing it to him.

Grandet eagerly seized the napoleon and slipped it into his vest pocket. "I'll certainly never give you anything again, not even this much!" he said, clicking his thumbnail under his front tooth. "So you despise your father! You don't trust him! Don't you know what a father is? If he's not everything to you, then he's nothing. Where's your gold?"

"Father, I love you and respect you, in spite of your anger, but let me humbly point out to you that I'm twenty-three years old. You've told me I'm of age so often that I can't forget it now. I've done as I pleased with my money, and you can be sure it's well invested."

"Where?"

"That's an inviolable secret," she said. "Don't you have your secrets too?"

"I'm the head of the family—can't I have my own affairs?"

"This is *my* affair."

"It must be a bad one, then, if you can't tell your father about it, Mademoiselle Grandet."

"It's an excellent one, and I can't tell my father about it."

"At least you can tell me when you gave away your gold." Eugénie shook her head. "You still had it on your birthday, didn't you?" Eugénie, whom love had made as crafty as avarice had made her father, shook her head again. "Who ever heard of such stubbornness, or such a theft?" continued Grandet in a voice which gradually rose to a crescendo and reverberated through the whole house. "What! Here, in my own house, my own home, someone has taken your gold, the only gold there was, and I'll never know who it was? Gold is a precious thing. The most honorable girls may make mistakes and give away I don't know what; it sometimes happens in great noble families, and even in middle-class families. But to give away gold! . . . Because you did give it to someone, didn't you?" Eugénie remained impassive. "Was there ever such a daughter before? Am I really your father? If you've invested it, then you must have a receipt. . . ."

"Was I free to do with as I saw fit or not? Did it belong to me or not?"

"But you're still a child!"

"I'm of age."

Dumbfounded by his daughter's logic, Grandet turned pale, stamped his foot and swore; then, finally finding words, he cried out, "Cursed serpent of

a daughter! Oh, ungrateful child, you know I love
you and you take advantage of it! You're torturing
your own father! By God, I'll bet you've thrown our
fortune at the feet of that worthless pauper in morocco
boots! By my father's pruning knife! I can't disinherit
you, damn it, but I curse you, your cousin and your
children! Nothing good will come of this, do you hear
me? If it was Charles that . . . But no, that's impossible.
What! Can that malicious young fop have robbed me?"
He looked at his daughter, who still remained cold and
silent. "She doesn't move, she doesn't flinch! She's more
of a Grandet than I am! At least you didn't give your
gold away for nothing, did you? Come on, tell me!"

Eugénie looked at her father with an ironical expression which offended him. "Eugénie, you're in my house,
in your father's house," he said. "To stay here, you must
submit to his orders. The priests order you to obey me."
Eugénie bowed her head. "You've offended me in what
I hold most dear," he went on. "I don't want to see you
again until you're obedient. Go to your room. You will
stay there until I allow you to come out. Nanon will
bring you bread and water. You heard me, go!"

Eugénie burst into tears and fled to her mother's
room. After walking around his garden a few times in
the snow, without noticing the cold, Grandet began
to suspect that his daughter was in his wife's room.
Delighted at the thought of catching her disobeying his
orders, he climbed the stairs with the agility of a cat
and walked into Madame Grandet's room as she was
stroking her daughter's hair. Eugénie's face was pressed
against her mother's bosom.

"Don't be too upset, my poor child, your father
will calm down. . . ."

"She no longer has a father!" said the cooper.
"Can it be you and I, Madame Grandet, who produced

such a disobedient daughter? A fine upbringing, and so religious, too! Well, why aren't you in your room? Go on, to prison, mademoiselle, to prison!"

"Are you trying to deprive me of my daughter, monsieur?" said Madame Grandet, her face flushed with fever.

"If you want to keep her, take her away with you— you can both clear out of my house. My God, where's the gold? What's become of the gold?"

Eugénie stood up, cast a haughty glance at her father and went into her room. The old man turned the key in the lock.

"Nanon," he called out, "put out the fire in the living room." Then he sat down in an armchair beside the fireplace in his wife's room and said to her, "She probably gave it to that wretched seducer Charles, who was only after our money."

From the danger threatening her daughter and from her feeling for her, Madame Grandet drew enough strength to remain outwardly cold, silent and deaf.

"I didn't know anything about all this," she said, turning her face toward the wall to avoid her husband's glowing eyes. "Your violence is making me suffer so much that, if my premonitions are right, I'll never leave this room alive. You should have spared me at this time, monsieur; I've never caused you any pain, at least I don't think I have. Your daughter loves you and I believe she's as innocent as a newborn babe, so don't torment her: revoke your sentence. It's terribly cold now; you might be the cause of a serious illness."

"I won't see her or speak to her. She'll stay in her room on bread and water until she's satisfied her father. What the devil! The head of a family ought to know what happens to the gold in his house! She had what may have been the only rupees in France, and genovines, and Dutch ducats. . . ."

"Monsieur, Eugénie is our only child, and even if she'd thrown them into the river . . ."

"Thrown them into the river!" shouted the old man. "Into the river! You're mad, Madame Grandet. I mean what I say, you know that. If you want to have peace in this house, make your daughter confess, get the truth out of her; women are better at that kind of thing among themselves than men are. No matter what she's done, I won't eat her. Is she afraid of me? Even if she covered her cousin with gold from head to foot, he's at sea now, so we can't very well run after him. . . ."

"Well, monsieur . . ." Made more perceptive by her nervous state, or by her daughter's misfortune, which heightened her tenderness and intelligence, Madame Grandet became aware of something sinister in the way her husband's wen twitched as she began to reply; she changed her mind without changing her tone. "Well, monsieur, do you think I have more control over her than you do? She's told me nothing; she takes after you."

"My God, how your tongue keeps wagging this morning! Ta, ta, ta, ta! I think you're trying to defy me! You're probably in league with her."

His wife stared at him intently and said, "Really, Monsieur Grandet, if you want to kill me, all you have to do is go on like this. I'm telling you, monsieur, and even if it costs me my life I'll go on repeating it, that you're treating your daughter unjustly. She's more reasonable than you are. That money belonged to her; she can only have put it to a good use, and God alone has the right to know our good deeds. I beg you, monsieur, bring Eugénie back into your good graces! . . . You'll lessen the effect of the blow your anger has dealt me and you may save my life. My daughter, monsieur, give me back my daughter!"

"I'm getting out of here," he said. "I can't bear to stay in my own house. My wife and daughter talk as if . . . Ugh! Pooh! You've given me a cruel New Year's gift, Eugénie!" he shouted. "That's right, cry! You'll be sorry for what you're doing, do you hear me? What good does it do you to eat the consecrated wafer six times every three months if you secretly give your father's gold to a lazy good-for-nothing who'll devour your heart when you have nothing else to lend him? You'll see what kind of a man your Charles is, with his morocco boots and his disdainful airs. He has neither heart nor soul, because he dares to carry off a poor girl's treasure without her parents' consent."

When the front door closed, Eugénie left her room, came back to her mother and said to her, "You were very brave for your daughter's sake."

"Now you see where improper conduct can lead us, my child. . . . You've made me tell a lie."

"Oh! I'll ask God to give me all the punishment for it!"

"Is it true, mademoiselle," asked Nanon in alarm as she entered the room, "that you've been put on bread and water for the rest of your life?"

"What does it matter, Nanon?" said Eugénie calmly.

"Oh, how could I eat jam when the daughter of the house is eating only dry bread? No, no!"

"Not a word about all this, Nanon," said Eugénie.

"I'll keep quiet; but you'll see!"

That evening Grandet had dinner alone for the first time in twenty-four years.

"Well, you're a widower now, monsieur," said Nanon. "It's very unpleasant to be a widower with two women in the house."

"I'm not talking to you, Nanon. Keep your mouth shut or I'll dismiss you. What's in that saucepan I hear simmering on the stove?"

"It's some fat I'm melting. . . ."

"I'm having company tonight, light the fire."

The Cruchots, Madame des Grassins and her son arrived at eight o'clock and were surprised to see neither Madame Grandet nor her daughter.

"My wife is feeling a little indisposed and Eugénie is staying with her," said the old winegrower, whose face betrayed no emotion.

After an hour had been spent in insignificant conversation, Madame des Grassins, who had gone up to pay a visit to Madame Grandet, came back downstairs and everyone asked her, "How's Madame Grandet feeling?"

"Not well at all," she replied. "Her condition seems quite alarming to me. . . . At her age, you ought to take every precaution, Papa Grandet."

"We'll see about that," replied the winegrower absentmindedly.

Everyone bade him good night. When the Cruchots were outside in the street, Madame des Grassins said to them, "Something's happened in the Grandet family. The mother is very ill, but she doesn't seem to know it. The daughter's eyes are red, as though she'd been crying for a long time. Can it be that they're trying to marry her to someone against her will?"

When Grandet was in bed, Nanon came silently in her slippers to Eugénie's room and showed her a pâté made in a saucepan. "Here, mademoiselle," said the kindly old maid. "Cornoiller gave me a hare. You eat so little that this pâté will last you at least a week, and in this cold weather it's sure not to spoil. At least you won't have to live on dry bread. That's not healthy at all."

"Poor Nanon!" said Eugénie, pressing her hand.

"I made it very good, just right; and *he* didn't notice anything. I paid for the lard, the bay leaves and everything else out of my six francs. After all, it's my money."

Then the servant hurried away, thinking she had heard Grandet.

For several months Grandet constantly came in to see his wife at different hours of the day, without ever mentioning his daughter's name, going to see her or even making the slightest allusion to her. Madame Grandet never left her room and her condition became worse from day to day. Nothing could soften the old cooper. He remained as unshakable, harsh and cold as a pile of granite. He continued to come and go as usual, but he stopped stuttering, talked less and behaved more implacably in business matters than ever before. He often made minor errors in his calculations.

"Something's going on in the Grandet family," said the Cruchotists and the Grassinians.

"What's happened in the Grandet family?" was a stock question that was asked in the course of all social gatherings in Saumur.

Eugénie went to mass escorted by Nanon. If Madame des Grassins spoke a few words to her as she was coming out of the church, she always replied evasively and without satisfying her curiosity. Nevertheless, by the time two months had passed it had become impossible to hide the secret of Eugénie's solitary confinement from either Madame des Grassins or the three Cruchots.

There came a time when there were no more pretexts to explain her constant absence. Then, although it was impossible to learn who had revealed the secret, everyone in town learned that ever since New Year's Day, by her father's orders, Mademoiselle Grandet had been kept in her room on bread and water, without a fire, that Nanon made delicacies for her and brought them to her during the night, and it was even known that the young lady could see and take care of her mother only when her father was out of the house.

Grandet's conduct was severely condemned. The whole town outlawed him, so to speak, remembered his treachery and hardness, and excommunicated him. When he walked past, people pointed at him and whispered to each other.

Each time his daughter came down the winding street, accompanied by Nanon, on her way to mass or vespers, all the people of the town came to their windows to examine with curiosity the rich heiress's bearing, and her face, which wore an expression of melancholy and angelic sweetness. Her confinement and her father's disgrace meant nothing to her. Could she not see the map of the world, the little bench, the garden and the stretch of wall? Could she not still taste on her lips the honey left there by the kisses of love? For some time she and her father were both unaware that people in town were talking about them. Pious and pure before God, her conscience and her love helped her to bear patiently her father's anger and vengeance.

But one profound sorrow silenced all others: her mother, that gentle, tender creature who was now made more beautiful by the light shining from her soul as she approached the tomb, her mother was wasting away from day to day. Eugénie often reproached herself with being the innocent cause of the slow, cruel illness that was devouring her. This remorse, though soothed by her mother, bound her still more firmly to her love. Every morning, as soon as her father had left the house, she came to her mother's bedside and Nanon brought her breakfast to her there. But poor Eugénie, sad and afflicted by her mother's suffering, silently drew Nanon's attention to her mother's face, wept and did not dare speak of her cousin. Madame Grandet was always forced to mention him first: "Where is he? Why doesn't he write?"

Neither she nor her daughter had any idea of the distances involved.

"Let's think of him, mother," replied Eugénie, "but let's not talk about him. You're ill, and you come before everything else."

"Everything else" meant "him."

"My child," said Madame Grandet, "I'm not sorry I have to die. God has protected me by making me look forward with happiness to the end of my miseries."

Her words were always saintly and Christian. When her husband came in to have breakfast with her and paced up and down her room, during the first months of the year, she always repeated the same words with angelic sweetness, but with the firmness of a woman to whom the approach of death gave the courage she had lacked during her life.

"Monsieur, I thank you for the interest you take in my health," she would reply to him after he had asked the most commonplace of questions. "But if you want to sweeten the bitterness of my last moments and lighten the burden of my sorrows, take our daughter back into your good graces. Show yourself a worthy Christian, husband and father."

When he heard these words, Grandet would sit down beside her bed and act like a man who sees a shower approaching and calmly takes shelter in a doorway. He listened to his wife in silence and made no reply. After the most touching, the most tender, the most pious supplications had been addressed to him, he would say, "You're a little pale today, my poor wife."

Complete forgetfulness of his daughter seemed to be engraved on his stony forehead and compressed lips. He was not even moved by the tears that streamed down his wife's white face when he made one of his vague replies, whose terms never varied appreciably.

"May God forgive you, monsieur," she would say, "as I forgive you myself. You'll need mercy some day."

Since his wife's illness he had no longer dared make use of his terrible "Ta, ta, ta, ta!" but his despotism was still not disarmed by that angel of gentleness, whose ugliness was vanishing from day to day, driven away by the expression of the moral qualities which now shone forth in her face.

She was all soul. The spirit of prayer seemed to purify and refine the coarser features of her face and make them radiant. Who has not observed the phenomenon of this transformation on saintly faces where the habits of the soul have finally triumphed over the most crudely fashioned features by imprinting on them that special animation which comes from the nobility and purity of lofty thoughts? The sight of this transformation brought about by the suffering that was consuming the remnants of his wife's physical being, affected, though weakly, the old cooper, whose character continued to be as hard as bronze. If his words were not disdainful, his conduct was dominated by an imperturbable silence which maintained his superiority as head of the family.

Whenever his faithful Nanon appeared in the market place, a few jeers and complaints against her master would suddenly whistle past her ears, but, although public opinion strongly condemned him, she defended him out of pride in the household.

"Well," she would say to the old man's detractors, "don't we all get harder as we grow older? Why shouldn't his heart get a little more callous too? Stop your lying gossip. Mademoiselle lives like a queen. She lives alone, but she likes it. Besides, her parents have their reasons."

Finally, one evening toward the end of spring, Madame Grandet, consumed more by grief than by illness and having failed, in spite of her prayers, to reconcile Eugénie and her father, confided her secret sorrows to the Cruchots.

"Imagine keeping a girl of twenty-three on bread and water!" cried Judge de Bonfons. "And for no reason! Why, that constitutes cruel and inhuman treatment, she can legally protest against it, as much in as upon . . ."

"Come, come, nephew," said the notary, "spare us your legal jargon. . . . Don't worry, madame, I'll put an end to this confinement tomorrow."

Hearing them speak of her, Eugénie came out of her room. "Gentlemen," she said, walking toward them with proud dignity, "I beg you not to intervene in this matter. My father is the master in his own house. As long as I live in it, I must obey him. His conduct must not be subjected to the approval or disapproval of the world; he's accountable for it only to God. I ask you in the name of your friendship for me to keep silent about this. To condemn my father would be to attack our own reputation. I'm grateful to you, gentlemen, for the interest you've shown in me, but I'll be still more grateful to you if you'll stop the offensive gossip that's going on all over town, and which I learned of by accident."

"She's right," said Madame Grandet.

"Mademoiselle, the best way to stop people from gossiping would be to give you back your freedom," replied the old notary respectfully, struck by the beauty which seclusion, melancholy and love had imparted to Eugénie.

"Well, daughter, you can let Monsieur Cruchot take care of the matter, since he guarantees the outcome. He knows your father and he knows how to handle him. If you want to see me happy during the little time I have left to live, you and your father must be reconciled at any cost."

The next morning, following a custom he had adopted since Eugénie's seclusion, Grandet went out to stroll around his little garden a few times. He had chosen for his walk the time when Eugénie was combing her hair. When the old man came to the big walnut tree he hid behind its trunk and stood for a few moments contemplating his daughter's long hair, no doubt vacillating between the thoughts suggested to him by the tenacity of his character and his desire to embrace his child. He often sat on the little worm-eaten wooden bench on which Charles and Eugénie had sworn eternal love to each other, while she also glanced at her father furtively, through the window or in her mirror. If he stood up and resumed his stroll, she would sit down complacently at her window and begin to examine the section of wall on which the prettiest flowers hung down, and from whose cracks grew maidenhair ferns, bindweed and a thick plant, yellow or white, a kind of sedum that is quite abundant in the vineyards of Saumur and Tours.

Monsieur Cruchot came early and found the old man, on a lovely June day, sitting on the little bench with his back against the dividing wall of the garden, absorbed in watching his daughter.

"What can I do for you, Monsieur Cruchot?" he asked when he saw the notary.

"I've come to talk business with you."

"Ah, do you have a little gold to give me in exchange for silver?"

"No, no, it has nothing to do with money—it's about your daughter Eugénie. Everyone's talking about her, and about you."

"What business is it of theirs? A man's home is his castle."

"Yes, of course, and a man is free to kill himself too, or, worse still, to throw his money out the window."

"What do you mean?"

"Why, your wife is very ill, my friend! You ought to consult Monsieur Bergerin, in fact; she's in danger of dying. If she should die without having received proper care, I don't think your mind would be at peace."

"Ta, ta, ta, ta! You know what's wrong with my wife. Once a doctor gets a foot inside your door, he comes five or six times a day."

"Well, Grandet, you can do as you like. You and I are old friends; there's no one else in Saumur who takes a greater interest in your welfare than I do, so I had to tell you this. Now I've said my say; you're over twenty-one and you know how to run your own life. Anyway, that's not why I came here. I want to talk to you about something that may be much more important to you. After all, you don't want to kill your wife, she's too useful to you. Just think of the situation you'd be in with regard to your daughter if Madame Grandet were to die. You'd have to render an account to Eugénie, since you and your wife hold your property in common. Your daughter would have a right to demand that you divide your fortune with her and sell Froidfond. In short, she'll inherit from her mother, which you can't do."

These words struck the old man like a thunderbolt. He was not as well informed in law as he was in business; the possibility of a division of property had never occurred to him.

"I therefore advise you to treat her gently," concluded Cruchot.

"But do you know what she did, Cruchot?"

"What?" asked the notary, eager to have Old Man Grandet confide in him, and curious to learn the cause of the quarrel.

"She gave away her gold."

"Well, didn't it belong to her?" asked the notary.

"That's what they all say!" said the old man, letting his arm fall in a tragic gesture.

"Because of a trifle like that, are you going to place obstacles in the way of the concessions you'll ask her to make to you when her mother dies?"

"Oh! Do you call six thousand francs in gold a trifle?"

"Well, my old friend, do you know how much the inventory and the division of your wife's estate would cost if Eugénie demanded it?"

"How much?"

"Two, three, perhaps four hundred thousand francs! The property would have to be sold at auction in order to determine its real value. But if you come to an agreement . . ."

"By my father's pruning knife!" cried the wine-grower. He turned pale and sat down. "We'll see about that, Cruchot."

After a moment of silence or of agony, the old man looked at the notary and said, "Life is very harsh! It's full of pain. Cruchot," he went on solemnly, "you wouldn't deceive me, would you? Swear to me on your honor that what you've been telling me is based on law. Show it to me in the law books, I want to see it in black and white!"

"My poor friend," replied the notary, "don't you think I know my own profession?"

"Then it's really true? I can be stripped bare, betrayed, killed, devoured by my own daughter?"

"She'll inherit from her mother."

"Then what's the use of having children? Oh, I love my wife. She has a strong constitution, fortunately; she's a la Bertellière."

"She has less than a month to live."

The cooper clapped his hand to his forehead, paced back and forth, cast a frightful glance at Cruchot and said, "What must I do?"

"Eugénie can purely and simply relinquish all claim to her mother's estate. You don't want to disinherit her, do you? But, in order to obtain such a concession, you mustn't treat her harshly. What I'm telling you now, my friend, is against my own interests. After all, my business consists of liquidations, inventories, sales, divisions of property . . ."

"We'll see, we'll see. Let's not talk about it any more, Cruchot. You're tearing my heart out. Have you received any gold?"

"No; but I have a few old louis, about ten of them. I'll give them to you. Make your peace with Eugénie, my good friend. Everyone in Saumur is talking about you."

"The scoundrels!"

"Come, come, government stocks have risen to ninety-nine. Be content for once in your life."

"Ninety-nine, Cruchot?"

"That's right."

"Well, well! Ninety-nine!" said Grandet, accompanying the old notary to the front door.

Then, too agitated by what he had just heard to remain at home, he went up to his wife's room and said to her, "Well, mother, you can spend the day with your daughter: I'm going to Froidfond. I want you both to enjoy yourselves. Today is our wedding anniversary, my dear. Look, here's sixty francs for your altar on Corpus Christi Day. You've been wanting to have one for a long time, so enjoy it! Have a good time, both of you, be happy, be healthy! Here's to happiness!" He tossed ten six-franc coins on his wife's bed, took her head between his hands and kissed her on the forehead. "You're feeling better, aren't you, my dear?" he asked.

"How can you think of receiving the God of mercy in your heart while you shut your own daughter out of your heart?" she asked with emotion.

"Ta, ta, ta, ta!" he said in a caressing tone. "We'll see about that."

"God be praised! Eugénie," cried her mother, flushed with joy, "come and kiss your father: he's forgiven you!"

But the old man had disappeared. He was hurrying off to his vineyards, trying to put his confused ideas in order. Grandet was just beginning his seventy-sixth year. In the past two years particularly, his avarice had grown as all persistent human passions grow. As is often the case with misers, with ambitious men, with everyone whose life is devoted to a single dominant idea, his sentiments had become fixed on one symbol of his passion. The sight and possession of gold had become his monomania. His despotic tendencies had increased in proportion to his avarice, and it now seemed *unnatural* to him to relinquish control of the slightest part of his property after his wife's death. Declare his fortune to his daughter? Inventory all his landed and personal property to be auctioned off to the highest bidder? "That would be like cutting my own throat!" he exclaimed aloud in the middle of a field where he was examining his vines.

Finally he made up his mind. He came back to Saumur at dinnertime, resolved to give in to Eugénie, to cajole and wheedle her, in order to be able to die royally, holding the reins of his millions in his own hands until he drew his last breath. Just as the old man, who happened to have taken his master key with him, was walking stealthily up the stairs to his wife's room, Eugénie had brought in the box containing the beautiful set of gold toilet articles and set it down on her mother's bed. During Grandet's absence, they were both indulging in the pleasure of evoking Charles's features by examining the portrait of his mother.

"That's his forehead and mouth exactly!" said Eugénie just as her father opened the door.

When she saw the way he was looking at the gold, Madame Grandet cried out, "God have mercy on us!"

The old man rushed toward the toilet kit like a tiger leaping on a sleeping child.

"What's this?" he said, picking up the treasure and walking over to the window. "It's good gold! Gold!" he cried. "A lot of gold! It must weigh at least two pounds. Aha! Charles gave you this in exchange for your pretty coins, didn't he? Why didn't you tell me? That was a good bargain, sweetie! You're my daughter, no doubt about that!" Eugénie trembled in every limb. "This belongs to Charles, doesn't it?" asked the old man.

"Yes, father. It doesn't belong to me. This case is a sacred trust."

"Ta, ta, ta, ta! He took your fortune; we must restore your little treasure."

"Father! . . ."

Intending to take out his knife in order to pry off a gold plaque, the old man was obliged to set down the case on a chair. Eugénie rushed forward to seize it, but the cooper, who was watching both his daughter and the case, put out his hand and pushed her back so violently that she fell onto her mother's bed.

"Monsieur! Monsieur!" cried the mother, sitting up in bed. Grandet had taken out his knife and was preparing to pry off the gold.

"Father!" cried Eugénie, falling to her knees and dragging herself over to him with her hands outstretched. "Father, in the name of the Virgin and all the saints, in the name of Christ who died on the cross, in the name of your eternal salvation, father, in the name of my life, don't touch that! That case is neither yours nor mine: it belongs to an unfortunate relative who left it to me as a sacred trust, and I must give it back to him intact."

"Why were you looking at it, then, if it's a sacred trust? Looking is worse than touching."

"Father, don't destroy it or you'll dishonor me! Do you hear me, father?"

"Be merciful, monsieur!" said her mother.

"Father!" cried Eugénie in such a piercing voice that Nanon ran upstairs in alarm.

Eugénie snatched up a knife that was lying within reach and armed herself with it.

"Well?" said Grandet calmly, with a cold smile.

"Monsieur, monsieur, you're killing me!" said his wife.

"Father, if your knife so much as scratches one bit of that gold, I'll stab myself with this one. You've already made my mother mortally ill, and now you're about to kill your daughter. Go ahead: a wound for a wound!"

Grandet held his knife over the case, hesitating as he looked at his daughter.

"Would you really do it, Eugénie?" he asked.

"Yes, she would," said her mother.

"She'd do just what she says!" cried Nanon. "Be reasonable, monsieur, for once in your life!"

For a few moments the cooper looked back and forth between the gold and his daughter. Madame Grandet fainted.

"Look, monsieur: madame is dying!" said Nanon.

"Here, daughter; let's not quarrel over a box. Go on, take it!" cried Grandet, throwing the toilet kit on the bed. "You, Nanon, go get Monsieur Bergerin. . . . Don't worry, mother," he said, kissing his wife's hand, "everything will be all right. We've made up. . . . Haven't we, sweetie? No more dry bread—from now on you can eat whatever you like. . . . Oh! She's opening her eyes! . . . Mother, little mother, mama dear, come now! Look: I'm kissing Eugénie. She's in love with her cousin, she can marry him if she wants to, and she can keep his little case for him. But go on living for a long time, my dear. Come on, try to move. Listen, you'll have the finest altar that was ever made in Saumur."

"In the name of God, how could you treat your wife and daughter that way?" asked Madame Grandet weakly.

"I'll never do it again, never!" cried Grandet. "You'll see, my dear." He went into his office, came back with a handful of louis and scattered them over the bed. "Here, Eugénie. Here, my dear, this is for you," he said, fingering the coins. "Come, my dear, cheer up, get well. You won't lack anything, and neither will Eugénie.

Here are a hundred gold louis for her. You won't give these away, will you, Eugénie?"

Madame Grandet and her daughter looked at each other in amazement.

"Take them back, father; we don't need anything except your affection."

"Well, all right then," he said, pocketing the louis, "we'll be good friends again. We'll all go down to the living room for dinner, and we'll play lotto every evening, for two sous. Have your fling! What do you say to that, my dear?"

"Alas, I wish I could, if it would make you happy," said the dying woman, "but I can't get out of bed."

"Poor mother," said Grandet, "you don't know how much I love you! And you too, Eugénie." He hugged and kissed her. "Oh, it's so good to kiss my daughter after a quarrel! My little girl. . . . There, you see, mother: we're reconciled now. . . . Go put that away," he said to Eugénie, pointing to the case. "Go on, don't be afraid. I'll never mention it to you again, never."

Monsieur Bergerin, the leading doctor of Saumur, arrived a short time later. When he had finished his examination he told Grandet categorically that his wife was gravely ill, but that great peace of mind, a mild diet and constant care might postpone her death until the end of autumn.

"Will it be expensive?" asked the old man. "Will she need medicines?"

"Not much medicine, but a lot of care," replied the doctor, who could not help smiling.

"Well, Monsieur Bergerin," said Grandet, "you're a man of honor, aren't you? I trust you. Come to see my wife as often as you see fit. Save my good wife for me. I love her a lot, you see, although I don't show it, because I keep my feelings inside myself and they eat my heart out. I'm full of sorrow. It began with my brother's death. I'm spending enormous sums for him in Paris, sums that . . . well, it's costing me an arm and a leg! And it goes on and on. . . . Good-by, monsieur. If it's possible to save my wife, save her, even if it costs a hundred or two hundred francs."

Despite Grandet's fervent wishes for his wife's recovery when the thought of losing part of her estate began to seem like a kind of preliminary death to him, despite the willingness he showed on all occasions to grant the slightest wishes of the astonished mother and daughter, despite the tender care lavished on her by Eugénie, Madame Grandet was rapidly approaching death. Each day she grew weaker and wasted away as most women do when attacked by an illness at that age. She was as fragile as the leaves of the trees in autumn. The light of heaven made her as radiant as leaves pierced and gilded by sunbeams. Her death was worthy of her life. It was a truly Christian death. Is that not equivalent to saying that it was sublime?

In October, 1822, her virtues, her angelic patience and her love for her daughter shone forth more brightly than ever; she passed away without the slightest murmur. A spotless, innocent lamb, she rose up to heaven, regretting the loss of nothing in this world except the gentle companion of her dreary life, for whom her last glances seemed to predict a thousand sorrows. She dreaded leaving her ewe lamb, as innocent as herself, alone in a selfish world that would seek to strip her of her fleece, her treasures.

"My child," she said just before she died, "there is happiness only in heaven. You'll learn that some day."

The day after her death, Eugénie found new reasons for clinging to that house in which she had been born, in which she had suffered so much, in which her mother

had just died. She could not look at the window and
the raised chair in the living room without shedding
tears. She felt that she had misjudged her old father's
heart when she found herself the object of his tender
care. He always came in and gave her his arm to take
her down to breakfast, he would look at her with an
almost kindly expression on his face for hours on end;
in short, he watched over her as though she were made
of gold.

The old cooper was so unlike himself, so subservient
to his daughter, that Nanon and the Cruchotists, who
observed his weakness, attributed it to his advanced age
and feared that his faculties might be deteriorating. But
the reasons for his conduct became clear on the day
when he finally put on mourning, after dinner, to
which Monsieur Cruchot the notary, who alone knew
his client's secrets, had been invited. "My dear child,"
the old man said to Eugénie after the table had been
taken away and the doors had been carefully closed,
"you're now your mother's heiress, and we have a
little business to settle between us. Isn't that right,
Cruchot?"

"Yes."

"Is it absolutely necessary to discuss it today,
father?"

"Yes, it is, sweetie. I can't stand this uncertainty
any longer. You don't want to hurt me, do you?"

"Oh, father!"

"Then we must settle everything tonight."

"What do you want me to do?"

"I can't decide that for you, sweetie. . . . Tell her,
Cruchot."

"Mademoiselle, your father doesn't want to divide
the estate, or sell his property, or pay enormous taxes
on any cash he may possess. If these things are to

be avoided, there must be no inventory of the fortune which you and your father now hold in common. . . ."

"Cruchot, are you quite sure of what you're saying, to talk that way in front of a child?"

"Let me go on with my explanation, Grandet."

"All right, my friend. Neither you nor my daughter would want to ruin me. . . . Isn't that right, sweetie?"

"But what should I do, Monsieur Cruchot?" asked Eugénie impatiently.

"Well," said the notary, "you'll have to sign this deed renouncing your inheritance from your mother and giving your father the usufruct of all the property you hold in common, without relinquishing your ownership. . . ."

"I don't understand a word of what you're saying," replied Eugénie. "Give me the deed and show me where I'm supposed to sign."

Old Man Grandet looked back and forth between his daughter and the deed, overwhelmed with such violent emotion that he had to wipe beads of sweat from his brow.

"Sweetie," he said, "instead of signing that deed, which would cost a lot of money to register, I'd prefer you to renounce purely and simply your poor, dear mother's estate and trust me to take care of the future. I'll give you a nice, fat income of a hundred francs a month. Then you'll be able to pay for as many masses as you like for those you have them said for. . . . Well, what do you say to that? A hundred francs a month, in *livres?*"

"I'll do anything you like, father."

"Mademoiselle," said the notary, "it's my duty to point out to you that you'll leave yourself penniless. . . ."

"Good heavens, what do I care about that?"

"Keep quiet, Cruchot. . . . Then it's settled, it's settled!" cried Grandet, taking his daughter's hand and
patting it. "You won't take back your word, will you,
Eugénie? You're an honorable girl, aren't you?"

"Oh, father . . ."

He kissed her effusively and hugged her until she
was breathless.

"My child, you've saved your father's life; but
you're only returning what I've given you: we're even
now. That's the way business ought to be done. Life is a
business. I bless you! You're a virtuous girl who loves her
papa. From now on you can do whatever you like. . . .
I'll see you tomorrow, Cruchot," he said, looking at the
horrified notary. "Be sure the deed is properly prepared
in the record office."

The next day at noon, Eugénie signed the document
whereby she deprived herself of all her property.

At the end of the first year, however, the old cooper
had not yet given her one sou of the hundred francs
a month he had so solemnly promised her. When she
finally mentioned it to him jokingly, he blushed in spite
of himself. He hurried up to his office, came back and
presented her with about a third of the jewelry he had
taken from his nephew. "Here, my girl," he said ironically, "would you like to take these for your twelve
hundred francs?"

"Oh, father! Are you really giving them to me?"

"I'll give you the same amount next year," he said,
dropping them into her apron. "So before long you'll
have all of *his* trinkets," he added, rubbing his hands
together, delighted at being able to make a profit on
his daughter's feelings.

The old man was still vigorous, but he nevertheless felt the necessity of initiating his daughter into the

secrets of the household. For two consecutive years he had her make out the daily menus and receive the rents in his presence. He taught her slowly, one after the other, the names and sizes of his various vineyards and farms. Before the end of the third year he had so thoroughly accustomed her to his miserly ways, so deeply instilled them in her as habits, that he gave her the pantry keys without fear and made her the mistress of the house.

Five years went by without a single event capable of brightening their montonous existence. The same actions were constantly repeated with the unvarying regularity of the pendulum of the old clock. Mademoiselle Grandet's profound melancholy was not a secret to anyone; but, while everyone felt sure of its cause, she never said a word that might justify the suspicions current everywhere in Saumur concerning the state of the rich heiress's heart. Her only company consisted of the three Cruchots and a few of their friends whom they had gradually introduced into the house. They had taught her to play whist, and every evening they came to play a game with her.

In 1827 her father, feeling the weight of his infirmities, was forced to initiate her into the secrets of his landed property. He told her that, in case of difficulty, she was to consult Cruchot the notary, whose honesty was known to him. Then, toward the end of that year, at the age of eighty-two, the old man was seized with a paralysis which developed rapidly. Monsieur Bergerin declared that he did not have much longer to live.

At the thought that she would soon find herself alone in the world, Eugénie drew closer to her father, clinging more tightly to this last link of affection. In her mind, as in that of all women in love, love was the entire world, and Charles was not there. She was sublime in the care and attention she devoted to her old father, whose faculties were beginning to wane, but whose avarice persisted instinctively.

Early each morning he had himself wheeled between the fireplace of his bedroom and the door of his office, which was no doubt full of gold. He stayed there without moving, but he glanced anxiously back and forth between his visitors and the iron-shod door. He demanded an explanation of every sound he heard and, to the notary's amazement, he could hear his watchdog yawning in the courtyard. He always roused himself from his apparent stupor on the day and at the hour when rents were to be received, when accounts were to be settled with his tenant farmers, or when receipts were to be given out. He would then laboriously move his wheelchair until he was in front of the door of his office. After ordering his daughter to unlock it, he made sure that she herself piled the bags of money in their hiding-place and locked the door again. Then he would silently return to his place as soon as she had given him back the precious key, which he always kept in his vest pocket, feeling it from time to time.

His old friend the notary, feeling that the rich heiress would necessarily marry his nephew the judge if Charles Grandet did not return, redoubled his care and attentions. He came every day to place himself at Grandet's disposal and went, on his orders, to Froidfond, the farms, the meadows or the vineyards, sold the crops and converted everything into gold and silver which was secretly added to the bags piled up in the office.

Finally the death struggle began. The old man's sturdy frame came to grips with the forces of destruction. He insisted on sitting beside his fireplace, facing the door of his office. He pulled off and rolled up all the blankets that were placed on him, saying to

Nanon, "Lock this up so nobody will steal it from me."

Whenever he could open his eyes, in which all his remaining life had taken refuge, he immediately turned them toward the door of his office, where his treasure was stored, and said to his daughter, "Are they still there? Are they still there?" in a tone which betrayed a kind of panic fear.

"Yes, father."

"Take good care of the gold. . . . Put some gold in front of me!"

Eugénie would spread out some louis on a table and he would sit with his eyes fixed on them for hours on end, like a baby which, when it first begins to see, stares stupidly at a single object; and, like the baby, he would occasionally smile painfully.

"That warms me up!" he would say sometimes, and a blissful expression would steal over his face.

When the parish priest came to give him the last sacrament, his eyes, which had shown no sign of life for several hours, became animated at the sight of the cross, the candlesticks and the silver holy water vessel. He stared at them intently and his wen twitched for the last time. When the priest put the silver-gilt crucifix to his lips so that he could kiss the image of Christ, he made a frightful effort to seize it, and this last effort cost him his life. He called Eugénie, whom he could not see, although she was kneeling in front of him and bathing his already cold hand in her tears.

"Father, give me your blessing," she said.

"Take good care of everything! You'll have to give me an account of it in the next world," he said, proving by these last words that Christianity ought to be the religion of all misers.

And so Eugénie Grandet found herself alone in the world in the old house, with no one but Nanon to whom she could turn with the certainty of being heard and understood, Nanon, the only person who loved her for herself and with whom she could speak of her sorrows. Big Nanon was a blessing to her. She was no longer a servant, but a humble friend.

After her father's death, Eugénie learned from Monsieur Cruchot that she possessed an income of three hundred thousand francs a year from landed property in the district of Saumur, six million francs in government stocks paying three per cent interest, purchased at sixty francs a share and now worth seventy-seven, two million francs in gold and a hundred thousand in silver, not counting the arrears still to be collected. Her total fortune was estimated at seventeen million francs.

"But where is my cousin?" she thought.

On the day when Monsieur Cruchot gave her a final account of her inheritance in terms of its cash value, Eugénie remained alone with Nanon, each of them sitting at one side of the fireplace in the living room, which now seemed so empty, in which everything evoked memories, from the raised chair which her mother used to the glass from which her cousin had drunk.

"Nanon, we're all alone!"

"That's right, mam'selle; and if I knew where he was, the darling young man, I'd walk there on my own two feet to bring him back."

"There's an ocean between us."

While the poor heiress was thus weeping in the company of her old servant in that cold, dark house which was the whole universe to her, everyone from Nantes to Orléans was talking about Mademoiselle

Grandet's seventeen million francs. One of the first things she did was to give Nanon a lifetime annuity of twelve hundred francs. Since she already had an annuity of six hundred francs, Nanon's marriage prospects became much brighter. In less than a month she went from spinsterhood to wifehood through the good offices of Antoine Cornoiller, who was appointed chief custodian of Mademoiselle Grandet's lands and estates. Madame Cornoiller had a great advantage over her contemporaries: although she was fifty-nine, she did not appear to be over forty. Her coarse features had withstood the attacks of time. Thanks to her monastic way of life, she defied old age with her ruddy complexion and her iron constitution. She had perhaps never looked better than she did on her wedding day. She had the benefits of her ugliness; she appeared big, stout and strong, with an expression of happiness on her indestructible face which made some people envy Cornoiller's fate.

"She's dyed in the wool," said the clothier.

"She's capable of having children," said the salt merchant. "She's as well preserved as if she'd been pickled in brine, if you'll excuse the expression."

"She's rich—Cornoiller is doing all right for himself," said another neighbor.

When she came out of the old house, Nanon, who was loved by everyone in the neighborhood, was showered with compliments as she walked down the winding street on her way to the parish church.

As a wedding present, Eugénie gave her a set of silverware for three dozen persons. Cornoiller, amazed at such lavishness, spoke of his mistress with tears in his eyes: he would have let himself be cut to pieces for her. Madame Cornoiller now became Eugénie's trusted assistant, and this gave her as much satisfaction as the possession of a husband. At last she had a pantry to lock and unlock, provisions to hand out in the morning like her late master. And she also ruled over two servants: a cook and a maid whose duties were to keep the household linen in repair and make Mademoiselle Grandet's dresses. Cornoiller held the combined offices of gamekeeper and steward. Needless to say, the cook and the maid chosen by Nanon were real "pearls." Mademoiselle Grandet thus had four servants whose devotion to her was boundless.

The tenant farmers scarcely noticed the old man's death, so firmly had he established the usages and customs of his management, which were scrupulously carried on by Monsieur and Madame Cornoiller.

VI

So Goes the World

At thirty, Eugénie had still known none of the joys of life. Her pale, sad childhood had slipped past beside a mother whose heart, misunderstood and wounded, had always been suffering. Departing from this life with joy, she pitied her daughter for having to go on living and left in her soul slight remorse and eternal regrets. Eugénie's first and only love was a source of melancholy to her. After spending only a few short days with the man she loved, she had given him her heart between two kisses furtively accepted and returned; then he had gone away, placing a whole world between them. This love, cursed by her father, had been one cause of her mother's death, and it gave her only sorrow mingled with frail hopes. Thus, so far in her life, she had pursued happiness in vain, exhausting her strength without being able to renew it. There is a breathing in and a breathing out in the life of the soul as well as in the life of the body: the soul needs to absorb the feelings of another soul, to assimilate them in order to give them back more abundantly. Without this sublime human phenomenon, the heart cannot live; it suffocates and withers away in pain.

Eugénie was beginning to suffer. For her, wealth was neither power nor consolation; she could exist only through love, through religion, through her faith in the future. Love explained eternity to her. Her heart and the Holy Gospels told her of two worlds awaiting her. Night and day she was absorbed in two infinite thoughts which, for her, perhaps, merged into one. She withdrew into herself, loving and believing herself to be loved. During the past seven years, her passion had seeped into everything. Her treasures were not the millions which continued to pile up interest, but Charles's toilet kit, the two portraits hanging over her bed, the jewels redeemed from her father and proudly spread out on a layer of cotton in one drawer of her dresser, her aunt's thimble, which her mother had used and which she now put on religiously every day to work on a piece of embroidery, a task as endless as Penelope's, undertaken only for the purpose of putting on her finger that gold full of memories.

It did not seem likely that Mademoiselle Grandet would want to get married during her mourning. Her sincere piety was well known. The Cruchots, whose strategy was wisely directed by the old priest, therefore contented themselves with closing in on the heiress by surrounding her with affectionate attentions.

Every evening her living room was filled with the most ardent and devoted Cruchotists of the region, all striving to sing the praises of the mistress of the household in every possible key. She had her court physician, her court chaplain, her chamberlain, her first lady in waiting, her prime minister, and above all her chancellor, a chancellor who sought to advise her in everything. If she had wanted a train bearer, one would have been found for her. She was a queen, the most skillfully flattered of all queens. Flattery never emanates from great souls; it is peculiar to little people who succeed in making themselves still smaller in order to enter more completely into the vital sphere of the person around whom they gravitate. Flattery implies self-interest. And so the people who congregated every evening in the living room of Mademoiselle Grandet, whom they called Mademoiselle de Froidfond, succeeded admirably in overwhelming her with compliments. This chorus of praise, new to Eugénie, made her blush at first, but gradually, despite the crude exaggeration of many of the compliments, her ear became so accustomed to hearing her beauty praised that if some newcomer had found her ugly she would have been more sensitive to the reproach than she would have been eight years earlier. Finally she came to like those sweet words, which she secretly laid at the feet of her idol. Little by little, she became used to letting herself be treated like a sovereign and seeing her court filled every evening.

Judge de Bonfons was the hero of this little circle, in which his wit, looks, education and charm were constantly praised. Someone would occasionally point out that he had greatly increased his fortune in the past seven years, that Bonfons, his estate, yielded an income of at least ten thousand francs a year, and that it was enclosed, like all the property of the Cruchot family, by the heiress's vast domains.

"Do you know, mademoiselle," one of the habitual visitors would say, "that the Cruchots have a combined income of forty thousand francs a year?"

"And don't forget their savings," remarked Mademoiselle de Gribeaucourt, an old Cruchotist. "Not long ago a gentleman came from Paris to offer Monsieur Cruchot two hundred thousand francs for his practice. He'll have to sell it if he becomes a judge."

"He wants to succeed Monsieur de Bonfons in the civil court, and he's already making preparations," said Madame d'Orsonval, "because Monsieur de Bonfons will become a councillor, then a presiding magistrate; with his abilities, he's sure to succeed."

"Yes, he's a very distinguished man," said someone else. "Don't you think so, mademoiselle?"

The judge had tried to make himself fit the part he wanted to play. Despite his forty years and his swarthy, unattractive face, withered and dry like most judicial countenances, he dressed like a young man, twirled a Malacca cane, never took snuff in Mademoiselle de Froidfond's house and always came there wearing a white cravat and a shirt whose pleated frill gave him a family resemblance to the turkey. He spoke familiarly to the beautiful heiress and referred to her as "our dear Eugénie."

In short, except for the number of visitors, the replacement of lotto by whist and the absence of Monsieur and Madame Grandet, the scene was essentially the same as the one with which this story began. The pack was still pursuing Eugénie and her millions, but it was now larger, barked louder and showed more coordination in its efforts to close in on the prey. If Charles had returned from the depths of the Indies, he would have found the same people and the same self-interest. Madame des Grassins, whom Eugénie treated with perfect kindness and courtesy, was still tormenting the Cruchots. But Eugénie would still have dominated the scene as before, and Charles would still have been sovereign there. Nevertheless there had been some progress. The bouquet which the judge had formerly given

Eugénie on her birthday had now become a more frequent occurrence. Every evening he brought the rich heiress a large, magnificent bouquet which Madame Cornoiller ostentatiously placed in a vase and secretly threw into a corner of the courtyard as soon as the visitors were gone.

Early in spring, Madame des Grassins tried to trouble the happiness of the Cruchotists by speaking to Eugénie about the Marquis de Froidfond, whose ruined family could rise again if the heiress would give him back his estate through a marriage contract. Madame des Grassins talked enthusiastically about the peerage and the title of marquise and, mistaking Eugénie's disdainful smile for approval, she went around saying that Judge Cruchot's marriage was not as certain as some people believed.

"Although Monsieur de Froidfond is fifty," she said, "he doesn't look any older than Monsieur Cruchot. He's a widower and he has children, it's true, but he's a marquis and he'll be a Peer of France. It's not easy to find a match like that nowadays! I know for a fact that when Old Man Grandet put all his money into the Froidfond estate he intended to graft his family onto theirs. He told me so many times. He was as shrewd as they come!"

"How can it be, Nanon," said Eugénie one night as she went to bed, "that he hasn't written to me once in seven years?"

While these things were taking place in Saumur, Charles was making his fortune in the Indies. To begin with, he had received a good price for his merchandise. He had quickly realized a sum of six thousand dollars. Crossing the equator made him lose a great many prejudices; he saw that the best way to make a fortune, in tropical regions as well as in Europe, was to buy and sell men. He therefore went to the coast of Africa and engaged in the slave trade. In addition to his traffic in human flesh, he also dealt in various kinds of merchandise which could be advantageously exchanged in the markets to which his interests led him. He devoted himself so completely to his business affairs that he never had a moment of free time. He was dominated by the idea of reappearing in Paris with all the splendor of a great fortune and regaining a position still more brilliant than the one from which he had fallen.

The experience of coming in contact with all sorts of men in various countries and observing their divergent customs had changed his ideas; he had become a skeptic. Having seen what was regarded as a virtue in one country condemned as a crime in another, he no longer had any fixed conceptions of justice and injustice. As a result of his constant preoccupation with business, his heart contracted, grew cold and dry. The blood of the Grandets did not fail to achieve its destiny. Charles became hard and greedy. He sold Chinese, Negroes, swallows' nests, children, artists; he practiced usury on a large scale. The habit of avoiding the payment of duty on his merchandise made him less scrupulous about his duty toward his fellow man. He would go to Saint Thomas, pay very low prices for merchandise stolen by pirates, then take it to places where it was scarce.

While Eugénie's pure and noble countenance accompanied him on his first voyage, like the image of the Virgin which Spanish sailors place on their vessels, and while he attributed his early success to the magic influence of the sweet girl's prayers and wishes, later on his memories of her, of Saumur, of her house, of their bench, and of the kiss stolen in the hall were obliterated by all the other women he had known— Egyptian dancing girls, Negresses, mulattoes, Javanese and white women—by his orgies of all kinds and by his adventures in various countries. He remembered only the little garden enclosed by old walls, for it was there that his hazardous destiny had begun. But he repudiated his family: his uncle was an old scoundrel who had cheated him out of his jewelry, and Eugénie had no place either in his thoughts or in his heart; she occupied only a place in his accounts as a creditor for the sum of six thousand francs. This conduct and these ideas explain Charles Grandet's silence. In the Indies, at Saint Thomas, on the African coast, in Lisbon and in the United States, the speculator had adopted the pseudonym of Sepherd, in order not to compromise his true name. Carl Sepherd could safely show himself everywhere as tireless, audacious and grasping, like a man who, resolved to make a fortune by fair means or foul, is in a hurry to be finished with infamy so that he can remain an honorable man for the rest of his life.

With this system, he made his fortune quickly and brilliantly. In 1827, therefore, he was on his way back to Bordeaux on board the *Marie-Caroline,* a handsome brig belonging to a Royalist firm. He had three stout kegs containing one million nine hundred thousand francs' worth of gold dust, on which he expected to make a profit of seven or eight percent by having it made into coins in Paris.

On this brig there was also a gentleman in waiting to His Majesty King Charles X, Monsieur d'Aubrion, a kindly old man who had been foolish enough to marry a woman of fashion, and whose fortune was in the Indies. He had gone there to sell his property in order to pay for his wife's extravagances. Monsieur and Madame d'Aubrion, of the house of d'Aubrion de Buch, whose last head had died before 1789, were now reduced to an income of no more than thirty thousand francs a year. They had a rather ugly daughter whom the mother wanted to marry off without a dowry, since her fortune was scarcely enough for her own life in Paris. This was an enterprise whose success would have seemed problematical to all society people, despite the cleverness they attribute to women of fashion. When she looked at her daughter, Madame d'Aubrion herself almost despaired of ever getting anyone to take her off her hands, even a man infatuated with the nobility.

Mademoiselle d'Aubrion was as long, thin and fragile as an insect; she had a disdainful mouth over which drooped a nose that was too long, thick at the end, yellowish in its normal state but bright red after meals, a kind of vegetable phenomenon more disagreeable in the middle of a pale, bored face than in any other. In short, she was all that a mother of thirty-eight, who was still beautiful and still had pretensions, could desire. But, to counterbalance these disadvantages, the Marquise d'Aubrion had given her daughter a very distinguished air, kept her on a diet which temporarily maintained her nose at a reasonable flesh tint, instructed her in the art of dressing in good taste, endowed her with gracious manners and taught her to cast those melancholy glances which interest a man and make him believe he has at last met the angel he has long sought in vain; she had taught her the maneuver of the foot, how to push it forward at the right moment, so that its smallness could be admired whenever her nose had the impertinence to turn red; in short, she had given her daughter every advantage possible under the circumstances. By means of full sleeves, deceptive bodices, carefully decorated billowing skirts and high-pressure corsets, she had obtained such extraordinary feminine attributes that she ought to have exhibited them in a museum for the edification of other mothers.

Charles became quite friendly with Madame d'Aubrion, and this was precisely what she wanted. In fact, several people claimed that, during the crossing, the beautiful Madame d'Aubrion neglected no means of capturing such a wealthy son-in-law.

After landing at Bordeaux in June, 1827, Charles, Monsieur, Madame and Mademoiselle d'Aubrion all stayed in the same hotel, then left for Paris together.

The d'Aubrion mansion was loaded down with mortgages; Charles was to free it. Madame d'Aubrion had already spoken of how happy she would be to let her daughter and son-in-law take over the ground floor. Not sharing her husband's prejudices on the subject, she had promised Charles Grandet that she would obtain from the good King Charles X a royal ordinance authorizing him to bear the name of d'Aubrion, to take the family coat of arms and, by establishing an entailed estate at Aubrion with a yearly income of thirty-six thousand francs, to take the title of Lord Buch and Marquis d'Aubrion. By combining their fortunes and living on close terms with each other, they would be able to concentrate an income of over a hundred thousand francs a year in the d'Aubrion mansion.

"And when a man has an income of a hundred thousand francs, a name, a family and a position at court (I'll have you appointed a gentleman of the bedchamber), he can become anything he likes," Madame d'Aubrion said to Charles. "You'll be able to take your choice: reporting magistrate, prefect, embassy secretary, ambassador. . . . Charles X is very fond of d'Aubrion; they've known each other since childhood."

She had aroused his ambition to fever pitch. During the crossing he had toyed with all these hopes, which were skillfully presented to him in the form of confidences poured out from one heart to another. Believ-

ing that his father's affairs had all been settled by his
uncle, he saw himself suddenly established in the Fau-
bourg Saint-Germain, where everyone wanted to live
in those days, and where, in the shadow of Mademoiselle Mathilde's blue nose, he would reappear as Count
d'Aubrion, just as the Dreux family reappeared one
day as the Brézés. Dazzled by the prosperity of the
Restoration, which had been in shaky condition when
he left, and carried away by the splendor of aristocratic
ideas, when he reached Paris he remained in the grip of
the intoxication that had begun on the ship. He resolved
to do everything in his power to attain the high position
which his selfish future mother-in-law had made him
visualize. His cousin was therefore only a minute point
in the brilliant perspective that lay before him.

He saw Annette again. As a woman of the world, she
urged him to go through with the marriage and promised
him her support in all his ambitious enterprises. She was
delighted to have him marry an ugly, boring girl. His stay
in the Indies had made him extremely attractive: his skin
was bronzed and he had developed the bold, decisive
manner of a man who is accustomed to direct action,
power and success. He felt more at ease in Paris now
that he knew he could play an important part there.

Des Grassins, having learned of his return, his
forthcoming marriage and his wealth, came to see
him to discuss the three hundred thousand francs
with which he could settle his father's debts. He found
him in conference with the jeweler from whom he had
ordered some jewelry as a wedding gift for Mademoiselle
d'Aubrion and who was now showing him some designs.
Despite the magnificent diamonds Charles had brought
back from the Indies, the workmanship and materials
of the silverware and heavy, useless jewelry ordered by
the young couple were going to cost over two hundred

thousand francs. Charles received des Grassins, whom he did not recognize, with the impertinence of a young man of fashion who, in the Indies, had killed four men in different duels. Monsieur des Grassins had already come three times before.

Charles listened to him coldly, then replied, without having fully understood, "My father's business isn't mine. I'm grateful to you for your efforts, monsieur, but I'm afraid I can't take advantage of them. I haven't piled up nearly two million francs by the sweat of my brow just so I could toss it into the laps of my father's creditors."

"And what if your father were to be declared a bankrupt a few days from now?"

"Monsieur, a few days from now my name will be Count d'Aubrion, so you can understand why it will be a matter of complete indifference to me. Besides, you know better than I that if a man has an income of a hundred thousand francs, his father is never a bankrupt," he added, politely pushing Monsieur des Grassins toward the door.

Early in August of that same year, Eugénie was sitting on the little wooden bench on which her cousin had sworn to love her forever, and on which she had breakfast whenever the weather was good. On this cool, cheerful morning, the poor girl was happily engaged in recalling the great and small events of her love, and the catastrophes which had followed it. The sun was shining brightly on the beautiful old wall; it was full of cracks and ready to fall into ruin, but the eccentric heiress had given orders that it was to be left alone, even though Cornoiller often told his wife that someone would be crushed beneath it some day.

The postman knocked on the door and handed a

letter to Madame Cornoiller, who came out into the garden shouting, "Mademoiselle! A letter!" She gave it to her mistress and asked, "Is it the one you've been waiting for?"

These words echoed as loudly in Eugénie's heart as they did between the walls of the courtyard and the garden.

"Paris! . . . It's from him! He's come back!"

Eugénie turned pale and held the letter unopened for a moment. She was trembling too violently to break the seal and read it.

Big Nanon stood with her hands on her hips, and her joy seemed to pour out like smoke through the crevices of her swarthy face.

"Go on, mademoiselle, read it. . . ."

"Oh, Nanon, why has he gone to Paris first when he left from Saumur?"

"Read the letter and you'll find out."

Eugénie trembled as she opened the letter. From it fell a draft on the firm of Madame des Grassins and Corret, of Saumur. Nanon picked it up.

"My dear cousin . . ."

"I'm no longer Eugénie," she thought; and she felt something grip her heart.

"You . . ."

"He used to say *tu*[*]!" Eugénie folded her arms, afraid to go on reading the letter, and large tears welled up in her eyes.

"Is he dead?" asked Nanon.

"He wouldn't be able to write if he were!" said Eugénie.

She read the entire letter:

---

[*] The intimate form of the second person pronoun, as opposed to the polite, formal *vous* which Charles has used in his letter.—L.B.

My dear cousin,

I think you will be glad to learn that my enterprises have succeeded. You have brought me good luck. I have become rich, and I have followed my uncle's advice. Monsieur des Grassins has just informed me of his death and my aunt's. The death of our parents is in the natural order of things, and we must carry on after them. I hope you have recovered from your grief by now. Nothing can withstand the power of time; I have learned that from experience. Yes, my dear cousin, unfortunately for me the time of illusions has passed. How could it be otherwise? While traveling through many countries, I have reflected on life. I went away as a child, I have come back as a man. I now think of many things which never occurred to me before. You are free, my cousin, and so am I; outwardly, there is nothing to stop us from carrying out our little plans, but I am too honest not to tell you the true state of my affairs. I have not forgotten my vows to you; I have always remembered, throughout my long wanderings, the little wooden bench . . .

Eugénie stood up as though she had been sitting on burning coals and went over to sit down on one of the steps of the courtyard.

. . . the little wooden bench on which we swore to love each other forever, the hall, the gray living room, my attic bedroom, and the night when, by your tactful generosity, you made my future easier for me. Yes, those memories kept up my courage, and I told myself that you

still thought of me as I often thought of you at the hour we had agreed upon. Did you really look at the clouds at nine o'clock? You did, didn't you? I cannot betray a friendship that is sacred to me; no, I must not deceive you. I am now planning a marriage which fulfills all the conditions I have come to regard as essential. Love, in marriage, is an illusion. Today my experience tells me that when one marries, one must obey all social laws and satisfy all the conventions imposed by the world. Now there is already a difference of age between us which might have a stronger influence on your future than on mine, my dear cousin. I will say nothing of your outlook on life, your education or your habits, which are out of harmony with Paris life and would probably not fit in with my plans for the future. I intend to maintain a large household and receive a great many guests, and I seem to recall that you like a quiet, peaceful life.

No, I will speak more frankly; I want you to judge my situation for yourself. You have a right to know it and form your own opinion of it. I now have an income of eighty thousand francs a year. This fortune enables me to marry into the d'Aubrion family, whose heiress, a young girl of nineteen, will bring me in marriage her name, a title, a post as honorary gentleman in waiting to His Majesty, and a very brilliant position. I confess, my dear cousin, that I am not the least bit in love with Mademoiselle d'Aubrion; but, in marrying her, I will be assuring my children of a social posi-

*tion whose advantages will some day be incal-
culable. Monarchical ideas are returning more
strongly to favor every day. Therefore, when
my son becomes the Marquis d'Aubrion, with
an entailed estate yielding an income of forty
thousand francs a year, he will be able to take
up any governmental position he chooses. We
must dedicate ourselves to our children.*

*You can see, my dear cousin, how frankly
I am describing to you the state of my heart,
my hopes and my fortune. It is possible that,
for your part, you have forgotten our childish
dreams after seven years of separation, but I
have forgotten neither your kindness nor my
promises; I remember them all, even the ones
that were given most lightly and which would
long since have been forgotten by a young man
less conscientious than I am, with a less youthful and honest heart. In telling you that my
only intention is to make a marriage of con-
venience and that I still remember our childish
love, I am placing myself entirely at your disposal, making you the mistress of my fate and
telling you that, if I must give up my social
ambitions, I will gladly content myself with
that pure, simple happiness of which you have
given me such a touching example. . . .*

"Tum, ta, ta; tum, ta, tee. Toom! Tum, ta, tee; tum,
ta, ta . . ." Charles Grandet had sung to the tune of *Non
Più Andrai* as he signed his letter:

> *Your devoted cousin,*
> *Charles*

"That's really doing it up brown, by God!" he had said to himself. Then he had looked for the draft and added the following:

> *P.S. I am enclosing a draft on the des Grassins bank, made out to your order and payable in gold, for eight thousand francs, which will cover the capital and interest of the sum you were kind enough to lend me. I am expecting a case from Bordeaux containing a few objects which I hope you will allow me to give you as a token of my eternal gratitude. You can send my toilet kit by stagecoach to the Hôtel d'Aubrion, rue Hillerin-Bertin.*

"By stagecoach!" exclaimed Eugénie. "And I'd have laid down my life to protect it!"

Terrible and utter disaster! The ship had sunk without leaving a single rope or plank on the vast sea of hope.

Some women, when they see that they have been abandoned, go off to snatch their lover from the arms of a rival, kill her and then flee to the ends of the earth, yield themselves to the scaffold or take their own lives. This is no doubt a noble course of action; the motive of such a crime is a sublime passion before which human justice stands in awe. Other women bow their heads and suffer in silence; dying and resigned, they weep, forgive, pray and remember until they draw their last breath. This is love, true love, angelic love, proud love, which lives from its anguish and finally dies of it. Such was Eugénie's feeling after reading the horrible letter. She raised her eyes to heaven and thought of the last words of her mother, who, as dying people sometimes do, had cast a clear, penetrating glance into the future. Then, remembering that prophetic life and death, Eugénie saw her whole destiny stretching out before her. From now on there was nothing for her to do but spread her wings, reach heavenward and live in prayer until the day of her deliverance.

"My mother was right," she said, weeping. "Suffer and die."

She walked slowly from the garden into the living room. Contrary to her habit, she did not go through the hall; but she found memories of her cousin in that gray old room, on whose mantelpiece there was always a certain saucer, which she used every morning at breakfast, along with the old Sèvres sugar bowl. That morning was to be solemn and eventful for her. Nanon announced the arrival of the parish priest. This priest, a relative of the Cruchots, was interested in furthering the cause of Judge de Bonfons. Several days earlier, old Abbé Cruchot had persuaded him to speak to Mademoiselle Grandet, on a purely religious plane, about her obligation to marry.

When she saw her pastor, Eugénie thought he had come for the thousand francs she gave to the poor each month. She told Nanon to bring the money, but the priest smiled and said, "Today, mademoiselle, I've come to talk to you about a poor girl in whom everyone in Saumur is interested and who, for lack of charity toward herself, isn't leading a truly Christian life."

"Good heavens, father, you've come to me at a time when it's impossible for me to think of my neighbor: I'm completely occupied with myself. I'm terribly unhappy and the Church is my only refuge; her bosom is deep enough to contain all our sorrows, and her compassion is so abundant that we can draw on it without fear of exhausting it."

"Well, mademoiselle, in concerning ourselves with

this girl, we'll be concerning ourselves with you. Listen to me. If you want to insure your salvation, you have only two paths to follow: either withdraw from the world or obey its laws; obey either your earthly destiny or your celestial destiny."

"Ah, you're speaking to me just when I wanted to hear a voice! Yes, God has sent you here, monsieur. I'm going to bid farewell to the world and live for God alone, in silence and seclusion."

"You must give a great deal of thought to that radical decision, my daughter. Marriage is life, the veil is a kind of death."

"Well then, father, I choose death, as soon as possible!" she said with frightening intensity.

"Death? But you have great obligations to fulfill toward society, mademoiselle. Are you not a mother to the poor, whom you supply with clothes and wood in winter, and work in summer? Your wealth is a loan which you must repay, and you've been saintly enough to accept it on those terms. It would be selfish of you to bury yourself in a convent; as for remaining a spinster, you mustn't do it. First of all, could you go on managing your enormous fortune alone? You might lose it. You'd soon have all sorts of lawsuits on your hands and become enmeshed in inextricable difficulties. Take your pastor's word for it: a husband will be useful to you, you must keep what God has given you. I'm speaking to you as one of the precious lambs of my flock. You love God too sincerely not to find your salvation in the midst of the world, of which you're one of the noblest adornments and to which you set a saintly example."

Just then the arrival of Madame des Grassins was announced. She had been brought to Eugénie's house by great despair and a desire for revenge.

"Mademoiselle . . ." she began. "Oh, I see you're

here, father . . . I won't say anything; I came here to
talk business and I see you're having an important discussion."

"Madame," said the priest, "I leave you in possession of the field."

"Oh, father," said Eugénie, "come back a little
later! I need your support very much right now."

"Yes, my poor child," said Madame des Grassins.

"What do you mean?" asked Mademoiselle Grandet
and the priest.

"You see, I know about your cousin's return and
his marriage to Mademoiselle d'Aubrion. . . . A woman
always has her wits about her."

Eugénie blushed and remained silent; but she decided that in the future she would wear the impassive
expression which her father had always been able to
assume.

"Well, madame," she replied ironically, "I apparently don't have my wits about me, because I don't
understand what you're saying. You can speak frankly
in front of the pastor; he's my confessor, you know."

"Very well, mademoiselle: this is what des Grassins
has written to me. Read it."

Eugénie read the following letter:

> *My dear wife,*
>   *Charles Grandet has returned from the*
> *Indies. He has been in Paris for a month . . .*

"A month!" thought Eugénie, letting her hand fall.
After a pause, she went on reading the letter:

> *. . . I had to wait in his anteroom twice with-*
> *out success before I was able to see the future*
> *Count d'Aubrion. Although everyone in Paris*

is talking about his marriage and the banns have
already been published . . .

"Then he wrote to me after he'd already . . ."
thought Eugénie. She did not finish, she did not cry out
"The swine!" as a Parisian girl would have done; but her
contempt was no less profound for being unexpressed.

> *. . . his marriage is far from certain. The Mar-*
> *quis d'Aubrion will not give his daughter to*
> *the son of a bankrupt. I went to inform him*
> *of the efforts his uncle and I had made to settle*
> *his father's affairs, and of the clever maneu-*
> *vers by which we had been able to keep the*
> *creditors quiet all that time. And the young*
> *upstart had the impudence to say to me, to*
> *me, who for five years have devoted myself*
> *night and day to his welfare and his honor,*
> *that his father's business was not his! A lawyer*
> *would have a right to demand a fee of thirty*
> *or forty thousand francs, at the rate of one per-*
> *cent of the money owed. But don't worry: one*
> *million two hundred thousand francs is quite*
> *legally owed to the creditors, and I am going*
> *to have his father declared bankrupt. I became*
> *involved in this matter on the word of that old*
> *crocodile Grandet, and I have made promises*
> *in the name of his family. Count d'Aubrion*
> *may care little about his honor, but I care a*
> *great deal about mine, so I am going to explain*
> *my position to the creditors. However, I have*
> *too much respect for Mademoiselle Eugénie,*
> *whom we hoped, in happier days, that our son*
> *might marry, to act before you have spoken to*
> *her about this matter . . .*

At this point Eugénie coldly handed back the letter without finishing it.

"Thank you," she said to Madame des Grassins. "We'll see about that. . . ."

"You sounded exactly like your father just now," said Madame des Grassins.

"Madame, you have eight thousand one hundred francs in gold for us," Nanon said to her.

"That's true; please be kind enough to come with me, Madame Cornoiller."

"Father," said Eugénie with a noble composure that was inspired by the thought she was about to express, "would it be a sin to remain in a state of virginity in marriage?"

"That's a point of conscience to which I don't know the answer. If you want to know what the famous Sanchez says about it in his treatise *De Matrimonio,* I can tell you tomorrow."

The priest left. Mademoiselle Grandet went up to her father's office and spent the rest of the day alone there, refusing to come downstairs for dinner, in spite of Nanon's entreaties. She appeared that evening when her usual visitors began to arrive. The Grandet living room had never been as full as it was that night. The news of Charles's return and foolish betrayal had spread all over town. But, despite the keenness of the visitors' curiosity, it was not satisfied. Eugénie had expected it and she did not allow her calm face to reveal any of the cruel emotions that were tormenting her. She was able to assume a smiling expression in reply to those who tried to show their sympathy by melancholy looks or words. She was able to cover her unhappiness with a veil of politeness.

By nine o'clock the whist games had ended and the players were leaving their tables, paying their losses and discussing the last hands as they came over to join those who had been engaged in conversation. Just as the company rose in a body to take leave of their hostess, there was a dramatic event which re-echoed first all over Saumur, then throughout the entire district and the four surrounding prefectures.

"Please stay, judge," said Eugénie to Monsieur de Bonfons when she saw him take his cane.

There was not one person in the large gathering who felt unmoved on hearing these words. The judge turned pale and was obliged to sit down.

"The judge gets the millions!" said Mademoiselle de Gribeaucourt.

"It's clear: Judge de Bonfons is going to marry Mademoiselle Grandet!" exclaimed Madame d'Orsonval.

"There's the best play of the evening," said Abbé Cruchot.

"It's a grand slam!" said the notary.

Everyone made his remark or his pun, everyone saw the heiress mounted on her millions as on a pedestal. The drama begun nine years earlier was now reaching its climax. To ask the judge to remain behind, in the presence of everyone in Saumur—was this not equivalent to a formal announcement of her intention to marry him? In small towns the conventions are so rigidly observed that an infraction of this kind constitutes a solemn promise.

"Judge," Eugénie said to him in a faltering voice when they were alone together, "I know what pleases you in me. If you swear that you'll leave me free for the rest of my life, that you'll claim none of the rights which marriage would give you over me, I'll give you my hand. Oh!" she exclaimed, seeing that he was about to kneel, "I haven't said everything yet. I don't want to mislead you, monsieur. There's already an inextinguishable love in my heart. Friendship will be the only feeling I can give to my husband: I don't want either to offend him or do violence to the laws of my heart. But you will have my hand only in exchange for a very great service."

"I'm willing to do anything at all," said the judge.

"Here's a million and a half francs, judge," she said, drawing from her bosom a certificate of a hundred shares in the Bank of France. "Leave for Paris, not tomorrow, not later tonight, but at this very moment. Go to see Monsieur des Grassins and find out from him the names of all my uncle's creditors, then call them together and pay all the debts still owed by his estate, including five percent interest from the day each debt was incurred to the day it's paid off. When you've done that, have them all sign a notarized receipt drawn up in proper form. You're a judge, so I trust you to handle the matter personally. You're an honorable and gallant man; I'll embark on the strength of your word and brave the dangers of life under the protection of your name. We'll be indulgent with each other. We've known each other so long that we're almost like relatives; I'm sure you wouldn't want to make me unhappy."

The judge fell at the feet of the rich heiress, palpitating with joy and anxiety. "I'll be your slave!" he said.

"When you have the receipt, monsieur," she went on, glancing at him coldly, "you will take it, along with all the proofs of indebtedness, to my cousin, Charles Grandet, and you will also give him this letter. When you return, I will keep my word."

The judge realized that he owed Mademoiselle Grandet's consent to a feeling of spite prompted by love; he therefore hastened to carry out her orders as quickly as he could, to avoid the possibility of a reconciliation between the two lovers.

When Monsieur de Bonfons had left, Eugénie sank into her armchair and burst into tears. Everything was settled now.

The judge took the stagecoach and reached Paris the following night. On the morning after his arrival he went to see des Grassins, then he summoned the creditors to the office of the notary with whom the proofs of indebtedness had been deposited. Not one of them failed to appear. Even though they were creditors, we must do them justice: they were punctual. Judge de Bonfons, in the name of Mademoiselle Grandet, paid each of them capital and interest. The payment of interest was one of the most startling events of the time in the Paris business world.

When the receipt had been registered and des Grassins had been given the fifty thousand francs which Eugénie wished to pay him for his services, the judge went to the d'Aubrion mansion, where he found Charles just returning to his apartment after being overwhelmed with reproaches by his prospective father-in-law. The old marquis had just told him that his daughter would never belong to him until the creditors of Guillaume Grandet had been paid off.

The judge handed him the following letter:

Dear cousin,

Judge de Bonfons has agreed to give you a quittance for all the debts owed to my uncle and a receipt acknowledging that I have received the money from you. There has been talk of a declaration of bankruptcy, and it occurred to me that the son of a bankrupt might not be able to marry Mademoiselle d'Aubrion.

Yes, cousin, you have correctly judged my mind and manners; it is no doubt true that

*I know nothing of the world; I understand
neither its calculations nor its customs, and I
could not give you the pleasures you hope to
find in it. Be happy, in accordance with the
social conventions to which you have sacri-
ficed our young love. To make your happiness
complete, all I can give you is your father's
honor. Farewell; you will always have a faithful friend in your cousin,*

Eugénie

The judge smiled at the exclamation which the
ambitious young man was unable to repress when he
received the official document.

"Each of us can now announce his marriage," he
said.

"Oh, you're going to marry Eugénie? Well, I'm
glad to hear it; she's a fine girl. . . . And," he went on,
suddenly struck by an illuminating thought, "she must
be rich. . . ."

"Up until four days ago," replied the judge ironically, "she had nearly nineteen million francs, but now
she has only seventeen million."

Charles looked at the judge in stupefaction and
stammered, "Seventeen . . . mil . . ."

"That's right, monsieur: seventeen million. After
our marriage, Mademoiselle Grandet and I will have a
combined income of seven hundred and fifty thousand
francs a year."

"My dear cousin," said Charles, recovering a little
of his self-assurance, "we'll no doubt be able to help
each other along in the future."

"Agreed," said the judge. "Oh yes, here's something else: Mademoiselle Grandet wanted me to give
you this little box in person," he added, setting down

on the table the case containing the gold toilet articles.

"Don't worry about what poor Monsieur d'Aubrion just said to you, my friend," said the Marquise d'Aubrion, entering the room without paying any attention to Cruchot. "The Duchess of Chaulieu had turned his head. Let me repeat to you that nothing will prevent your marriage . . ."

"Nothing, madame," replied Charles. "The debt of three million francs which my father once owed was paid off yesterday."

"In cash?" she asked.

"Paid in full, capital and interest. I'm going to rehabilitate his memory."

"How stupid!" cried his future mother-in-law. "Who's this gentleman?" she whispered, noticing Cruchot.

"My agent," Charles replied in a low voice.

The marquise bowed disdainfully to Monsieur de Bonfons and left the room.

"We're already helping each other along," said the judge, taking his hat. "Good-by, cousin."

"He's making fun of me, that stupid cockatoo from Saumur!" thought Charles. "I'd like to give him six inches of steel in the belly!"

The judge left Paris. Three days later, back in Saumur, he announced his marriage to Eugénie. Six months later, he was appointed councillor of the royal court in Angers.

Before leaving Saumur, Eugénie had a goldsmith melt down the gold of the jewelry she had cherished so long and had it, along with the eight thousand francs she had received from her cousin, made into a gold monstrance which she presented to the parish church in which she had so often prayed for *him*!

She divided her time between Angers and Saumur.

Her husband, who had proven his loyalty in a political situation, became a judge in the superior court, and finally, several years later, a presiding magistrate. He was impatiently awaiting the next general election in order to obtain a seat in the Chamber. He already had his eye on a peerage, and then . . .

"And then will the king be his cousin?" asked Nanon, Big Nanon, Madame Cornoiller, a middle-class lady of Saumur, when her mistress told her of the heights to which she could expect to rise.

VII

Conclusion

However, Judge de Bonfons (he had finally abolished the name of Cruchot altogether) did not succeed in carrying out any of his ambitious plans. He died a week after being elected deputy from Saumur.

God, who sees everything and never strikes amiss, had no doubt punished him for his calculations and the legal skill with which he had drawn up, *accurante Cruchot,* his marriage contract, in which both parties gave each other, in case they should have no children, "all their property, landed and personal, without exception or reservation, in full ownership, dispensing even with the formality of an inventory, it being understood that the omission of said inventory shall not be employed to the disadvantage of their heirs or executors, and that this donation *inter vivos* shall be . . ." etc. This clause may explain the deep respect which the judge always showed for Madame de Bonfons' wishes and privacy. The women of his social circle cited Judge de Bonfons as one of the most considerate of men. They pitied him, and often they went so far as to condemn Eugénie's sorrow and passion. Their censure was expressed, as it frequently is when one woman censures another, in terms of cruel solicitude.

"Madame de Bonfons must be quite ill to leave her husband all alone. Poor little woman! Will she get well soon? What's the matter with her, anyway? Is it gastritis? Cancer? Why doesn't she see a doctor? Her complexion has been quite yellow lately; she ought to go and consult the specialists in Paris. How can it be that she doesn't want a child? They say she loves her husband—how can she refuse to give him an heir, in his position? It's really terrible, isn't it? And if it were only because of a whim, it would be unforgivable. . . . Poor judge!"

Endowed with that keen perception which the person who lives in solitude derives from his unceasing meditation and the clarity with which he sees the things that fall within his sphere, Eugénie, accustomed by unhappiness and her final disillusionment to guessing the concealed truth of things, knew that the judge desired her death so that he could come into full possession of that enormous fortune, augmented still further by the estates of his uncle the notary and his uncle the priest, whom God had, for some reason, seen fit to call unto Himself. The poor recluse felt sorry for the judge. Providence avenged her for the calculations and infamous indifference of a husband who respected, as being the strongest possible guarantee, the hopeless passion with which she was consumed. If she had given birth to a child, would it not have meant the death of the selfish hopes and glittering ambitions which the judge cherished?

And so God showered still more gold upon His prisoner, who cared nothing for gold and yearned for heaven, who lived, pious and good, in holy thoughts, and who was always giving aid, secretly, to those in distress.

Madame de Bonfons became a widow at the age of thirty-three, with an income of eight hundred thousand francs a year, still beautiful, but with the kind of beauty usually found in women who are nearly forty.

Her face is pale, relaxed and calm. Her voice is gentle and serene, her manners simple. She has all the noble qualities imparted by sorrow and the saintliness of a person whose soul has never been sullied by contact with the world, but she also has the rigidity of an old maid and the petty habits engendered by the narrowness of provincial life. Despite her income of eight hundred thousand francs, she lives as the poor Eugénie Grandet once lived; she lights a fire in her bedroom only on the days when her father used to allow her to light a fire in the living room, and she puts it out in conformity with the schedule in force during her younger years. She is always dressed as her mother was. The house in Saumur, sunless, cold, always dark and melancholy, is the image of her life.

She carefully accumulates her income, and she might seem parsimonious if she did not disprove the accusation by the noble use she makes of her wealth. Pious and charitable foundations, a home for the aged, Christian schools for children, a richly endowed public library— these things bear witness each year against the charge of avarice which certain people bring against her. The churches of Saumur owe a number of embellishments to her generosity.

Madame de Bonfons, jokingly referred to as Mademoiselle, is held in reverent respect by nearly everyone. Her noble heart, which once beat only for the most tender of feelings, was fated to be trampled underfoot by the calculations of human selfishness. It was fated that money should communicate its cold glitter to that saintly life and arouse mistrust of the feelings in a woman who was all feeling.

"You're the only one who loves me," she used to say to Nanon.

This woman's hand heals the secret wounds of countless families. Eugénie continues on her way to heaven, accompanied by a train of good deeds. The greatness of her soul overshadows the narrowness of her education and the habits she acquired early in life.

Such is the story of this woman who is in the world but not of it, who, born to be a magnificent wife and mother, has neither husband, children nor family.

For the past few days there has been talk of another marriage for her. The people of Saumur are speculating about her and the Marquis de Froidfond, whose family is beginning to close in on the rich widow as the Cruchots did in the past.

Nanon and Cornoiller are said to be helping the marquis, but nothing could be farther from the truth. Neither Big Nanon nor Cornoiller is clever enough to understand the corruptions of the world.

Paris, September, 1833

Bantam Classics bring you the world's greatest literature—books that have stood the test of time—at specially low prices. These beautifully designed books will be proud additions to your bookshelf. You'll want all these time-tested classics for your own reading pleasure.

Titles by Mark Twain:

☐ 21079-3	**ADVENTURES OF HUCKLEBERRY FINN**	$2.50
☐ 21128-5	**ADVENTURES OF TOM SAWYER**	$2.25
☐ 21195-1	**COMPLETE SHORT STORIES**	$5.95
☐ 21143-9	**A CONNECTICUT YANKEE IN KING ARTHUR'S COURT**	$3.50
☐ 21349-0	**LIFE ON THE MISSISSIPPI**	$2.50
☐ 21256-7	**THE PRINCE AND THE PAUPER**	$2.25
☐ 21158-7	**PUDD'NHEAD WILSON**	$2.50

Other Great Classics:

☐ 21274-5	**BILLY BUDD** Herman Melville	$2.95
☐ 21311-3	**MOBY DICK** Herman Melville	$3.50
☐ 21233-8	**THE CALL OF THE WILD & WHITE FANG** Jack London	$2.95
☐ 21011-4	**THE RED BADGE OF COURAGE** Stephen Crane	$1.95
☐ 21350-4	**THE COUNT OF MONTE CRISTO** Alexander Dumas	$4.95